Praise ...

'The commu... ...
a joy to read ... ... to read the
everyday effects of brutal government policies that seem awfully
recent. The history has been meticulously researched, and the
result is Heiss's great achievement: the reader is transported in
place and time.' – *The Australian*

'With deftness and a lightness of touch . . . Heiss's strengths as
a writer are on full display: the blossoming romance presenting a
complex view of cross-cultural relationships' – *The Conversation*

'History with heart . . . Love defies the cultural boundaries of
war' – *The Daily Telegraph*

Praise for *Tiddas*
'Brisbane through jacaranda-tinted glasses, the river and a
group of loud-mouthed, big-hearted girlfriends flowing through
it. Generous, witty, a paean to BrizVegas, friendship and
sophisticated urban Aboriginal life: only Anita Heiss is writing
this new contemporary women's story.' – Susan Johnson

'This enjoyable and human story is impressively interwoven with
historical and contemporary Aboriginal issues.' – *The Sun Herald*

Praise for *Not Meeting Mr Right*
'Heiss creates the genre of Koori chick lit in *Not Meeting
Mr Right*' – *The Sydney Morning Herald*

'Anita is Aboriginal Australia's answer to Whoopi Goldberg.'
– Jackie Huggins

Praise for *Manhattan Dreaming*
'Captures all the wide-eyed excitement of Manhattan:
the sights; the shopping; the history; and – of course – the men.
It's a contemporary romance with spunk.'
– *Australian Bookseller and Publisher*

Barbed Wire
AND
Cherry Blossoms

Also by Anita Heiss

Fiction
Not Meeting Mr Right (2007)
Avoiding Mr Right (2008)
Manhattan Dreaming (2010)
Paris Dreaming (2011)
The Tightening Grip,
written with the students of St Laurence's College, Brisbane
(2012)
Tiddas (2014)

Nonfiction
Sacred Cows (1996)
Dhuuluu-Yala: Publishing Indigenous Literature (2003)
I'm Not Racist, But . . . (2007)
Am I Black Enough For You? (2012)

Young adult and kids
Who Am I? The Diary of Mary Talence, Sydney 1937 (2001)
Yirra and Her Deadly Dog, Demon,
written with the students of La Perouse Public School (2007)
Demon Guards the School Yard,
written with the students of La Perouse Public School (2011)
Harry's Secret (2015)
Matty's Comeback (2016)

Poetry
Token Koori (1998)

Anthology (ed)
Macquarie PEN Anthology of Aboriginal Literature,
edited with Peter Minter (2008)
Life in Gadigal Country (2002)

ANITA HEISS

Barbed Wire
AND
Cherry
Blossoms

**SIMON &
SCHUSTER**

London · New York · Sydney · Toronto · New Delhi

BARBED WIRE AND CHERRY BLOSSOMS
First published in Australia in 2016 by
Simon & Schuster (Australia) Pty Limited
Suite 19A, Level 1, Building C, 450 Miller Street, Cammeray, NSW 2062
This edition published 2017

10 9 8 7 6 5

Sydney New York London Toronto New Delhi
Visit our website at www.simonandschuster.com.au

National Library of Australia Cataloguing-in-Publication entry
Creator: Heiss, Anita, 1968 – author.
Title: Barbed wire and cherry blossoms/Anita Heiss.
ISBN: 9781925184853 (paperback)
            9781925184860 (ebook)
Subjects: Erambie Aboriginal Reserve (NSW) – Fiction.
            Prisoner-of-war escapes – New South Wales – Cowra – Fiction
            Prisoners of war – Japan – Fiction.
            Prisoners of war – New South Wales – Cowra – Fiction.
            Women, Aboriginal Australian – New South Wales – Cowra – Fiction.
            Man–woman relationships – Fiction
            Love stories.
Dewey Number: A823.3

Cover design: Christabella Designs
Cover images: Australian Scenics/Getty Images, Winai Tepsuttinun/Shutterstock,
AVprophoto/Shutterstock
Typeset by Midland Typesetters, Australia
Printed and bound in Australia by Griffin Press

To all those who call Cowra home

Barbed Wire
AND
Cherry
Blossoms

Prologue

5 August 1944

Hiroshi is wide awake and waiting when the bugle sounds across the camp at two am. Not long after, a couple of gunshots are fired by a guard. It's time to honour his Japanese heritage and no longer bring shame upon his family. It's time to run with his countrymen and break free from the confines that have given him both refuge and grief over the last twelve months.

He rises, fully clothed, and becomes part of the chaos that consumes B Compound. Japanese soldiers are bellowing and running with frantic purpose to fulfil what they had all agreed to less than twenty-four hours before. They are breaking out.

Six hundred men sprint up the stretch of sealed road known as Broadway. It is lit up like the famous New York City street that Hiroshi knows little about, but he knows America because he is a fan of baseball. He also knows America is his enemy in the war he has fought and will probably die in. He knows he should die with honour rather than live with the shame of failure. Bringing shame on their families is what is driving these men to break out of Cowra's prisoner of war camp.

'Tenno Heika Banzai!' men yell as they run. 'Long live the Emperor!' They are dressed in surplus Australian First World War uniforms. The uniforms are dyed maroon but most are faded, as the Japanese have boiled the garments to wash the much hated red out. Many of the men have blankets tied in strips around their legs and some carry baseball gloves they have made themselves. These will be used to protect their hands when climbing the barbed-wire fence. But blankets and baseball mitts will not be enough to protect them from bullets.

The screams of pride and duty are lost among cries of pain as some hit the ground, yelling, 'Okasan!' – calling for their mothers. They are the same shrieks Hiroshi knew in New Guinea. The war has come to them in Cowra.

Hiroshi is carrying a bread knife that has been ground down to razor sharpness. He hopes he won't have to use it against anyone. He hopes he doesn't have to use it against himself. He is not ready to commit suicide as others are, although he knows his obligations: a duty to the emperor and his family. He is running for his family, not only to save them from shame, save them from the pain of following Shinto rituals once they believe he is dead, but because he desperately wants to see them again. Some of his comrades are carrying baseball bats and heavy sticks as weapons, and while the Australian guards are caught off-guard, eventually gunfire will render bats and sticks as useless as the blankets and mitts.

There are a number of ways to escape: the prisoner of war camp is divided into four quarters, making twelve sides. Most of the men take Broadway, the road running north to south. A few others head along the unsealed road known as No Man's Land. *It's too much of a risk to be in a smaller group. Safety in numbers,* Hiroshi tells himself, just as he did when the men voted on whether or not to attempt an escape.

Only hours ago, each hut leader had ordered his men to vote. Hiroshi wanted to mark 'X' on the ballot; he didn't want to do what he was now forced to do: run, risking death rather than the ongoing dishonour of being held captive as a prisoner of war. He knew there were other men who didn't want to escape either, but they were not the majority. Like most of the others, he did the only thing he could with his ballot paper, voted in favour, and handed it over, yet he remained naïvely hopeful there would not have to be a breakout at all. The pressure was on all of them – they had only two options: die an honourable death or return home alive. Hiroshi knew that he must no longer bring shame upon his family, even if the stain of being held captive would still be there regardless.

Hiroshi does not like his chances of survival. Once it had been agreed they would break out, though, he knew he needed a strategy. If he could get out and away alive, then he would make sure he had the best chance at staying that way. He values his heritage and the traditions that come with being Japanese, but he values his life and the family he so heartbreakingly misses more. He will follow the river, because at least he can catch fish to eat if needed. If he can keep himself fed and alive then there is some hope.

Smoke fills the cold night air and Hiroshi's lungs. It's not the smell of log fires warming Cowra homes, though, it's the burning of fear and hatred and the huts the men had stacked fire wood under and set alight as part of the breakout. Hiroshi is agile, lean, running with speed and strength but others aren't as light-footed or balanced. He can tell by the way some of them are zigzagging that they are still affected by the home brew they'd drunk when saying their farewells in the hours leading up to this moment. Hiroshi hadn't drunk any of the Cowra Masamune, named after the famous sake of Kobe. He said goodbye sober, wanted a clear head if and when the escape began. But his head is far from clear – it is filled with terror and turmoil about what will happen. Other men surround Hiroshi when he reaches the fence where the No. 2 Vickers gun is stationed, in the northeast corner near F Tower. The gun is mounted on a trailer and there are two Australian soldiers there firing rounds. Japanese soldiers fall and Hiroshi's ears are filled with the cries of pain, which are somehow more deafening than the blasts of artillery. He tries to block the noise of the men who are already lying wounded.

His heart beats frantically as he looks around. With each step he imagines he will be the next to fall. He can't see his closest friend, Masao, but he hasn't got time to wait. He throws his blanket over the barbed-wire fence, scrambling up and over it quicker than others. He runs as fast as his legs will carry him. He runs like he did in his university days when his studies were mixed with sport. He runs like the child he was with his cousins, the very family he wishes he could see right now. He runs so fast he becomes conscious of his heartbeat, pounding like the taiko drum his father made him listen to when preparing for war; he knew the drums were used in past times to scare the enemy but also to issue commands. *What do Australians use to scare the enemy? What is their war cry?* he wonders momentarily. But the beating of the taiko calls his mind to attention as if the drum is right in front of him, sending a message for him to run, to escape, and to be smarter than the enemy this time.

In minutes Hiroshi finds himself alone, already away from the compound, his friends, Masao, and the night seems suddenly darker. It's the blackest night sky Hiroshi remembers seeing. There are millions of stars but the moon is low. He is grateful for that; less chance of being seen as he runs. A bead of sweat drips down his face and he slows his pace slightly, focusing his eyes on his surrounds, looking for a sign in the distance to suggest somewhere to hide. He's not sure what he's looking for, but he knows he needs to keep moving – the only plan he has right now is to stay alive. He must find and follow the river and use it as a navigation point, perhaps to the sea. He doesn't know the landscape, the geography, how far away the ocean that could carry him home is. Some of the men thought they could get to a port, but Hiroshi wasn't so sure. He still isn't.

He continues to run to the sound of gunfire behind him and his mind moves at the same speed. The ground is hilly but not too steep. He remembers the mountainous terrain of his island home and the farmers to the north growing rice and barley and wheat. He knows there are farms nearby where the Italian soldiers used to work but he doesn't know how many hills he might have to run up and down tonight.

Deep breathing turns to deep thought as Hiroshi's own life flashes past in vignettes as if he is flicking through an old black and white photo album. Memories flood his thoughts like the tears his mother cried the day he left. All he can see are images of the people he loved, the people he *still* loves, the life he misses back home. Each lunge he takes into the darkness of the unknown town he is now running the outskirts of, brings new recollections. His heart is filled with pain and joy at the same time.

This is the last time he will see the compound, because he knows that whatever happens, he will not return to the camp. He can't. He's been a prisoner since June 1943 and he's seen the four seasons come and go and start to come again. He's heard the kookaburras in the gum trees at daybreak, and the barking owls at dusk, and enjoyed embellished stories about snakes in huts even though he's never seen one himself. He's been told there's good fishing in the nearby Lachlan River, but that's all he knows, and he's prepared for even less.

Hiroshi trips, stumbles, takes a deep breath and looks around. He can see the twinkle of lights ahead of him and fires burning behind. He hears the faint cries of his countrymen and the ongoing ringing of gunfire. He starts to run again and tries to drown out the sounds of his heavy breathing and beating heart with thoughts of home, of why he wants to live, why he will risk both death and dishonour just to see his family again. He keeps running because he wants to hug his mother's tiny frame once more and relieve her of the worry he knows she will have. His mother is kind and loving – unlike his father, who urged him to take his physical examination for the army on his twentieth birthday. At the time Hiroshi was at university studying English. He knew that he could get a reprieve until his studies were done but his father was not impressed and when he finally left for military camp at the age of twenty-two, his father put one hand firmly on his shoulder and said, 'If you go to war, please die.' Hiroshi knew what he meant. It is better to die with honour than live with shame.

This is why the memory of his mother and her peaceful approach to life has always remained the strongest for him. She detested war but could never express it; it was not the Japanese way. 'Please come home,' she'd whispered in her son's ear the last time he saw her. It is for his mother that he continues to run until the fear of what is behind him and what is ahead of him makes him collapse.

Hiroshi begins to hyperventilate, panicking to the point of shaking, a wave of nausea causing him to gag and double over with cramps. He hears more gunshots but he is paralysed with fear, with the reality that he is alone and his fellow soldiers and Masao are probably dead. He slows his breathing and picks himself up like the soldier he was trained to be. He stands to attention and immediately begins quietly chanting the Senjinkun – the military creed – because he knows that is what he is supposed to do: 'Strong is he who comprehends shame. Be always mindful of the reputation of your community and family, while making every effort to fulfil their expectations. Do not in death leave to posterity a stain on your honour by having suffered in life the disgrace of being a prisoner.'

He wasn't prepared for the escape. Then again, he was never prepared for the capture – it was not something that was expected to happen to Japanese soldiers and therefore none had been trained in what to do if they were. It is why he had been like other soldiers and given information readily to the Australian guards, who had always treated him with respect, after some initial rough handling that was exacerbated by anxiety and distress.

Some of the Australian officials interrogating Hiroshi and the other Japanese soldiers had remarkable skills in the Japanese language, and this impressed Hiroshi, and made it easy for him to cooperate. Hiroshi wasn't considered to be difficult or militant and mutual respect was shown between the captor and captive. Some of the soldiers were tricked though, manipulated by being offered a cigarette or sugary treat. Australian soldiers would get the information they needed by asking, 'When was the last time you had sugar?' and pushing a sweet towards them. The thoughts of the capture, the need for sugar, the memories of the sweet mochi rice cakes his mother used to make are all too real for Hiroshi. He can taste them now.

Of course there were lies too. Hiroshi, like many others, did not give his real name so that his family would not be able to trace him back to a camp. He would never be traced back to the prisoner of war camp in Cowra; he could never be known to have been a prisoner of war *anywhere*. That is where the shame would start. He lied about his position too. His university background meant he was an officer in the Imperial Japanese Army. He did not tell the truth about his rank, and therefore did not go to D camp with other officers, who did not break out. He claimed he was just a soldier – feeling it was better to be held back with his friends, with Masao, than be separated in an already shameful situation.

He knew the truth, though: in this bloody war, life in the compound was utopia compared to life on the warfront, to life in military training. The Japanese government had left their soldiers starving in New Guinea so they were forced to fight for food as well as fighting the enemy. Hiroshi respected the Australian soldiers who fed and treated them all well. He was still lean but he'd gained weight while in B Compound.

New Guinea is a lifetime away for Hiroshi as he hits the river where people are camping. The camp is under the railway bridge and near the quarry. There are about six huts strung out between the river and the road south of the bridge, and another four huts north of the bridge and a few more between the bridge and a fence line that Hiroshi can just make out. The huts remind him of the traditional wooden architecture scattered throughout Shikoku. He wonders if there are local fishermen here who cast nets into the river like the men do back home.

It is quiet except for a barking dog. He decides to run to the second set of huts and rest, because even though there's no way of telling how long he has been running or how far he is from the camp, he knows it's still not far enough away. He keeps moving with the little energy he can muster. He imagines running from one base to another, like he did playing baseball back in university and at the camp. He focuses on a specific point as if it is a base he is running to. *Find somewhere to hide*, he tells himself.

His clothes are soaked with the sweat of fear and exertion when he reaches the second group of huts, small like the ones in B Compound. He is exhausted and slows his pace in the hope he might find some refuge. He quietens his breathing and uses his military training to move like the kitsune, a spiritual entity with superior intelligence likened to the fox. He moves around the huts until he finds one with a verandah to crawl under.

The sun is rising just as Hiroshi's eyelids fall, heavy. Anxiety and adrenalin have kept him awake till now, but he is emotionally drained and exhausted from running. He's been alert for hours, and that too has been a strain on his mind. The cold and frost make it hard to feel comfortable. He wishes he had the warmth of the camp to protect him.

After what seems like only minutes he wakes to see first light. He smells tobacco and hears a man's voice. He listens closely and thinks it's strange there's only one voice, before realising the man is talking to a dog sitting three feet from where Hiroshi lies. The dog sticks its head under the verandah and growls. Hiroshi panics, thinking it is one of the dingoes he's heard about, and sits up abruptly. He hits his head on a wooden beam and groans loudly and the dog barks. He panics even more.

'Shh, KB, you'll wake everyone up. We don't need the goothas running around yet,' the brown-skinned, black-haired man with a cigarette stuck to his bottom lip whispers to his four-legged mate, who is making more noise than either the man or Hiroshi want.

The fella has long legs, but one doesn't bend at all, so he struggles to get down low to see what the dog is growling at. The men's eyes meet, Hiroshi's full of fear, the other's oddly full of warmth.

'What have we got here then?' the man says, blowing smoke into Hiroshi's face, an inquisitive look on his own.

1

Four Aboriginal men who look older than their years sit around a small wooden table in mismatched chairs. It's Banjo Williams' home and he's there with Sid Coe and Fred Murray, who both come from a long line of respected leaders in the community. Fred's cousin Doolan Murray was a main leader at Erambie for twenty years and was the force behind setting up the school on the reserve. Since he passed, Fred has carried the mantle for the family. Fred and Sid work at the local cannery and King Billie, the Manager at Erambie, has a lot of respect for them, as does everyone else. Banjo is a carpenter and has built most of the furniture in the houses at Erambie as well as the verandah his family enjoys. He has done some work at the prisoner of war compound, but has had no contact with any of the prisoners first hand. Banjo's brother Kevin, a drover and buckjump rider who works around New South Wales, is the fourth in the group.

The men look tired from long days of hard work and years of worry about protecting and caring for their women and children. Except for Kevin, whose cheeky eyes and smile have somehow helped him maintain his youthfulness. He's not only got a reputation with the goothas across the Riverina for being an engaging storyteller, but also has a reputation for being a bit of a ladies' man, wooing women with his dance moves, smooth singing voice and charm. Banjo doesn't like his brother's philandering ways and Kevin doesn't like the fact that some men travel across country to Cowra because the town is known for its beautiful Black women.

The men are listening to Banjo, who is usually good for a yarn and a laugh, but today the mood is serious.

'I'm just sitting there, having my morning smoke, and KB starts making a racket, which isn't unusual but you know a man needs some quiet time in the morning.' Banjo taps his tobacco pouch on the table and the other men nod. 'I tell the mirri to be quiet but he's sticking his nose under the hut and growling. Of course I think it's going to be a rabbit, or another mirri or maybe a snake, but he just keeps going, so I crouch down as best I can with this gammy leg, and you won't believe what I saw. What I found.' Banjo can see high expectations on the other men's faces. He looks around to check there's no one else in earshot. 'It was a Jap,' he says. 'A Japanese soldier, from the camp up there,' and he points in the direction of the camp miles away.

'What?' Kevin asks loudly.

'Shh,' Banjo implores. 'He's on the run, obviously.'

'Where is he?' Kevin asks.

'I've hidden him,' Banjo says with a frown at how loud Kevin is speaking.

'You did what?'

'Will you stop it, Kev? I didn't know what to do. He was terrified. I mean, he looked terrified – we didn't speak. I just took him quickly to the air raid shelter and made him climb down there. My leg won't let me get down the ladder. You know it's never been the same since that tree fell on it when we were out cutting.'

Kevin shakes his head in disbelief. 'But why d'ya do that with the Jap?'

'I didn't know what else to do. He needed my help. If he's on the run, I'm not going to put him in. That's not our way. It's over four miles from the camp to here in a direct line – *if* he's on the run and came the long way round, skirting the east of town around Taragala, he would've run over six miles. The man deserves a medal for that.' Banjo speaks fast, almost without taking a breath.

'And some rest!' Sid adds, rubbing his large belly.

Kevin clenches his fists. 'We can't hide him here! No one in the community will want to hide a Jap.' When no one responds, he raises his voice. 'We're at war with these mongrels.' He looks at Sid and Fred, blood boiling, and slams his fists on the table. 'We've got our own fellas at war. Are you mad?'

Banjo's wife, Joan, comes cautiously into the hut carrying clean bed sheets she's washed by hand in a galvanised tub out the front. The windy day has dried them quickly. 'Shh, I can hear you outside. King Billie will be here if you don't

3

keep quiet,' she says, looking at Kevin. She walks over to her husband and leans low to whisper, 'Where is he?'

'He's in the air raid shelter,' Banjo whispers back. 'He's safe.'

'*He's* safe!' Kevin slams both fists on the table again. '*He's* safe! What about *us*? Are *we* safe?'

Joan walks around the table and puts her hands on the shoulders of her brother-in-law and says, 'Kev, we need to be united on this.'

Kevin is momentarily placated, lowering his voice out of respect for Joan. 'We have to be united the other way round.'

'What do you mean?' Sid asks.

'We shouldn't even be talking about this. The Japs are the enemy in this war. Do you think they're treating Australian soldiers well? I heard the Australian soldiers captured by the Japs were sent to Singapore and other places to work for their army! Our men are being forced to work for the enemy. And you, you want to work for *their* army! Traitors, all of you!'

Banjo knows that Kevin is right in most respects, as does everyone else. Australia is at war and there are Wiradjuri men fighting too.

'Jim told me that it's common knowledge the Aussies are beaten with leather whips and clubbed with bats to make them talk, even if they have no information to give. They are brutal, and this fella you want to save, he'd probably do the same, given the chance.' Kevin keeps shaking his head.

Banjo doesn't believe that; he saw the man's eyes, saw the fear and warmth in them.

'We've got nearly a dozen men – *our* people – in this war.' Kevin looks each man in the eye. 'We don't even know where they are. You think the Japs are protecting them? They're probably bloody eating them. The *bastards*.'

Joan shakes her head at Kevin and his suggestion that the Japanese are cannibals. Kevin has always been the dramatic one in the group, so Joan lets the comment pass without a reaction, as do the others.

Banjo is quiet. He has always been the thoughtful one and as his younger, more aggressive, sibling rants, he is thinking of how to respond in a way that will dull the fire in his brother's belly.

'What do you reckon we should do then?' he asks, knowing that giving Kevin a chance to offer suggestions is the right thing to do.

His brother leaps at the opportunity. 'Why don't we ask old Tommy Mack what he thinks? Ask someone who's actually *been* to war what *they* think about hiding an escaped Jap prisoner.' There is so much venom and sarcasm in Kevin's tone that the room becomes uncomfortable. The likelihood of the escaped prisoner lasting even one more hour is dwindling rapidly, the way the conversation is headed. '*Or* why don't we ask the Coes what they think? They lost men to war in the past – I bet they won't want to hide any of the enemy in *this* war.' Again he looks at Banjo, Fred and Sid one at a time, waiting for a response.

'And why don't we ask the Newtons about Dooley and Bibby,' Kevin continues, referring to Lindsay and Reuben, the brothers who are both fighting in the war. 'Bibby's in Malaya, but no one's heard from him for yonks.' He stops short of suggesting the man is dead, but everyone already believes that. 'Rueben's in Bougainville, or is he? He could've been fighting the bloody Jap you're hiding.'

'Shh,' Joan says angrily. 'The goothas might hear you. They play with the Newton kids and I don't want any of that getting back to the family.'

They all remember the two Coe men, and each Anzac Day the whole community pays tribute to them. The men remain well respected and will always be remembered for fighting a war for a country that denied them the right to be Australian citizens, or to earn equal wages or marry without permission of the Manager.

'You mob are traitors,' Kevin repeats. 'Where's your loyalty to your own people? Sometimes I can't believe we're related.' He lights up another cigarette. 'Aren't we going to respect our brothers?'

Banjo finally speaks. 'This fella is someone's brother, Kevin. What if he was *our* brother?' He puts his hand to his heart. 'What if our brother escaped from a POW camp like this bloke? Wouldn't you want someone to look after him and treat him like a human being?'

Unconvinced, Kevin stands up and pushes his chair so hard it falls over. He can't believe what he's hearing, and blows smoke through his nostrils.

'And wouldn't *you* want to escape the prison if you could? Wouldn't you escape *this* prison if you could?' Banjo addresses all three men. He knows what he's doing, he just needs the others to understand and agree. 'This fella just wants his freedom and probably wants to see his family.'

'Can't argue with that,' Fred says, gently.

One down, two to go, Banjo thinks. He already knows Joan is with him.

'The government is fighting the Japanese – the same government we are fighting. We're fighting for a better life. I feel like I'm at war every day with all those who control our lives. I'm sick of living in this hut without water. I want the same wages as the whitefellas doing the same job. I'm tired of us living in fear of having our kids taken away, while white people don't have to worry about anything: they have enough food and they have water and electricity and get paid properly for their work.' Banjo's voice is not loud but it is firm. 'If *we* are at war with this government, then, to my mind, this fella and I are on the same side.'

Banjo has conviction in his voice and Joan has never been more proud of her man.

Sid and Fred look at each and raise their eyebrows in understanding and agreement, but Kevin is not giving up easily. 'Okay, well, let's vote then,' he says.

Banjo nods and says, 'I vote we protect him. All in favour, raise your hands.'

Sid and Fred slowly put their hands in the air, but a belligerent Kevin shoots both his arms straight to the ground like a child. 'You win again,' he says, which is a vague but ongoing reference to the fact that they both once competed for the woman Banjo married. Kevin has never stopped loving Joan and the three of them know it. She is still the only one who can calm him down when he gets aggressive. The only one he will listen to. The only one he could never have because of his wild ways.

'Three votes to one,' Banjo says. 'So it's agreed – we'll hide him in the air raid shelter for as long as we can. For as long as it's safe, and if that's until the end of the war, then so be it.'

'What are we going to feed him, then?' Kevin asks, knowing there is little food to go around and that rations are already stretched beyond what's acceptable. 'It's bad enough we have to work for our rations – the bread and tea and sugar – but now you want to give it away?'

'We share, Kev, you know that. We always have. Sharing is not new to us. Stop acting like we're doing something bad here. We're being ourselves. This is what we do.' Joan's voice quivers.

Banjo puts his arm around his wife's shoulder. 'We'll get by,' he says. 'We have the vegie garden and we can spare a little each, enough to keep him alive.'

'There's only potatoes in that patch, and not a lot of them!' Kevin argues, walking to the window.

'We have pumpkin and cabbage too,' Joan says. 'You're just never around long enough to enjoy them.' Even Joan is getting testy with her brother-in-law's insistence on being difficult.

'We can't tell anyone,' Sid says anxiously. '*I* understand your logic, Banjo, but there will be some who don't and King Billie will tar and feather us if he finds out.'

'I agree, we tell no one, not even your wives.' Banjo looks at Fred because everyone knows Fred's wife, Marj, is the queen of the Black grapevine and if she knows what's going on, then it's all over. Fred and Marj live next door, and Marj has eyes in the back of her head – she knows who's doing, saying, thinking what. And with no fence between the huts, she can see right down to the opening of the air raid shelter at the back of the Williams' lot. Everyone loves Marj, but they also know she has a mouth, a big, uncontrollable mouth, and sometimes a bitter tongue. Fred loves his wife, but even he knows she's got the loosest lips this side of the Great Dividing Range.

'I won't tell Marj,' he promises.

'I won't tell Ivy either, but what about Jim?' Sid asks of the local Wiradjuri lad who'd returned from the First World War and was now part of the 22 Battalion acting as a guard at the POW camp. 'We need Jim to find out information about what's going on, how this fella got out and why, but he can't know we are hiding an escapee.'

'I think he needs to know,' Kevin says. 'Surely he has a right to know.'

'No! We can't compromise his livelihood,' Banjo says. 'We can't put him or his job in danger with the authorities. What do you think they'll do to him if they find out he knows about this? They'll court martial him.'

'There's also that other Aboriginal fella who leads the Italians out to the farms,' Fred offers.

'He's a Charles,' Fred says.

'That's him, he'd have to know something about what's going on. I hear he also rolls cigarettes for the soldiers, so he must get on well with them.'

'I don't understand why there's no real security around the Italians,' Kevin says. 'It's like they run this town – bike riding, going to the movies and the pubs. I even heard they've got grappa stills in the camp and the guards swap leftover meat for alcohol. I'd trade some rabbit or some watermelon for some grappa, that's for sure.'

Banjo wishes his brother would just stick to the issue at hand instead of mouthing off about everything that upsets him. Before he gets the chance to get back to the Charles fella, Kevin is off again.

'I've even heard that they built a proper stage and made costumes and printed programs for shows they do in there. And they get given musical instruments and supplies to paint. Can you imagine, that? They're prisoners and they're treated better than us. I wonder how that Charles fella feels about that, seeing them having a good life and all.'

'We need to leave him out of this,' Banjo says adamantly. 'We need to keep this as quiet as possible, can't go snooping around too much and drawing attention, especially if anyone is working at the camp.'

'Well, how long do you reckon we can hide him in the air raid shelter? What if there's a bloody air raid?' Kevin will not concede defeat without making it difficult for his brother. The rivalry is one-sided, but it is there. He sees Joan frowning. 'Sorry,' he says, knowing that profanity and blasphemy are not allowed in her home.

'The war isn't coming to Cowra,' Joan says with a twinkle in her eye. She pulls him up when she deems it necessary, when no one else would even try.

'We could hide him at Ryan's Place. It might be safer there than having him here on the mission,' Fred offers.

'Yeah, let's put him down where he can have fun, singing

and dancing with the mob there. Bloody parties most of the time.' Kevin's bitterness flows easily. 'He can even get a drink down there too!'

'You'd know,' Joan says with a hint of sarcasm.

'What?' Kevin assumes shocked innocence but if he's going down, he's taking his brother with him. 'It's not just me – Banjo's been there too. And I'm sure I've seen you both dancing there.' Kevin doesn't like Joan judging him even though he still needs her approval all these years later. 'Anyway, there's nowhere to hide him there, with only those few huts.'

The door bursts open and the Williams kids race in full of energy and laughter. The adults immediately stop talking. Mary, the eldest daughter, is seventeen years old. It took a long time for Banjo and Joan to fall pregnant with Mary, and they didn't think they would again – it was nine years before the next girl came along, and then another two, before the only boy was born.

'Take the goothas into the other room,' Banjo instructs Mary. 'Mum will come get you all in a minute. We just need to finish some business here first.'

Mary knows something is up but she obeys her father and walks the kids out of the front room which is the kitchen, through the lounge room of sorts to the bedroom, which leads to the back sleep out. Banjo and Joan sleep out the back with the kids: Betty, Dottie, Jessie and the baby of the family, James, who was a surprise to them all three years ago. Mary sleeps in the front room, which has a fire place, so she's warm in winter. Compared to other huts, Banjo's is one of the best, with a fence, a small vegie garden and morning glory vines hanging on the verandah and around the hut to offer protection from the sun in the summer and the wind in the winter. The tap at the front of the hut provides all the water the family needs for cooking, cleaning and washing. The bare corrugated iron walls don't provide much insulation from the frosty winter weather, but the black stove in the kitchen offers some warmth.

As soon as Mary and the kids leave the room, Banjo leans across the table and says in a low voice, 'It's settled, he'll stay in the air raid shelter. It's the only place they won't look given it never gets used, and people outside of Erambie wouldn't even know it's there. Joan'll gather whatever leftovers she can without suspicion. We've got more mouths to feed than you lot and it's normal for people to share with us. Mary can take them down to him at dusk each night when she comes back from King Billie's.'

'Why Mary?' Sid asks. 'Is it safe for her to do that? I thought we weren't going to tell anyone else.'

'Yeah,' Kevin growls, 'you just finished ordering us not to tell anyone, and now you're breaking your own rule. Why don't you or Joan or one of these fellas take it down?' He points to Sid and Fred.

Banjo taps on his gammy leg. 'I can't climb down a ladder with this leg. And you fellas seen in our yard a lot will only draw suspicion.'

'But why Mary? She's so young,' Sid says, concerned.

'Yes, she's young, but King Billie trusts her, everyone trusts her. If there's ever any suspicion here they will never look at Mary.'

'Banjo!' There's a thump on the door. 'Banjo! Open up, it's John Smith!'

'What does he want?' Kevin mouths to Sid and Fred, who both shrug their shoulders.

John Smith is the Manager of Erambie. Behind his back, everyone refers to him as King Billie. There is a version of King Billie on every reserve and mission in the country. Few Managers understand the resentment that Blacks have towards them, and even fewer would care if they did – being a mission Manager requires one to have no sense of human rights or justice. It's only Black humour and making fun of the Manager that sustains the locals at Erambie through the misery being no one in your own land can bring.

Everyone sits to attention as Joan looks around her kitchen to check it's tidy.

'It's not Manager's Day,' she says to her husband, referring to the nominated days that the Manager and/or his wife could go through their huts. Joan, like the other women on the mission, knew the authorities – the Smiths and the police they brought sometimes – were always looking for a reason to say the Blacks were unfit parents. A speck of dirt on the floor. Beds not made perfectly. Kids not clean enough.

Joan looks at the meat safe, the cast iron pots hanging over the fire and the kerosene hurricane lamp, which has been polished. She checks and double-checks the wooden floors she scrubs with sandstone soap on a regular basis. Everything looks clean and tidy as Banjo opens the door.

'What's going on here?' King Billie says, looking over Banjo's shoulder to the men at the table. 'Stop-work meeting?'

The men laugh awkwardly but say nothing.

'Everyone is to stay indoors until further notice,' he orders.

'What's up, John?' Banjo asks, hoping it has nothing to do with the morning's events.

'There's been a breakout at the Japs' camp, and I want everyone indoors until I say so.' King Billie has the shits, as if someone has put a spanner in his works. 'Jim is up at the compound as you know, but I don't want you talking to him. I don't want you talking to *anyone* about it. We don't want people getting hysterical. Let the army sort this mess out.' He speaks directly to Banjo. 'You just keep to your own business here. I'll let you know when things have settled down.

'And you lot,' he finally addresses the other men, 'you do the same, and if you see anyone out and about, you know to give them this order. Right. Go.'

Kevin, Fred and Sid get up, all pushing their chairs in slowly to bide time while King Billie leaves. When they can see him marching towards another hut, they shake hands and cement their decision before heading off.

'Mary!' Banjo calls out.

She enters the room with the kids and little James runs straight to his mother and squeezes between her legs, as he often does. The three younger girls look frightened.

'What did he want?' Mary asks, trying not to sound disrespectful.

'We all have to stay inside for a few hours at least, until Mr Smith comes back.' Banjo rarely uses the term King Billie in front of the kids in case they let it slip in front of the Manager. 'Come with me,' he says, leading his daughter out to the verandah and leaving the others inside.

He lights up a cigarette and looks to see if anyone is outside the hut. 'This morning, a visitor arrived here. A Japanese soldier. It turns out he escaped from the camp up the road.'

Mary listens, sipping a mug of black tea.

'And, well, we, the Elders, have decided we'll give him shelter here.'

'You're hiding him?'

'Yes, we are. We don't know what happened, but John Smith said there was some kind of breakout, so he must be one of the ones who got away. Now, Mary, I want us to look after this fella, he's probably been through a lot in the war, like our own fellas have. He probably has a family just like us. He looked scared.'

'What will everyone say, though, Dad? Everyone here hates the Japanese. Mr Smith is saying stuff about them all the time.'

'I know, but we aren't filled with that hate. You know in our house we treat people the way they treat us, right?' He looks straight into his daughter's eyes.

'Yes.' She nods.

'So we will take care of him as long as we can.' He takes a drag on his cigarette then blows smoke before adding, 'And there's two things you're responsible for.'

Mary's eyes light up. 'What? What can I do?'

'Firstly, you can't tell anyone about him, no one. If Smith finds out, or your Aunty Marj, then we could be in a lot of trouble.'

'I understand.'

'And you're also responsible for taking his food down every day. It won't be much, but we'll give what we can.'

15

'But why me?'

'You're the only one who won't attract attention or suspicion.'

'When will I take it down?'

'We won't risk doing anything tonight, but tomorrow you will take whatever we can pull together and head to the shelter.'

'Okay.'

'Are you nervous?'

'Not yet,' she says although she laughs anxiously.

'You sure?'

'I feel proud you all trust me to do this. It's much more exciting than doing the Smiths' laundry.' She laughs softly.

Later that night, against his better judgement Banjo sends Mary to get a group of young fellas, including her cousin Claude Williams, who are at the Theatre Cowra in Kendal Street. They somehow didn't get the message to stay indoors, but Mary knows they probably would've snuck out anyway. When she arrives, she sees Jim in uniform.

'What are doing here, Mary? You should be back home,' he says.

'Yes, I know, I just came to get Claude and some of the other fellas,' she replies nervously.

'Okay, hurry up, the film's about to start.'

As usual the boys have entered the theatre by the side entrance and are segregated by a rope from the whites. They

16

sit up the front of the cinema close to the screen, necks craned as they watch. As Mary walks into the theatre just before the movie begins, an announcement is made: 'There has been an outbreak from the prisoner of war compound, it is recommended that everyone return to their homes and stay indoors until further notice.'

The lads are all trying to be tough but Mary can tell by the speed of their departure from the theatre how scared they really are. They've only ever heard bad things about the Japanese – the newspapers often have cartoons that paint the enemy in a bad light. They've heard phrases like 'yellow peril' at school but never really knew what it meant. They've never seen any of the soldiers in real life because the Japanese aren't allowed out into the community like the Italian prisoners, who work on properties and in homes in town. Banjo often gets angry that the local whites would prefer to have the Italians they are at war with work for them than the local Blacks. The day he heard that the Italian prisoners working at Mulyan got midday meals and had electricity and running water, he nearly hit the roof, literally: he threw a punch in anger and missed the ceiling by an inch. It was an unusual display of aggression that scared Joan and the kids.

Mary follows the boys closely, half worried, half laughing, as they run at speed all the way back to the station. As they cross the golf course there are shrieks and giggles, the odd attempt at scaring each other, and every time there's a strange noise, one of the lads asks fearfully, 'What's that?'

After a while, the group slows down to a fast walk, almost breathless from running, fear and laughter. Claude is at the back of the pack as he is the least fit. He doesn't play football like the other lads. Mary walks alongside him but says nothing. She suspects there's some damage to his ego as the others are way ahead and Claude is panting and breathless. She doesn't want to make it harder for him.

Only minutes from Erambie, in the still of the cold night, Claude has slowed his pace considerably and so Mary walks ahead, eager to get home and out of the cold.

Alone, Claude feels a hot breath on the back of his neck and stops in his tracks, too terrified to move or to speak. He tries to sing out to Mary but she's too far away and his voice won't cooperate anyway – he cannot muster the slightest sound and his mates are still walking ahead. Claude is convinced he will die, that a Japanese soldier is about to kill him, probably with a machete or a karate chop. If not that, he will definitely goonan his pants. And then he hears a familiar sound, a gentle neigh, and realises the hot breath on his neck was from a local horse.

Lying in bed that night, Joan is worried. 'We really don't have enough food, Banjo, and we could lose the children if anyone finds out. You know they're looking for reasons to say we're bad parents.'

Banjo doesn't respond. He shares his wife's concerns but the last thing he wants to do is add more worry to her life.

'Father Patrick has always been good to us,' Joan continues. 'St Raphael's helps the poor. I'll just have to ask for more.

I can take some of the clothes they're going to throw out and mend them for him. I do it for the kids all the time.' She knows there's no room for shame when it comes to asking for food and clothes. She needs to keep everyone alive, even if she has to go without.

Banjo pulls his wife closer to him, her body warm against his in the cold night. His lean but muscly arms are firm around her frail frame.

'You're right, love, food is scarce and I really want to just fatten you up. But we will manage, we always do.' He nuzzles into the nape of her neck.

I married the right brother, Joan thinks as she dozes off to sleep.

2

'**D**on't let the goothas anywhere near the river today,' Banjo orders Joan. He's shaking as he lights a cigarette and pulls a chair out to collapse onto. It's the morning after Hiroshi has appeared and they haven't yet risked getting any food to him. For all they know, he has escaped his hiding spot.

'What is it?' Joan has never seen her husband so shaken. She sets some water on the wood stove to boil for a cup of tea, grateful there's plenty of chopped wood thanks to young Claude being busy the last few weeks.

'I saw them,' he says softly, taking a long draw on his cigarette then resting his head in his hands as he exhales. In the early hours of the morning, Banjo had taken a walk down to the river and around the local area to see what he could find out. He'd planned on asking anyone he saw if they knew anything. He didn't expect to find death on his doorstep.

'Saw who?'

He looks up, eyes watery, distressed. 'Hanging in the trees. I saw them.' He drags again on the rollie as if it is the only thing that will give him comfort. 'Bloodied soldiers on the ground too. They killed themselves, and they must've killed each other.' He puts his head back in his hands and feels the tears well. It's not a sight he could've imagined and not one he'll forget soon.

Joan puts her arms around her husband's broad shoulders and neck. She can feel the tension in his body as she hugs him close, but says nothing. What can she say to make what he saw any easier? What words could possibly remove the memory of what he's seen? She rubs his shoulders, trying to draw out some of the misery from his body.

'King Billie was right to keep everyone in. Don't let the kids out till this is sorted,' he says softly, choking back emotion.

'I don't understand why,' Joan says. She makes the sign of the cross as she stares at the ceiling and says a quiet Hail Mary.

'I don't know why they did it either. Surely life in the compound wasn't that bad? Jim reckons they eat real good tucker, they play sport and they are treated well.' He closes his eyes and sighs. 'Suicide just doesn't make sense.'

'They were still locked up, Banjo. That's no life either. And they've been at war, seen things we will never know or understand.' Just as her own husband has just seen something *she* will never know.

Mary walks in the door with three eggs. 'Mrs Smith gave them to me,' she says, handing them to her mother. 'Says the hens are laying faster than they can eat them and Mr Smith is sick of eating eggs.' Mary wishes John Smith would just stop eating all together and die, but she'd never say that out loud. When Mary prays that's the kind of thing she asks God for.

Joan takes the eggs from her daughter and looks at Banjo, who is still too choked up to speak.

'We'll give one of these to that fella,' Joan says. She puts the eggs into the pot of water on the stove. 'You'll have to go down tonight, Mary, as soon as it looks like the Smiths have settled in for the night. You'll know better than anyone when that is.' Without trying or wanting to be, Mary Williams is the person closest to the Smiths. She knows their daily routine, their eating habits, when Carmichael wets the bed, when Mr Smith is in a foul mood, when Mrs Smith is on her rags. She knows more than she wants to, but all that knowledge now means she can help her parents and the Elders help this Japanese soldier.

She nods.

It's dark by six pm and quiet on the mission. Families are sitting in their huts, woodstoves burning to keep them warm. Many are eating rabbit stew thanks to Claude and some of the other young fellas, who have caught a few on the other side of the train lines. Everything is shared between the local families. Kids are getting ready for sleep, making their own fun and keeping warm with four bodies, sometimes more, in one bed. Mary sits at the kitchen table for what seems like hours, just waiting. She has a belly full of butterflies, having rehearsed a thousand times what she will say to the stranger, and how she will pass the food over. She has been feeling sick all day about seeing the Japanese soldier for the first time. She understands the logistics of what lies ahead: getting food to the Japanese man and keeping him alive and hidden. But she is feeling nervous and nauseous about making a mistake, even though being appointed the food messenger by the Elders also makes her feel important and special. What if she gets caught? His presence could bring trouble to them and everyone at Erambie, and she doesn't want to be responsible for that.

At well past eight o'clock, Joan puts a hard-boiled egg and some damper into a hessian bag and wraps it tight for Mary to slip under her coat, which barely keeps her warm over the calico dress underneath.

'I want you there and back in five minutes, Mary, okay?'

'Yes, Mum.' Mary understands her mother's concern and respects her wishes.

'Don't make me worry. Just go down, give him the food and come back. That's all you are to do. That's all!'

'Be careful,' Banjo says as he walks his daughter to the back door. 'I'll stay here and have a smoke.'

'What if someone sees me?' Mary asks, looking at Fred and Marj's hut. Everyone knows Marj has eyes on every window but no one knows how.

'Keep looking around and if you think you see anyone, just go to the lav,' Banjo suggests. The lavatory is also up the back of the yard right near the entrance to the air raid shelter. 'You better go,' Banjo urges his daughter with a gentle pat on her back.

Mary walks gingerly down the back of their lot. She tries not to look suspicious but checks slyly whether anyone is out and about, and possibly watching her. She is really only concerned about Aunty Marj, and perhaps a dog barking, which might draw attention to her. All the huts have lights on and it's early, but it's too cold for anyone to be outside, other than Claude, who she sees smoking in the distance. Her heart is racing and she can feel the beats in her chest as if it is about to burst through her skin.

A dog barks and she stops walking but her heart keeps racing, faster. She looks around; there are no people and the dog stops. When she gets to the shelter, she struggles to move the sheet of corrugated iron that covers the entrance and when she finally slides it across, it's noisy in the still of the night. She's convinced someone will hear her. She looks around nervously; her father is still at the back door of their hut. No one seems to be around so she climbs in, pulls the sheet of iron across again and makes her way down the unsteady ladder into the dark pit. She counts the rungs so it's easier the next time: ten rungs then one foot on the ground.

When she reaches the bottom she feels around for the lantern her father had told her is hanging at shoulder height on the left. She lights a match and then the lantern and there, in the corner, she sees a man whose slumped body conveys his fear and gratitude. He watches her with hollow eyes that she believes must hold the horrendous stories of war. The man's face is filled with desperation, but it is also gentle as he looks at Mary and sees a saviour. At that moment she feels sorry for him.

The man stands slowly. He is weak but respectful. He bows.

Mary is startled, unsure of the custom, then bows in response. She hesitates to make eye contact, feeling self-conscious that she has never been alone with a man in any space before other than her father – and Mr Smith, but that experience is always terrifying. There is so much about this moment that is new to Mary and she is thrilled and nervous at once.

She doesn't realise that the man feels the same, awkward in her presence, a member of the enemy nation. And yet he stays, perhaps not knowing a better place to be while away from home, and not wanting to go back to being an official prisoner.

Mary takes the parcel of food from under her coat, unwrapping it and handing it to him. 'Here,' she says, not expecting him to understand English. 'To eat. An egg and some damper.' She motions her hands to her mouth and realises immediately how stupid she must look. Of course it is food and he will know that.

'Thank you,' he says. Hiroshi has eaten eggs before but not damper, but he doesn't care what it is as he's starving and is grateful for any food at all. He is desperate to eat but too polite to do so while she is there.

For all the stereotypes she has heard about the Japanese, the one that was missing is that they are incredibly polite. He speaks English and although she is intrigued and wants to know how and why, she is conscious that she has already been here longer than the five minutes her mother had given her. 'I must go,' she says, folding the hessian bag and putting it under her coat again. She pauses. 'There is a lavatory, a toilet up the ladder.' She points to the sky. 'To empty the bucket.' She looks towards the corner where a faint stench comes from. 'Be careful, be fast. Don't stay up there. My parents will get angry. No one knows you are here. We are keeping you safe.'

He nods, trying to understand so much, so quickly, feeling embarrassment and shame about everything.

'I'll be back tomorrow and will bring something for you to wash with and some more food,' she says as she turns to blow the lamp out.

On the first rung of her climb back to the top, she hears the man repeat faintly, 'Thank you.'

Hiroshi's first two nights have been restless due to hunger pangs and anxiety. The shelter is damp and cold and he has only the dirt to sit on. It is pitch black and fear of the unknown is making him depressed. At least in the camp there was routine and daylight and people to keep the insanity at bay; here there is nothing but darkness with hints of sunlight through the holes in the iron sheet above. And the endless silence means he has nothing to focus on but his fear and regret and that is dangerous. Hiroshi is desperate to know what is happening outside the bunker he is hiding in. How the others are, how many survived and got to a place of safety like he did.

It's hard for him not to think about what he would be doing back in the camp.

Hiroshi spends the long hours waiting, thinking about how he is going to survive, where he is and what will happen if he is caught. He wonders if he should try to escape again, but what opportunities will there be to get home to his family? He feels guilty about not being the warrior his father wanted him to be. He knows he should already have committed suicide, but he still doesn't see this final action helping anyone – himself, his family or the Emperor.

He is full of regret about dishonouring his family, about how his mother will already be mourning him, believing that he is dead. He wishes he could write to her and tell her he is alive, that he *will* return one day.

He wishes too that he could at least read the newspaper as he did in the camp, if not to the others then at least to himself. Because of his English skills he was one of a few men granted the privilege of reading the newspaper to the men in B Compound. It also meant he knew what was going on in the war, but now he is so lost. He wants to know what has happened to his countrymen, where the war is up to, what chance he has to get home to his family. As a matter of priority he wants to know how many are dead, and if his best friend Masao is still alive. He wonders if he should ask the girl if he can have a newspaper when she reappears. It would be a greedy act, asking for something beyond the shelter and food they have already provided so generously, but the newspaper will hold some answers that the girl might not have; answers to questions he doesn't even know if he should ask. But even the girl's presence makes him uncomfortable.

Hiroshi is confused about where he is, who the people hiding him are, why they are feeding him and whether or not they are Australian. They don't look like the soldiers at the camp, who were mostly white. He saw one brown soldier and sometimes he'd see a dark person make deliveries to the compound, but here the two people he's met – the man and the girl – have both been very dark. He is suspicious as to why these dark people are helping him and where they actually come from.

3

Thoughts of the man under the ground help Mary get through the day working at the Smiths' house. She has been thinking as hard and fast as Hiroshi, and she has so many questions she wants to ask him. The mundane chores are done automatically: make the beds; wash the clothes; sweep the floors; help Mrs Smith cook; clean up after the Smith children, Catherine and Carmichael. The two children are at school all day but Mary is responsible for walking them the three miles to and from St Raphael's, because it is too far for Mrs Smith to walk. Mrs Smith is very English, and an elegant English woman does not walk in the street that distance, or so Mr Smith told Mary when he first gave her her list of duties. Some people think that working for Mr Smith must be the worst job in the world, but it gives Mary more freedom than others, as she gets to go into town every day, even if it's only to walk to the school and back. Sometimes she even sees the Italian prisoners riding bikes through town, throwing lollies at kids and grownups. She always grabs a couple if she can, and gives them to her sisters. The domestic duties and the long walks twice a day, five days per week, coupled with living on rations, means Mary is thin, very thin. But she is fit.

Mrs Smith likes Mary, and will often send her home with leftover food that she is never to tell Mr Smith about. Mr Smith is the opposite of his wife – if Mary is there at mealtimes she must sit in the kitchen and wait until the family is finished before she clears the dishes. She is never to sit at the same table as the Smiths to eat – or the tables of white people generally, she is told.

Before she leaves the Smiths' house, she hears the wireless being turned on and Mr Smith telling everyone to be quiet. She stands silently as ordered and listens with the others to a well-spoken man reading the news.

'An international incident has occurred in Cowra, in the central west of New South Wales. One thousand, one hundred and four Japanese prisoners have escaped. It is not clear how many have been captured, how many are still at large, and there is no tally on the death count as yet. There have been many reports of aircraft converging on Cowra from Parkes and Wagga. It is believed the aircraft are British-built Spitfires and Australian-built Wirraways and that crews are hunting prisoners of war who have escaped from the Cowra Prisoner of War Camp.'

John Smith grunts and leaves the room, mumbling something about the 'Japs not winning the war'. Mary doesn't take much notice – she is very tired, as she is after most days spent

32

at the Smiths'. Tonight, though, there is exhaustion mixed with the nervous adrenalin that has been bubbling away inside her at the thought of seeing the stranger again.

When she walks in the door, her mother has just finished wrapping a boiled potato and some more damper for 'the hidden one'. This time at least the logistics of getting to the bunker are sorted: she knows how to slide the sheet of corrugated iron gently to minimise noise, how many rungs there are on the ladder, where the lantern is situated on the wall. The family's faithful mirri, KB, is walking with her tonight, and she hopes he doesn't bark.

As Mary lights the lantern, Hiroshi waits patiently, standing still, trying to silence his anxious breathing. He is as grateful for the human contact as he is for the food that she carries. She hasn't looked at him yet and as she gets the parcel from under her coat, he says, 'Hiroshi.'

She looks up in surprise at a word she's never heard before.

'My name is Hiroshi,' he says, pointing to his nose. 'Hiroshi.'

'My name is Mary,' she replies, handing over the food with the tiniest hint of a smile and a blush.

'Mary,' he repeats. He wonders what the name Mary means. It sounds a little like the Japanese name Mari, which means 'truth child'. He hopes Mary is named so because she is a truth child.

'I am twenty-five,' he offers, and Mary thinks he looks much older, with lines around his eyes. She can even see a few grey hairs in the light of the lantern. He is very skinny but he has muscles. She thinks there is something attractive about him, although she is not sure what. She's really only ever looked at the local Aboriginal boys, and never had a boyfriend, but tonight she notices what Hiroshi looks like.

'How old are you?' he asks, trying not to look her in the eye.

'I am seventeen.'

Hiroshi thinks Mary looks much younger than her years – she is slim and small like his sister.

'Do you have brothers and sisters?'

'I have two sisters, they are young like you.' Hiroshi stops there, refraining from telling Mary that because he is a prisoner it will affect his sisters: they may not be able to marry, they may be ostracised in their jobs, they will be made to feel ashamed of him. That thought is unbearable, but too personal to share with a stranger.

'I have three sisters and one brother and lots and lots of cousins.' Mary laughs but Hiroshi doesn't know it's because everyone at Erambie has a big family.

'I am Japanese,' he says with pride. 'Yamato.'

She giggles a little because she knows he is Japanese but doesn't know what Yamato means. She says it back to him, hoping she's pronouncing it properly. 'Yah-mah-toe.'

'Yes.' Hiroshi relaxes his shoulders at the sound of Mary's voice. It is soft and gentle and brings peace to his troubled mind. It is a voice that makes him feel safe and warm inside. But it is awkward, unusual for him, a Japanese man to be talking to a Westerner *and* a woman, in such close promiximity and about his personal life. But war makes a man desperate and he is just a man, and there have been no female voices for so long. No women to talk to, to look at, to smell, to share anything of life with. He becomes suddenly aware of how much he misses female company and the comfort it brings. Masao has been his only close companion since he's been in Cowra, and now he could be dead. Masao, his loyal confidant in the camp, was true to the meaning of his name – righteous – and Hiroshi knows his friend would do what was morally right and commit suicide.

'What is Yah-mah-toe?'

'Yamato are the main people in my country. We are the people who come from Japan, not like other peoples who have settled there in many regions of my country,' Hiroshi says with pride. Although he is ashamed of being a prisoner of war, he will always be proud to be Yamato. 'The Koreans and the Taiwanese in my country are sometimes called Japanese but they are not Yamato. There were Koreans in the camp too, Mary. Here, in Cowra, and I think maybe the guards might have thought they were Japanese too. Some people think we look the same and so they say we are all one people.'

'Ah, I see,' Mary says, but she doesn't really understand and she walks towards the lantern. 'I will see you tomorrow,' she says, 'with more food.'

'I will see you tomorrow,' Hiroshi repeats, already counting down the hours and minutes to more contact with the outside world. With Mary and her food. Maybe tomorrow he will ask for the newspaper, but right now he is grateful for the girl who is simply being kind to him.

8 AUGUST 1944: PRISONERS ESCAPE FROM CAMP
A number of prisoners of war escaped from the internment camp at Cowra at an early hour on Saturday morning. The district is being thoroughly patrolled by members of the military and police forces.

Individuals may attempt to secure assistance and evade capture. Any person approached for help in this way should immediately inform the military or police authorities.

Mary reads the *Cowra Guardian* spread out on the large oval dining table she is supposed to be polishing. Mr Smith is out and Mrs Smith is having a lie down – she has a headache. Mary assumes it's from having to live with Mr Smith, because he'd give anyone a headache. She keeps reading and learns that the censorship authorities have said that the media are not to report anything about the breakout beyond the statement issued by the prime minister, which is yet to be released.

Any person approached for help should immediately inform the military or police authorities. Mary rereads the line and knows how much trouble her family will be in if anyone finds out about Hiroshi. Mary knew enough about her family's history to know why her parents were hiding him. She also knows her parents would never go to the gundyibuls – ever. It was the gundyibuls who took her mum's sisters and brothers away years ago. No one knew that the police had the power to do that, they thought only the Welfare Board stole children. But since that day, when Mary's mum was only a child, Joan had said she would never help the gundyibuls with anything.

Mary memorises as much of the information as possible to report back to her parents before she finishes polishing the table and repositions the paper exactly where she found it. The locals rarely have newspapers in their homes and if someone manages to get their hands on one, it gets passed around, which means sometimes the news may be days old by the time they get to read it. As she recounts the facts in her head, Mary feels like a spy – a good spy – even though she knows the Japanese are doing evil things in the war, they are Allies with the Germans, who are doing bad things in Europe. But still she wants to outsmart the authorities. She knows enough to know that war is tragic. It rips families and nations apart. War scars the bodies and minds of innocent individuals forever. Mary is pretty sure nothing good has ever come of war, but she can't help feeling a little grateful for war bringing Hiroshi to Erambie. Hiroshi has already made her life more interesting.

On the way home, Mary bumps into Aunty Marj, who is standing at the front of her hut, alone.

'Hello, my girl, how was King Billie today?'

'Oh, all right, I guess.' Mary prefers not to talk about the Manager at all, and she wonders why her Aunt doesn't call him John Smith in front of her like her father does.

'You be careful walking around this place alone, now, you know about that breakout, don't you?'

'Yes, Aunt, Dad told me.'

'Well, those Japs, they're a real threat to Australia.'

'Yes, Aunt.' Mary is anxious to move on and not talk about anything related to the Japanese.

'They are the most dangerous of all the enemy forces,' Marj whispers. 'And it's us against them.'

'I better get home, Aunt.' Mary kisses Marj on the cheek and walks away.

'Mum, Dad,' she says as soon as she gets home. 'I have some news.' She wants to tell them before she forgets what she's read.

The three of them sit at the kitchen table as she shares her news in a low voice. 'The military authorities have said that the escape happened at two am on Saturday but they don't know yet how many prisoners broke out.' Mary looks at her father, who says nothing.

Joan parcels up Hiroshi's food. 'We don't have much for you to take down tonight, Mary. There's nothing in the garden and only a small bit of damper, and a tiny apple Sid dropped in. It'll have to do.' She hands the package to Mary. 'There's nothing from Fred, and I reckon that's because he's worried about Marj getting suspicious. Here's a jar of water, the lid's on tight. Get him to drink it while you are there so you can bring it back.'

'Hiroshi will be grateful,' Mary says, glad there is something to take so she can at least see him again. Her parents look at her in shock and she realises she hasn't told them she knows his name. 'That's his name. He speaks English.'

'What?'

'Really?' Banjo says. 'He never said a word when I found him and raced him to the shelter – I just assumed he only spoke his own lingo and when we walked down the lot, I just did this.' Banjo puts his finger up to his lips. 'How good is his English then?'

'I don't know, he just said his name was Hiroshi and that he was Japanese, Yamato. It means the original people of Japan. Like us, I guess.' Mary is surprised at how much she remembers and how interested she has become in wanting to know more. She is an intelligent and inquisitive young woman but having to leave school to work for the Smiths means there is a lot of education she's missed out on. What she knows about the world generally is what she reads sporadically in the newspaper.

'You're not supposed to be spending too much time there, Mary. I told you, just deliver the food, get him to drink the water, be kind, and leave.' Joan will help Hiroshi but she doesn't want her daughter being anything more than hospitable. There is no need for it, and nothing good that can come of it. 'You don't have to be friends,' she adds sternly.

Mary thinks her mother is overreacting, considering all she did was learn his name. She is a good girl, a good Catholic girl, she was even baptised at St Raphael's. Mary still says her nightly prayers without any prompting from her parents. Even so, sometimes she thinks that even her very Catholic mother can have some un-Christian ways.

Visiting Hiroshi is easier than the night before: she has a name now, she knows he speaks English. 'Hello,' she says as she lights the lantern.

Hiroshi is waiting for her. The day has been long and lonely but he knew that at the end of it, she would come with food and with her caring face and kindness. And here she is.

'Konnichiwa,' he says quietly. 'It is hello in my language,' he says, patting his chest. 'Kon-eech-ee-wa.' He sounds out the word slowly so she has a chance to hear it again.

'Kon-eech-ee-wa,' Mary says, happy to learn a new, greeting. She smiles because she feels like she mastered it quickly. 'I'm sorry, we do not have much to give you tonight, Hiroshi.' She likes the sound of his name – exotic, different, close to the sound of 'hero'. 'Here is some damper, an apple and some water.' She hands him the wrapped food and the jar she carried in her pocket.

Hiroshi bows with respect. 'Please don't say sorry. *I* am sorry to be a burden, to take your family's food. Thank you for everything, the shelter.' He waves his hands to point out the safety of his surroundings, and although he wants to wait until she is gone to eat, he is starving and unwraps the food straight away. He sits down without looking at her. The food barely touches his tongue, is almost swallowed whole. It disappears so quickly Mary feels sorry for him, wishing she had more to give. He drinks and hands back the jar without her instructing him to do so.

'Do you like the damper?'

'This taste is new to me. It is –' he smacks together lips that are dry from the doughy food, '– is it a little bit sweet?' He isn't sure how to describe the taste. 'Can I ask you something?' he says shyly.

40

'Of course.'

'Where am I?' He looks upwards.

'This is Erambie Station,' she says. 'Some people call it a mission, it used to be a reserve where Black people camped.'

'Erambie,' he says.

'Some people reckon Erambie means yabbie.'

Hiroshi frowns and repeats, 'Yab-bee.'

'My dad says Erambie means waterhole, because we are so close to the Lachlan River.'

'Who lives here? Are they all . . .' He pauses. 'Are they all like you?' He rubs the skin on his arm.

Mary laughs. 'Yes,' she says. 'Everyone who lives here is Black.'

Hiroshi nods, suddenly more interested in this place so close to the prisoner of war camp that has only Black people living in it. His experience with white people at war had been horrific, except for the guards in the compound, who, for the most part, treated him well. Other than that he knows that white people call the Japanese yellow people. He doesn't think he looks yellow. He wonders what other colour people might be in this country.

'This land, here where we are, around town, all of Cowra, and where you were up at the camp –' Mary struggles to find the words to explain the enormous size of Wiradjuri land. 'All the land around this area for hundreds of miles belongs to Aboriginal people. This is Wiradjuri land. You are called Yamato; we call the original people here Wiradjuri. Aboriginal people.' She puts a hand to her chest. 'Have you heard of Aboriginal people before?'

'Yes, I have read the word in the newspaper but I do not really understand anything about the people or what Aboriginal really means.'

'Erambie is a place where Aboriginal people live, it's thirty-two acres in size, so sometimes we just call it 32 Acres. It's a mile from town, so you probably ran about four miles or more to get here.' Mary isn't sure about the distance or if he understands everything she is saying, or if she is going into too much unnecessary detail, but she keeps talking because she rarely gets the chance to talk about being Aboriginal or living on Erambie to anyone who's white, even though she knows that the Japanese aren't really white. She thinks they are yellow too, because that's what the newspapers and people in town always say, even though Hiroshi doesn't really look yellow to her. She too wonders how many colours of people there are in the world.

'We live on the land in the hut that you were hiding under. It's known as Number Sixteen. Most of the people living here are Wiradjuri people from around this area. Most of the families are local but others have come from Tumut, Brungle, Griffith and Yass, also Wiradjuri country. Some people have married into the Erambie community. My Uncle Kevin reckons some people come to Cowra searching for the good-looking women here. He reckons we are famous for them.' Mary blushes. She doesn't want Hiroshi to think she means she's good looking.

'We have a boss, a Manager called John Smith. He tells us what to do, where we can go. He decides whether we can leave here and who is allowed to visit, who we can marry, what time we have to be at home, if we can go to the city.' Mary lists all the restrictions in one breath. 'So it's kind of like being in a prison, like you were up there, because we have rules and regulations with someone in charge to boss the "captives" around. Like POWs, Blacks are constantly supervised, checked and rechecked, we have little or no income and much of our food is given to us. They're called rations.'

Hiroshi is overwhelmed with all the information about the other prison camp Mary lives in. He's also a little surprised the girl talks so much to a stranger, a Japanese soldier, but thinks maybe the people at this place are very different to other places. She is not like Japanese women who would never give so much information to a stranger, and certainly not a man. But he is thankful for her openness, making his circumstances just a little less tragic.

'Do you work?'

'I work for Mr Smith. I clean his house and help his wife, Mrs Smith. Most of the women here do domestic work, washing or cleaning at people's places. My mum works at the convent and the church. Sometimes I help her if there's lots of work to do. It's all they think Aboriginal women are good for.'

Mary sounds angry, and Hiroshi wonders if he asked the wrong question. 'I'm sorry,' he says.

'I have to go,' Mary says abruptly. 'My mother will probably be cranky with me for staying here too long.'

Hiroshi nods. 'Please,' he says pleadingly, 'can you bring me a newspaper, so I can read?' He doesn't say he wants to know about the war, and he doesn't consider how it will be possible to read in the dark, but he asks anyway. 'A newspaper will give me company,' he adds, which is not a lie.

Mary doesn't know if it will be possible, so without promising anything, she says, 'I'll try.'

As she walks at speed back to the hut, Mary has already worked out a plan to get Hiroshi a newspaper. She will ask for the newspaper at the end of her working day and tell Mrs Smith that she wants to practise her reading. It's only a part-lie because she will read the newspaper before passing it on to Hiroshi – and the more she reads, the better she will get.

When Hiroshi is alone again he thinks of the Black people of Cowra and how he hadn't heard about Aboriginal people when he was at university, but then he never heard much of anything of Australia before. The talk with Mary forces him to think about the Ainu people, the Indigenous people of both Japan and Russia, but in Japan they don't get talked about much. He wishes he had taken more interest in what he'd read in the paper while at the compound. Hiroshi is just as confused about the issue of heritage and people with Ainu backgrounds as he is about Australian people. He doesn't know that the Aboriginal people of Cowra don't get talked about much either.

11 AUGUST 1944: FOOLED AGAIN! REFERENDUM PROPOSALS WILL NOT GIVE ORGANISED MARKETING

Mary reads an article to her parents about a referendum Australians will vote on. It's about the marketing of produce. She plans on giving the paper to Hiroshi later, although she has decided not to tell her parents what she has agreed to do; she knows her mother won't approve. Just like the excuse she told Mrs Smith, this is not really a lie because she is just not saying anything. She rationalises in her Catholic mind that 'partial lies' for a good cause are a Christian act, just like feeding Hiroshi. Mary wishes she could get books for Hiroshi, but there are no books near her to be gotten. She knows there is a Literary Institute in Brisbane Street, but it's not free to borrow books from there.

'Bloody voting! If I had the right to vote, I'd vote out this blasted government and give us some rights,' Banjo proclaims, distressed at the reminder that he has no rights to his own land.

Mary and her mother say nothing. They let Banjo wrestle with his own thoughts, knowing full well there is nothing either of them can say or do to appease him or change the reality for their mob, voting in a referendum or anything else.

When Mary makes her trek to the air raid shelter again, she has an apple and a jar of water to give Hiroshi. It seems like the food is already dwindling and it's only been a few days. Theirs is the only family contributing regularly. The newspaper is stuck in the band of her apron and she's hoping it doesn't fall out as she walks faster than usual. She's also got a wet rag for Hiroshi to wash with. Frost is due to set in overnight, and she wonders how cold Hiroshi must be every night with no fire and only one thin blanket. She starts to think about how she can get him something to make life in the shelter more comfortable. New clothes would be a start.

Hiroshi is waiting as usual. His strict, tall posture makes the moment feel more official than Mary had planned, or hoped for. 'Um, I only have an apple for you tonight,' she says, handing it over with the jar of water from her pocket.

Hiroshi receives both graciously, and for a fleeting moment he forgets everything about the day, about his own awkwardness and the reason he is there. The gesture of kindness overwhelms him. He's spent the last hour listening for the sound of the corrugated iron sheet being moved as his signal to stand up in readiness for Mary's entry. While he is eager for her arrival, he still feels the cultural awkwardness that any Japanese man would in the same situation, but wartime and desperation change the expectations and behaviours of everyone.

'I have this for you too,' Mary says, pulling the newspaper from under her coat and dropping the wet rag at the same time.

Hiroshi's eyes light up as if the newspaper is a block of gold that will buy him freedom and help him travel back home. 'Thank you,' he says, then, 'arigatō. Thank you, in my language.'

He becomes completely preoccupied with reading the paper, hunger and thirst momentarily forgotten until Mary points to the jar. He gulps the water with a passion she's never seen before.

He hands the jar back and they both stand there. He doesn't want to talk any more, he just wants to read the paper.

'I must go,' she says and turns to the lantern.

'Please,' Hiroshi says desperately, 'please can you leave the lantern on so I can read?'

Mary knows the bunker will be dark without it and she is torn. How will she explain the need for more kerosene when it runs out more quickly than expected? It doesn't matter. What kind of person offers someone a newspaper and then leaves them in the dark? Not a Christian, she tells herself.

'Of course,' she says. 'I will see you tomorrow.'

'I will see you tomorrow,' Hiroshi repeats then adds, 'arigatō.'

'Arigatō,' Mary says over and over to herself as she walks back home.

The next night, when Mary hands over a parcel of food, there is an apple and an orange. Hiroshi takes them enthusiastically, along with the newspaper.

'Where in Japan are you from?' she asks.

Hiroshi is surprised that anyone is interested in where he is from, and the question makes him homesick. 'My home is Shikoku Island; it means four countries.'

Mary immediately wonders if Japan is divided up like Australia, with tribal land like Wiradjuri and Yorta Yorta land further south, but she doesn't want to confuse Hiroshi by asking, so she just lets him keep talking.

'There is Ehime, Kagawa, Tokushima and my home province is Kochi.' Hiroshi proudly talks about his home. 'Shikoku is Japan's fourth largest island, and many men at the camp are from where I call home. Most of them went to the war in New Guinea.'

Mary is trying to imagine what Hiroshi's home looks like. 'Is the land like it is here?' she asks.

'I don't really know what the land is like here, Mary,' he says, not wanting to make her feel silly, but still compelled to tell the truth. When he broke out it was pitch black and after he was discovered under the hut, he took little notice of what anything looked like as he was rushed down the yard to the bunker. 'But maybe if I tell you about my home you can tell me if it sounds the same?'

'Yes,' Mary says enthusiastically.

'My island has very high mountains and steep slopes. Because it is so hilly there is not a lot of farming but we do have rice and vegetables, and we grow fruit.'

'We have farms too, but we don't have that many mountains here,' Mary says. 'We have Billy Goat Hill,' she continues quickly, feeling a little silly saying it, because it's just a hill, but she hasn't been anywhere else to see big mountains. 'Maybe when the war is over you will be able to see more of the land around here. My mum calls it God's country.' At that Mary is reminded that her mother will be counting the minutes. 'I'm sorry, I really must go now Hiroshi, but we will talk again.' Hiroshi offers a respectful nod of acknowledgement even though he is disappointed that their conversation has been cut short again.

As she walks back to the hut Mary is eager for the night to be over and the new day to start so she can look at the Smiths' atlas. She wants to see how far Hiroshi's home is from hers, what the fourth largest island of Japan actually looks like and if it is bigger than Australia. She also wants to know where New Guinea is. Mary is aware that she's never even thought about other countries much before. Life at Erambie, working for the Smiths every day, means she's missed out on a lot. But she now has a new found thirst for knowledge and for that she thanks Hiroshi.

4

Banjo has landed a carpentry job rebuilding a barn for a local farmer. It's a big job and there's a couple of other Aboriginal men and some local whitefellas there too. The Aboriginal men are chosen for the job because they are good craftsmen.

Working together provides a chance for the men to whine about their wives, talk about what's happening in town, who's playing the best football and today, most importantly to Banjo, to hear what people know about the breakout. There is still nothing in the papers but rumours are flying around town and, like everyone else, he has no idea how long the war will go on, so any more information he can get will be useful.

As the men put their woodworking skills into action and the smell of sawdust fills their nostrils, Bill, a local whitefella, starts to speak. Banjo's ears prick up.

'I hear they haven't caught all those bloody Jap bastards yet,' Bill says. 'I've got the wife locked inside when I'm not there, and a bloody shotgun at the ready.'

'Me too,' another whitefella chimes in. 'Bad enough they kill our men in action and treat them like dirt as POWs, but the nerve of them to break out into our town. Shoot on sight, I say.'

Banjo wants to say, *It's not your town, this place belongs to us*, but he doesn't want to draw unwanted attention to himself.

'Us whites are smarter than those yellow bastards,' Fat Bobbo says, 'and so we should've known this was going to happen.' He lights a cigarette.

'Why?' Banjo asks, ignoring the 'us whites' comment.

'Cos it'd already happened over in New Zealand – a place called Featherstone. There was a mutiny over there. The Jap bastards just refused to work or follow any orders they were given, and when the fella in charge fired a warning shot, the Japs went crazy, throwing stones at him, and then all hell broke loose. But they killed forty-eight of the yellow bastards, so that's good. Pity one of the guards died, though, and that was just unfortunate, as he was hit by a ricocheting bullet.'

'Do we really know how bad they are?' Banjo asks vaguely, sanding back a piece of wood.

'Well, I know!' Fat Bobbo fumes. 'The Allies are being tortured right now as we stand here! They use our men as target practice. *Target practice!* God knows what else is happening there. And if you don't reckon that's disgusting, then that makes you a Jap lover. Are you a Jap lover, Banjo?' Fat Bobbo asks accusingly. 'The Japs are worse than the Germans, but they're all in it together.' Some of the other men nod in agreement.

Banjo can't believe what he's hearing but doesn't want to say too much more for fear he won't be able to argue well enough without raising suspicion.

'I hardly even thought about the camp until the breakout,' a whitefella named Johnno says. 'I mean, why would I? It's not like anyone ever heads this way. And the Ities are okay, I reckon. They do the gardening at my mates' places, and I never heard of anyone having a problem with them.'

'Yeah, the Ities are okay,' Fat Bobbo says. 'Everyone knows they'd rather be here than on the warfront, that's no secret – they've got it easy. They make their own grog, they call it grappa, and they sing to the women, but I don't reckon they'll ever get any – can't go past an Australian bloke.' Fat Bobbo scratches the fat white gut that's poking through the buttons of his stretched shirt as he speaks, as if he is the most prized possession a woman in Cowra could have. 'But I don't care about the Ities at all, they'll be gone as soon as the war is over, and at least they're growing fruit and vegetables and are working at the cannery too. They make good use of themselves.' He sits down. 'Now, the Japs, on the other hand, are animals, the whole race are terrible people.'

The other men nod in agreement, but even if they didn't, no one is brave enough to argue with him because although he's unfit, everyone knows he can pack a punch and would KO anyone he threw his fist at.

'There was the bombing of Darwin, Changi, the Thai–Burma Railway, *and* the Sydney Harbour submarine attack.'

'They are literally on our doorstep,' Bill adds. 'We *should* be worried!'

'And think about Pearl Harbor,' Fat Bobbo continues, looking specifically at Banjo. 'You know about that, don't you?' Fat Bobbo thinks the Blacks are dumb and useless and sighs when Banjo gives no response. 'The Japs bombed Pearl Harbor in 1941! They killed about two and a half thousand Yanks. It was the worst fucking attack in history.'

'Where do you get all these details?' Johnno asks.

'I listen to the broadcasts on my wireless, it's a Stromberg Carlson valve radio. It's top of the line, probably the best wireless in Cowra. I hear the Japanese propaganda and Tokyo Rose too. All the anti-US stuff. So yeah, I listen to the enemy broadcasts – gotta keep one step ahead of those bastards.'

When no one says anything, Fat Bobbo goes on, preaching confidently. 'This is shit we need to be on top of, chaps. We need to know about what's going on in the world. How else are we going to keep ourselves safe from the yellow peril if we aren't one step ahead of them?

'The Japanese are the most hated race on earth and we need to fight them now, because they might invade here. They purposely crash their planes into ships. It's called a Kamikaze attack.' He does a nosedive with his hands and makes a splash and explosion sound. 'They'll do that to our ships just like they did with the Americans, and they'll start in Darwin.' Fat Bobbo is almost spitting, he is talking so fast and so passionately. He is a little scary to the other men, who still just listen and watch.

'We don't want the yellow peril here. We're *white* Australia,' Fat Bobbo states.

'But,' Banjo interrupts, 'we're not white.'

Fat Bobbo doesn't correct himself, just shrugs his shoulders. 'I reckon they should have electric fences at the camp and then the bastards can't escape. Or at least they'd get electrocuted trying to!' And he laughs his big, fat, belly laugh as if death by electrocution is hilarious.

Banjo is trying to contain the anger he can feel building up. He doesn't want to get in an argument with the whitefellas and he doesn't want to wind up the Blacks, but he's willing to take the risk. He remembers the sad, gruesome site of the dead Japanese soldiers he saw the morning after the breakout and his own sense of humanity takes over. He wasn't raised to speak with such hatred, and he doesn't want to be around it. He wonders how the hearts and minds of some people have been poisoned to such extremes.

'War is hideous, but we need to remember that soldiers, even the enemy, are human. They are men like you and me who do their best for their country. And the Japanese aren't the only ones fenced in around here. Erambie,' he says, and the white men roll their eyes. For the first time, Fat Bobbo starts to put his hammer to a nail. 'All I'm saying is that, as far as I'm concerned, there are two prison camps in Cowra. And neither of us want to be where we are, living under someone else's rules.'

'At least the Japs get fed well,' George, another Aboriginal builder, says. 'They're not on rations, are they? They get more than sugar, flour and tea. I'd rather be in *that* camp than ours.'

The men stop work and listen. Even Fat Bobbo, who's already tired from two swings of the hammer.

'How do you know that?' Banjo asks.

'Jim told me. And apparently most of them are fatter than when they arrived. And the Japs, they get rice with most meals and their fish is from New Zealand. Our fish from the Lachlan isn't even good enough for them.'

'So they are treated too good then!' Fat Bobbo says. 'They should be on rations too.'

'No one should be on rations!' Banjo is furious and forms a fist that he wants to put into Fat Bobbo's head. 'Everyone, including the prisoners of war, should be treated like human beings.'

'But look how they treat our men!' Fat Bobbo yells.

'I know what you're saying about our POWs, but you're missing my point, Bobbo! My argument is about how we are treated like prisoners too, at Erambie. We shouldn't be on rations. We should all be paid the same for the same work and have enough money to buy food for our families – not just flour, tea and sugar rations and whatever we can hunt or manage to grow. It's not fair for anyone. The prisoners of war are just like us.'

'There used to be heaps of camps around town when I was young,' George says. 'The football ground in West Cowra was a camp. So was Taragala and there was another in North Cowra.'

The other workers – except for Fat Bobbo – nod in acknowledgement; they all know the truth, they just don't talk about it much.

'And then Erambie was created, to round up all the Blacks together.'

'Oh, come on, it's not all bad,' Fat Bobbo says. 'I thought you liked living together.'

The truth is they do. And people follow other family members to Erambie to live together.

'The thing is, Bobbo, Erambie was my family home before we had to live under a Manager. My grandparents were born in Brungle but my parents were born here. This was home for them before it was turned into a reserve twenty years ago. It's home for me, it always will be. Even if we are trapped by the Manager.'

'What the hell are you saying, Banjo?' Johnno asks. 'Sometimes you speak in riddles.'

'I'm saying that this government treats its prisoners better than it treats us and so we should be angry at the government, not the Japanese POWs. These fellas are just doing their duty to their country, like Aussie soldiers are. War is not any soldier's fault.'

'We get rations given to us out of an old horse stable and what gets handed out is very little,' George adds.

'It was only a few years ago that Erambie was overcrowded with over two hundred people living on thirty-two acres.' Banjo is rubbing his lower back, which is sore from being hunched over, sanding. 'Our life is different to places like Cummeragunga; they had the same number of people living on a twenty-seven-hundred acre station.'

Fat Bobbo, obviously bored with Banjo's history lesson and the Blacks complaining generally, changes the topic. 'Did you hear the story about Walter Weir's missus at their farmhouse at Rosedale?'

'Nah, what happened?' Johnno asks, equally disinterested in Banjo talking about Erambie's history, or Erambie anything, for that matter.

'Apparently she offered some of the escaped prisoners fresh scones and tea, while their daughter Margaret went to alert the cops.' Fat Bobbo speaks as though the words leave a bitter taste in his mouth.

Banjo keeps listening, knowing that his wife would've provided the same hospitality, *was* providing the hospitality, and sending their daughter to provide food, not to dob anyone in.

Johnno jumps in with, 'That's nothing, I heard Alf Bourke and his son found a group of six Japs while they were out on a rabbiting trip near Claremont. Reckons he shot two dead in self-defence.'

Fat Bobbo pretends to fire a gun. 'I reckon he shot them dead cos he hates the Japanese bastards.'

The site supervisor walks over to see where things are up to and the men stop talking immediately. Johnno starts whistling and Fat Bobbo says, 'I'm off for a piss, when's smoko?'

'When I say so,' the supervisor says angrily, having been watching them from afar.

5

21 August 1944

When Mary takes the paper home from the Smiths' she has already decided that she won't tell her parents that twice as many voters in Cowra were against the proposed referendum changes than for them. She's fairly sure they won't care about the result – it will only start another distressing discussion about how Aboriginal people don't have the right to vote. As she walks across the mission to home, she sees a group of kids huddled around something and squealing. She starts to walk faster. When she realises Jessie is throwing up across the way, she starts to run towards her.

'What's wrong?' Mary asks, bending down and pulling the child's hair back. She smells the vomit before she sees it all over Jessie's clothes. Jessie has tears streaming down her face and when Mary wipes them away, she notices her sister is burning up. 'What's she been eating?' she asks Dottie and Betty frantically.

Dottie shrugs. 'Dunno,' she says.

'She ate too many of those nuts from the pine trees,' Betty dobs. 'She's probably sick because she didn't want to share.' She bends down and whispers in her sister's ear, 'Mum always says to share. See what happens when you're a greedy guts?'

'Stop it, Betty. Let's get her home.' Mary picks her young sister up, demonstrating a physical strength she didn't even know she had.

'*Mum*, Jessie's chucking *uuuupppp*,' Betty screams at the top of her lungs and Joan, walking back from the church where she's spent the morning cleaning, starts to run, trying not to drop the clothes Father Patrick has given her for the goothas and an old pair of pants he was throwing out. She intends to mend the hole in the bottom of them and give them to Hiroshi, who has been in the same clothes for over two weeks.

By this time there is a circle of kids making vomiting noises and laughing, and a few of the teenage boys have appeared at their hut too.

'Go find your Uncle Banjo, and tell him we're taking Jessie to the hospital,' Joan instructs Claude Williams, and he takes off with his mates in tow. He runs as fast as his legs will carry him.

'You can wait in here,' a short, round nurse says to Joan with a frown when she arrives at the hospital with Jessie.

Joan looks around. It's the linen room. She knows they isolate the Blacks at Cowra Hospital, but she's never been put in the linen room before. Once when Mary got sick at the Cowra Show they just put her in a separate room at the back of the hospital. But this is a new kind of segregation and Joan's worried about how Banjo will react when he arrives.

Jessie is asleep in her mother's arms when the doctor finally walks in to offer his services. Blacks are also the last to be seen, it seems. He takes the child's temperature and says very little before mumbling to a nurse by his side.

Joan feels like she is invisible, and asks, 'Will she be all right?'

'Temperature's down, and she hasn't vomited for –' he looks at the chart, '– two hours, so yes, I think the worst has passed.' The doctor turns to the nurse and offers instructions. 'She will bring something for the child, and you can stay here till the morning, just in case.'

Just in case what? Joan worries to herself but says nothing. All she needs to know is that the worst has passed.

Hiroshi starts to panic when Mary misses an evening visit. Is it all over? Have they changed their minds about protecting him? Are they planning to hand him over? Should he try to escape and, if so, where would he go now? He is still no better off than he was when he first left the POW camp. He has torturous hunger pangs and he spends hours pacing the small space. He loses count of how many sit-ups he does just to keep moving. He tries to do push-ups but his arms are weak from lack of nutrition and only eggs for protein. He stretches out his entire body, sore from no real exercise since the night he ran here.

When he hears the sheet of iron above move, his feelings are a mix of relief and fear. As Mary's legs appear on the ladder, his heart lifts, glad that she has returned.

'I'm so sorry,' she says, handing him some damper and a jar of water. 'Jessie was very sick at the hospital and I had to stay with the other goothas.'

Hiroshi frowns.

'Oh, children, goothas means children. I had to stay with them and couldn't come down last night. You must be starving.'

Hiroshi unwraps the damper and eats it instantly. The water disappears quickly too.

'I'm sorry Jessie was sick. What was wrong?'

'She had poisoning. She ate some nuts off a pine tree and you're not supposed to eat them. She had to stay in the hospital, which is never a good experience for Aboriginal people. Mum said they made her wait in the cupboard with all the linen – the sheets and blankets.'

'That doesn't sound right.'

'It gets worse,' Mary says. 'At the Cowra hospital there's a ward out the back for the Black people, that's where they put the Aboriginal women if they come in to have babies. My Aunt said that when she was there it had the word "ABO" written in capital letters on the sheets and the towels. It's so they don't accidentally give them to white people to use.'

'No!' Hiroshi exclaims in disbelief. 'This is how Australians treat other Australians?'

Mary gets the newspaper out of her waistband. 'I nearly forgot, here's the paper.'

Hiroshi takes it, eyes wide, always grateful. He flicks through it quickly while Mary is still there and stops.

'What is this?' Hiroshi asks Mary, pointing to the headline COWRA v. CANOWINDRA.

'Oh, that's a story about football,' she says. 'It talks about my dad's cousin Doug Williams.'

Hiroshi starts reading, '"He chased down an opposition player, bringing him down in a flying tackle."'

'Yes, that means he ran after the man with the ball and grabbed him, pushing him to the ground. That's a tackle.' Mary moves like she is going to tackle an invisible footballer. Hiroshi chuckles at the dramatics.

'The Black Diamonds are from here, Erambie,' she says proudly. 'They're legends across the region. Everyone knows about Dicky McGuinness, Viney Murray, Archie Bamblett, Harold Carberry and Doug Williams. They're our local heroes, and we're all related in some way, either by blood or by marriage, and always by this land around here.'

Hiroshi just nods, still trying to understand how everyone can be related. He thinks Mary has a very big family.

'Here in Cowra, football – footy – is very popular.' Mary loves her football as much as the others at Erambie. It's a time when all the community can have some fun, although the men are very competitive and sometimes the women too, and on occasion there's fisticuffs, as her dad calls it. 'We don't have much money here, but one ball can keep us entertained for hours.'

'Football,' Hiroshi says the word for the first time.

'Footy.'

'Footy. I like the sound of football,' Hiroshi says, then corrects himself, 'Footy.'

They both grin widely.

Mary wants to tell Hiroshi more about the Erambie Allblacks, who played their last game in 1940, and that it's the new players that are known as the Black Diamonds. But she doesn't have time to go into the history of football and simply says, 'I'll see you tomorrow.'

'Ashita mata,' Hiroshi replies. 'See you tomorrow.'

'There's the bell,' Joan sings out to her children two days later. 'School's on!'

The kids all stagger out of their bedroom, whining about having to go to school. It's only across the mission but the Williams kids drag their feet every time. The kitchen is warm and the air smells sweet and that's where they'd rather stay.

'Here's some porridge, eat it quickly and then be off,' Joan says.

Mary hopes her mother has managed to pick the weevils out of the oats. She tries her best but sometimes she doesn't have enough time and the goothas start up about it. This morning they are too concerned about having to go to school, which isn't an everyday occurrence.

'I like the days when Mr Smith is too busy for school,' Dottie says.

'Me too, the days when the bell *doesn't* ring are the best!' Jessie agrees, having fully recovered from her hospital visit.

'Just finish your breakfast and go,' Joan says, trying to get around with James stuck to her leg. 'And be polite!' she instructs. Joan doesn't have much faith in the mission school, it's hit and miss and she believes it's second-rate teaching. 'The government must think it's good enough for the Black kids,' she's been known to say when the kids are at home for days on end.

'It's a waste of time, we don't learn anything. Mary would be a better teacher than Mr Smith or his wife,' Betty grumbles as she ushers her younger sisters out the door. She isn't a fan of the school and some days when she goes home for lunch, she convinces her mother to let her stay home and help clean.

Mary crosses the mission to the Manager's house. It's a blue-sky day but the cold wind stings her face; she had some porridge but it wasn't enough to warm her properly. She sees a magpie and stops in her tracks. She recalls the saying that Uncle Kevin has taught her, has taught them all: One for sorrow, two for joy, three for girls, four for boys, five for silver, six for gold, seven for stories that have never been told.

She knows she has to see another magpie quickly so that there is joy, not sorrow. She spends the whole day looking out the window as often as she can to see a second magpie, hoping there won't be any bad news about Hiroshi being found, or anyone she knows getting sick, or worse, dying.

As she finishes washing the dishes that night there is a knock on the Smiths' door. It's a young Murray fella, her second cousin about the same age as Betty, who is usually very quiet. He's been crying and is breathing heavily when Mr Smith opens the door.

'What is it then?' Smith says coldly, not acknowledging the lad's distress.

'My mum had a baby,' the boy sobs, 'but it died.' And he pushes himself into the belly of the Manager for comfort.

Mary drops the metal bowl she's drying. 'One for sorrow,' she says out loud. She knows she will be the one to break the news to her parents when she goes home.

Smith puts one hand on the boy's shoulder momentarily and then steps back.

The next day the community is in mourning. A stillbirth is something difficult for people to fathom, but there is no decent medical help for pregnant women at Erambie. Many of them don't go to the hospital to give birth, and most babies are born in the huts. There is a funeral at the Baptist church on the mission and everyone is solemn, even the kids who are usually boisterous and noisy are behaving themselves. Joan hasn't stopped crying since Mary broke the news.

'We had a funeral today, a little baby girl, who never got to breathe at all. She was born dead,' Mary tells Hiroshi when she goes to see him. A single tear drops from her eye.

'In the hospital?' Hiroshi asks. 'Was it the hospital's fault, because they don't treat your family properly?'

'No, we really only go to the hospital if it's an emergency, like when Jessie was poisoned,' Mary says softly. 'It is so very sad, but I knew something bad was going to happen. We have ways of knowing things will happen. We have messengers, animals. There is a small bird called a willy wagtail, it's black with a white belly. They usually have white eyebrows and little white whiskers too. It always wags its tail, that's where it got its name from. We believe if you see one of these willy wagtails, if it comes and sits on the fence, for example, then it usually brings bad news. That we will get bad news.'

'And did you see this bird?' Hiroshi asked.

'No, I saw another bird, it's called a magpie, and it has a lot of meanings. It can bring different messages. There is a saying: One for sorrow, two for joy, three for girls, four for boys, five for silver, six for gold, seven for stories that have never been told.' Mary breaks down, sobbing.

Hiroshi doesn't quite know what to do. It has been a long time since he saw a woman cry, not since he said goodbye to Benika, and that was completely different. He could comfort Benika, put his arms around her. He cannot do this with Mary. He stands awkwardly, waiting for her tears to stop. When they do, he talks about the magpies back in Japan.

'In my country we have a story about magpies as well. It is related to the Star Festival, the Tanabata, and it celebrates the meeting of two stars. It is the story of the Weaver Girl and the Cow Herder. There is a weaving princess, she is the daughter of the sky, and her name is Orihime. She weaves beautiful clothes, she worked very hard to weave and her father loved her work. But then she was sad because she worked so hard and never had time to meet anyone, so her father arranged for her to meet a cow herder by the name of Hikobishi, who lived on the other side of the Amanogawa River from her. They fell in love instantly and married quickly.

'But Orihime stopped weaving and Hikobishi let his cows roam all over, so the weaving princess's father separated them back to opposite sides of the river. Orihime cried so much her father said that if she worked hard enough he would let the two meet on the seventh day of the seventh month. But there was no bridge to cross for them to meet. This is where the magpies come into it. A flock of magpies knew that Orihime kept crying so they decided to use their wings to make a bridge across the river, and then she could cross and be with her love. Legend has it that if the weather is bad on Tanabata, if there is too much rain, then the magpies won't come and the two lovers must wait for another year to see each other.'

Mary is crying again by the end of the story. 'That is really beautiful,' she says. She cannot believe that a man who has been to war, who has been a prisoner in the camp in Cowra, who is living in the dark under the ground, is also capable of telling such a beautiful story. Mary loves Hiroshi's magpie story. She imagines she and Hiroshi are like two magpies connecting worlds and wishes she could sit and listen to his stories all night. Mary knows Hiroshi has been through so many terrible things and yet he knew just what to say to make her feel better.

When Mary walks back into the hut she has made sure her face is not flushed from seeing Hiroshi and listening to the story he told. The ladies are all there playing cards. One way to deal with grief is to sit together with cups of tea and play cards. Cooncan is the most common game played. Marj is known as a hustler, Ivy is the cautious one and Joan is the peacemaker when there is conflict. There are often about six women around the table and on those nights the men are outside, preferring to leave the women to themselves.

The mission kids love it when all the Aunties get together and play cards, as they gossip and talk about who's kissing who and tell stories and laugh really loud. Aunty Marj has the biggest laugh because she has the biggest belly, or so Kevin says, and the kids agree.

'Now, you know I'm not one to gossip,' Marj says in her butter-wouldn't-melt-in-her-mouth tone. 'And you know I love Banjo like my own brother,' she adds to Joan. 'But, someone in town told someone else who told Rosie down at Ryan's who told me just this morning, that Banjo was defending the Japanese to whitefellas at work.'

'Don't be silly,' Joan says, glancing at Mary. 'Banjo doesn't even know any Japanese. Why would he be defending them?' She looks at her cards but Mary can tell her mother isn't focused on the game at all.

'Should I put the kettle on, Aunty Marj?' she interrupts.

'Yes, thank you, my girl,' Marj answers, still staring at Joan. 'Now, I'm not saying that this is true, or that this is right or wrong, Joan, no, I'm not. Far be it from me to offer judgement on anyone, Black, white or brindle – or yellow, in the case of the Japs – but I did feel it was my role as a good friend and neighbour to you and Banjo, and because, well, we don't keep anything from each other ever, now, do we? So I thought that

I should tell you what *someone* was saying about your husband. Because you know, it reflects on all of us, being friends and relatives. Not that I care one bit about gossip or what other people think or say, as you'd both know, because people who gossip have nothing better to do with their time, as we know, and . . .'

Mary is rolling her eyes as her Aunty Marj is rambling, but no one can see her. She wishes that if her Aunt had something to say, she'd just say it.

'Rummy,' Ivy says, putting her cards on the table, taking the pennies from the middle and saving Joan and Mary from any more of Marj's blathering.

Marj gets up in a huff at losing. 'Where's my tea?' She starts fussing with the kettle and looks out the back window. 'Who's that?'

Mary panics – her Aunt has spotted Hiroshi. She looks out the window and sees him roaming the yard with his shoes off. He's smiling like he's enjoying the touch of the dried grass under his feet.

'Fred, Fred!' Marj is squealing hysterically. 'Fred, come quickly!'

Mary drops the kettle on the floor, it's all she can think to do to distract Marj. 'Argh!' she screams, although the hot water has not hit her.

'What have you done, Mary? *Fred!*' Marj yells.

Ivy, Joan and finally Marj make their way to Mary's side, trying to clean the water up, as Fred walks in.

'What is wrong, woman, a man can't have a quiet smoke with the other fellas without you bellowing across the mission? Everyone can hear you.'

'Outside.' Marj motions to the back door. 'Look outside!'
By the time Fred gets to the back door, Hiroshi has gone.

'We saw you today,' Mary says with a hint of anxiety and anger in her voice. 'Walking around up there.' She points to the outside world. 'You can't do that, Hiroshi, it's too dangerous.' There is desperation in her voice as she recalls her Aunt Marj calling out to Uncle Fred.

Hiroshi hangs his head like a chastised child. 'I am sorry,' he says softly. 'I am sorry.'

Mary doesn't know what to do. She wants to touch his arm gently, to apologise for her tone, but she knows that would be inappropriate. But she needs him to understand how reckless his actions were. 'Hiroshi, not everyone knows you're here. If other people see you they will call the police. Why were you up there?'

Hiroshi sighs and smiles. 'The fresh air, Mary, the soft grass, the sunshine and blue sky.' He looks around the dark, damp space. 'I am going a little crazy in here. I can only smell myself and feel the dirt. I just had to go outside. I am sorry.' He hangs his head again.

'We will figure something out, I promise.' Mary puts her hand on his shoulder, hoping the action is more sisterly and less intimate than a touch to the bare skin of an arm or hand.

6

On 1st September, Mary reads a war bonds advertisement in the *Guardian* out loud to her parents. "'Journey's End for a Japanese,'" she begins, and they all peer at the newspaper and the photo of a plane plummeting into the ocean. They listen intently as she continues, hands wrapped around their mugs of black tea. "'Crashing into the sea, with its torpedo undischarged, the Jap torpedo plane is yet another we won't have to worry about on our way to Tokyo. This sort of thing has been happening on the sea, on the land, and in the air, from the time that our bonds provided the equipment our men needed to beat the Jap wherever they met him.

"'We will have to down thousands more planes like this, sink more Jap ships, and dig many more Nips out of foxholes before we win victory. We've got the men to do it – and all that we have to do is to see that they have the equipment that the job needs.

'"Our money has been fighting – and it has to keep on fighting until victory is won. Make an advance subscription to the Second Victory Loan."'

When Mary stops reading, the three Williams all feel the same level of discomfort at the language the paper uses – 'Japs' and 'Nips' – and even though they feel uncomfortable with it, no one really knows how to voice their opinions. Banjo has been called a 'Black bastard' on the job, and Joan has been referred to as a 'Black gin' more than once; it is language that is normal in town, but normal doesn't mean it's right or that they remain unaffected by it. Either way, name-calling, such as that in the newspaper, is not something any of them approve of.

'Even if I had the money, I wouldn't donate to war bonds,' Joan says, taking another sip of tea.

Banjo blows smoke through his nose and says, 'Fat Bobbo was talking about the "yellow peril" at work the other day. Apparently, we're supposed to be concerned about the possible threat of hordes of Asians heading our way.'

'I understand some of our mob are upset, we can't just ignore they bombed Pearl Harbor, or what's happened in Malaya.' Joan pauses. 'It's all horrible. The Newtons will never get over Bibby not coming home.' She shakes her head and swallows, starting to cry. 'Everyone is angry, everyone. It's only natural people are going to be afraid of the Japanese. What are we doing, Banjo? Maybe Kevin was right.'

Banjo stands as fast as his dodgy leg will allow and puts his strong arms around his wife.

Mary knows her parents nearly always agree on things, and if her mother is having second thoughts and wants to turn Hiroshi in, then her father will most likely go along with it. She says nothing.

'Love, Hiroshi may be a Japanese soldier, but he has done us no harm. We are doing the right thing.'

Joan nods into his chest.

When Mary sees Hiroshi waiting patiently that night, the story, its disturbing language and the image of death that accompanied it are forgotten, and she is glad. She feels like a food angel, and has brought with her some jasmine from the Smiths' garden. She hopes it will help to make the small space smell better in light of Hiroshi's recent escape into the fresh air and daylight.

In only a month they have reached a place where silence is comfortable but rare, where the exchange of food and a newspaper is secondary to the exchange of a smile or a warm glance, where the sound of Hiroshi's voice brings peace to an existence that is far from peaceful.

Mary hands the paper over gently, as if there are only peaceful stories in it, and not the advertisement she has felt ill about while walking over. She thinks about the planes diving into the sea, glad that Hiroshi is safe from what is continuing in the Pacific. She carefully passes him a parcel of still warm rabbit stew.

'Some of the young fellas caught some rabbits. Locals reckon that's why they're so good at football, cos they're quick on their feet when they chase the rabbits with sticks. Anyway, my mum makes the best stew around,' she says proudly, convinced Hiroshi will love it as much as she does.

'Rabbit,' Hiroshi says. He has never eaten it but doesn't care, because he is hungry and eating far less than he did in the compound. He opens the package and takes a mouthful, savouring the taste on his tongue, chewing the meat over and over again to make it last. 'Mmm,' he says. 'I have never tasted anything like this before, Mary. It is . . . strange.'

'Oh,' Mary says, disappointed.

'No, strange is the wrong word, it is different, it tastes different from what I know, that is all. It is different, but very good.'

'What do you normally eat?' she asks, as Hiroshi puts another piece of rabbit to his lips. He swallows quickly so he can answer.

'At home I ate rice and fish and vegetables.'

Mary's stomach begins to grumble. She would love some rice and fish and more vegies, something other than potatoes. All at once, if she could. She doesn't remember the last time she felt really full.

'The Shimanto River where I live is full of shrimp and sweet fish,' he continues.

'Fish from the river, like the river here?' Mary asks.

'Yes, but we also get fish from the sea, and sometimes we don't cook the fish.'

'You mean you eat it raw?' Mary asks, screwing up her face.

'Yes, raw,' Hiroshi repeats. 'We eat raw fish. And my father is from the Kagawa prefecture, and they eat udon noodles with soy sauce, so my mother makes that a lot too.' Hiroshi is talking about food like a man who hasn't eaten well for a long time. Mary feels as if she has never eaten well *ever*. Both their stomachs grumble and Mary's mouth waters at the thought of eating shrimp and udon noodles even though she has no idea what either of them are.

'What about rabbit?' Mary asks. 'And other meat?'

'No, we don't eat a lot of meat, Mary, and definitely not rabbits. We have a story in Japan about rabbits.' Hiroshi thinks back to his childhood and the tale he heard that had been passed on from generation to generation for centuries.

'I love stories,' Mary says.

'If you look at the moon, when it is big,' Hiroshi says, moving his hands to make a circle.

'Full, when it is a full moon.' Mary gestures to make a full circle too.

'When it is a full moon, you can see a shadow where there is a rabbit pounding a mochi rice cake.' Hiroshi experiences a hunger pang at the thought of the glutinous rice cake he remembers enjoying most as a child, especially at Japanese New Year. He loved watching his mother pound the rice into a paste and then mould it into a special shape, usually a rabbit. When his father wasn't looking, she would create something else, like a cat or a star. 'Autumn is the best time to look at the moon and see the rabbit,' Hiroshi says.

'Really? I will look very hard at the next full moon and see if I can see the rabbit.'

They stare at each other for a few seconds, until both feel uncomfortable with the intimacy of the moment and glance away.

'It's time,' Mary says, disappointed that each visit seems to go faster than the one before. She climbs up the ladder.

On the way back to the hut, Mary looks at the sky in the hope of seeing the moon and the rabbit pounding the mochi cake, but the sky is blanketed in clouds and she sees nothing.

She will look again tomorrow and the next night, and keep looking until she can see what Hiroshi sees. She will search for the two stars also. She wants to see the same sky that Hiroshi has seen. She hopes they can both see the sky together one night soon.

The scent of jasmine lingers and soothes Hiroshi to sleep, but he is soon woken by a violent nightmare, drenched with sweat. The war bonds advertisement that caused Joan to cry has also brought to the surface Hiroshi's painful memories of his role in the war: the military training he endured with all the other eligible Japanese men between twenty and forty years of age. Hiroshi was glad that students like him were given a reprieve for the compulsory medical and that it didn't happen until after he had at least finished his degree. But it didn't matter how old he was or how long it had been delayed, the training still offered the same torture, the same physical and psychological trauma to each and every man. He knew some men who died in training and many more who were treated worse than in war. Some of the memories of training were fiercer than those of combat, because it was his own men inflicting the pain.

When Hiroshi passed his physical examination, he was classified as 'adequate for soldier', and then ordered to enlist. He wasn't like Masao, who joined the army voluntarily at fifteen – Hiroshi was still at school and enjoying teenage life when he was fifteen; he didn't believe in war, and he didn't want to be a soldier. He'd never once imagined being in the Japanese Army. He dreamt of being an artist, a writer; he loved poetry, he read poetry, he recited poetry, and when he was in the camp, he would occasionally write poetry.

In the dark of night, trying to bring peace to his mind, Hiroshi attempts to remember lines of his favourite works, the Haiku that he read in the library and with his girlfriend, Benika. His favourite Haiku poet had always been Japan's most famous, Bashō, and he starts reciting out loud:

> *The smoke at the place*
> *where, on this day of o'bon,*
> *death, and life reborn*

The words make him think of the burning huts at the compound. Even though he didn't help put the firewood underneath them, all the Japanese soldiers knew the plan to burn them down. He wonders how many of his own men died that night; if any managed to escape fully. He tries to believe that Masao is still alive, but there are no guarantees, and no news. His eyes well with tears that have been building for months, years – perhaps his whole lifetime. He sits there shivering as the cold air from above penetrates the shelter, the corrugated iron doing little to protect him when it hits his sweaty clothes.

Hiroshi knows the only thing that will soothe his mind is writing a letter to his parents, to confess the shame of not dying in the war. A letter to relieve himself of the burden of the shame he carries. A letter to relieve his mother of her heartache, to tell her that her son is alive.

He lies down and waits for sleep to find him. He thinks about how he will eventually get home. Will he have to wait until the war is over? Should he ask Mary for help to get to a boat? When will he be able to feel the sunshine on his face again? He wants his chaotic mind to stop – stop thinking about war and death, and stop stealing hope from him. He thinks of Mary, picturing her handing him food, offering him comfort, and that thought puts his mind and body at ease. He thinks he is a different man when he is with her. He breathes in the jasmine again. He feels the tension drain from his neck and recites out loud another of Bashō's Haikus while he thinks of her, wishing he was living Bashō's words:

> *The irises, they*
> *do too, tell of the pleasures*
> *of the sojourn, no?*

Mary's heart sinks the minute she lays eyes on Hiroshi the next day. It is clear that he has had little sleep: his face looks tired, eyes bloodshot, and his smile is slower to form than on previous days. He slumps when he stands to welcome her.

'Are you all right?' she asks, knowing full well that no one could be all right in his circumstances. Mary wishes she could give him a hug. She is on the brink of tears looking at him.

'Can I have some paper please?' he says softly. 'To write a letter to my mother.'

'Yes, I'll bring you some paper tomorrow.' Mary's heart aches for Hiroshi. She can't begin to imagine how much he must miss his family. She is determined that she will get some paper and more kerosene for the lantern and some matches, but she knows she will have to steal it all. This fact does not deter her at all. Stealing in this instance will be the right thing to do.

She does not stay long; the mood in the shelter is intense and sad, and she is wise enough, even at her age, to know that sometimes people need to be left alone, even when they are alone most of the time. She hands Hiroshi more of the rabbit stew her mother says they'll be eating for weeks – and bounding like bunnies afterwards.

He takes it gratefully, and she leaves without another word.

It's 3 September 1944, and Mary skims the newspaper for her own interest before she gives it to Hiroshi. There's plenty about dances, theatre, meetings, balls, and a boring gossip column, but absolutely nothing about the loss of life on Cowra's doorstep.

But no coverage means no mention of the soldier still missing and this is the daily relief that she requires. It's as if the army hasn't yet realised that Hiroshi has not been found, dead or alive. She's grateful anyway; it's better for him to be invisible in the big scheme of things, that way there is more hope for the future.

The most interesting thing in the *Guardian* is a story about Cowra beating Orange in the football. The names Murray, Bamblett and McGuiness are mentioned and when she shows him, Hiroshi seems as pleased as she is that they are highlighted in the paper. He has never met any of these men but, thanks to Mary, he understands that they are important to the community and most of them, in some way, are her family. He has lost track of how many cousins and second cousins she has, but loves that her family is so large and so close, even though it's a sad reminder that his isn't.

'In the compound,' Mary begins bravely and somewhat boldly, 'what did you do for entertainment? Did you play sport?' She knows this might be a stupid question, but surely they were outside during the day and she really wants to know what life in the compound was like. She rarely sees Jim, the only Aboriginal guard up there, so there's no one else to ask.

'We played a lot of baseball,' Hiroshi says.

'Baseball?' Mary asks. 'I've heard of baseball, but I don't know the rules.'

'It's an American game, with a bat and a ball, and men run around a diamond.' He draws a diamond in the air with his finger.

Mary sees a connection and is excited. 'We have a game here called rounders, it sounds a little like your baseball. You hit the ball with a wooden bat, sometimes we use a cricket bat that my dad made out of wood, but some of the boys will just use a broom handle if they have to. You have to hit the ball and then run from base to base and get there before the ball is thrown there. Is that the same as baseball?'

'Yes, that sounds a lot like baseball. It's called rounders?'

'Yes.' Mary doesn't understand how or why the Japanese are playing American baseball. 'How do you know this American game, though, and aren't you at war with the Americans?'

'We played baseball when I was at university. We have been playing baseball in Japan for many, many years. It is very popular. We had a baseball team in the 1880s but the year I was born, in 1919 is when Japan first got two professional teams. It's strange now; Japan and America are at war. We hate each other. I don't know if we will have baseball again when I go home.'

Mary is taken aback by the comment. Hiroshi talking about going home upsets her; she doesn't want him to leave. But Hiroshi hasn't seen the change in her expression and keeps talking.

'Back home I followed the Yomiuri Giants. We called them the Tokyo Giants.' Hiroshi laughs for the first time in months. He shakes his head. 'Tokyo Giants is so American. We are so much like the country we are at war with.'

'And you played baseball in the camp?'

'Yes, we made the baseball gloves ourselves from old boots, and masks for the catcher. We would take one grille out of the Kendo masks we used in our own Japanese martial arts and we would turn it into a catcher's mask.' Hiroshi puts his hands up to his face.

Mary doesn't ask about Kendo because she is conscious of time and wants to know more about the Japanese playing

American baseball with other soldiers. 'Did you play sport with the Italians?' Mary asks, knowing that they were the first prisoners to arrive in Cowra. 'Everyone says they are very funny.'

'No!' Hiroshi says aggressively, a tone that Mary has not heard him use before. He sees her reaction to his voice, and repeats more softly, 'No. I am sorry, no, we didn't.'

There's silence for a few seconds and then he adds, 'We did not mix with the Italians. We had our separate places of living.'

'Yes, but surely they would let you play baseball against each other?'

'We did nothing with them,' Hiroshi says, conscious that Mary might judge him for hating the Italians as well as the Americans. Hiroshi hasn't really heard Mary speaking about hating anyone. He thinks Mary is a nice girl who is too young and probably too sheltered to understand anything of life in a prisoner of war camp, regardless of how much she might like to try. 'They are very different to us. They sing a lot and play instruments.'

'What instruments did they play, and what did they sing?'

Hiroshi is not eager to respond, he did not and does not care for the Italians. Like most of the Japanese soldiers, he feels an unspoken level of contempt for them, perhaps because they were allowed out into the community while the Japanese weren't. Or perhaps it is because they were happy to wait the war out in Australia and didn't wear the pressure of shame for being a prisoner of war. He is sure the Italians don't have an Emperor or a centuries-old philosophy of dying with honour. He has read that the Italians had signed an armistice with the Allies, which makes him hate them more. In Hiroshi's eyes they have no shame, which also means that he and the other Japanese soldiers think they are better than the Italians.

The Italians were held in A and C Compounds and the hardline fascists were held in D Compound. He doesn't want to tell Mary that even though the Japanese enjoyed operas and dramatic performances in B Compound every month, the Italians were thought to do it better and had their own opera society and band. It irks Hiroshi that the Italians also played soccer and created their own field to play on.

Hiroshi also partly resents the fact that the guards always considered the Italians cheerful. 'Why aren't you more like the Italians?' he'd heard more than once. He's never seen it, but knows the Italians had building skills and many were artisans back home. Unlike the Japanese, the Italians had turned their camp into a place like their home country: there were garden beds between the mess halls, and the men used their skills as cobblers to turn old car tyres into sandals to sell in the community.

Either way, it is not easy to explain the reality of life in the POW camp with Mary here in front of him with eyes wide and a warm smile that could make any man soft in the heart. He just wants to see her smile more. 'I think they are called saxophones.' He gestures to blow into a pretend pipe-like instrument and fingers imaginary keys.

Mary loves her father's banjo playing, and Uncle Muddy on the piano accordion is fantastic and when the Williams boys play their guitars, it's like a party, but something new, something from another country, that is special, and her face lights up.

'The guards told us the Italians, they play something called a mandolin . . . it is like a small guitar,' he says, gesturing to indicate the size of the instrument.

'My Uncles play the mandolin too, but gee, it would be wonderful to see the Italians play it. I guess they have different songs,' Mary says cheerfully.

Hiroshi knows that she simply does not understand that nothing about the Italians is wonderful.

There has been silence between them now for the longest time, both lost in their own thoughts of Italian prisoners of war.

'It's time to leave,' Mary suddenly declares. 'But before I do, I have a surprise for you.' She watches Hiroshi's face as she hands him the writing materials. Mary has shown initiative and told Mrs Smith she wants to practise writing. This has landed her a notebook and two pencils, which Hiroshi gently takes with both hands.

His heart wells with happiness and gratitude but also the fear of penning the truth of his existence to his parents, even though he doesn't expect they will get to read it.

As she walks through a gentle mist that will later turn into a heavy downpour, Mary is proud of the charity she is offering Hiroshi and hopes the notebook gives him something to pass the time in the long hours he is alone in the shelter. She also hopes that Mrs Smith doesn't ever ask to see the notebook again, because that will require another lie and she has already lost track of how many lies she has told in the last month. She's glad that even though she has been baptised, she has never been expected to go to confession at St Raphael's, because she would need to be in the confessional for a very long time. While her mother would like to go to church more often, Mary is glad that Aboriginal people from Erambie only go to church on special occasions like weddings and funerals.

By the dim light of the kerosene lamp, Hiroshi begins to write, but it is far harder than he thought it would be. He is already feeling the heartache and pain of the words he must pen to his parents. It takes him almost an hour before he can write something other than the opening greeting. But then the words flow and so do his tears.

Dear Mother and Father,

I know this letter will come as a shock. I know that you have been told I am dead, killed in action. I know reading this will be even harder for you to accept than losing your son at war. But here I am, writing to you, which means I am alive. I am in a place called Cowra. In Australia. I am living with a family here, until I can see you again. I beg you for forgiveness. I have become a prisoner of war. I am sorry I am not the brave warrior you wanted in a son. I do not want to bring shame on the family, on you, my loving parents. I honour my family, my nation, and you have my loyalty, but I am a better man in life than in death. Mother, please do not cut your hair in mourning, for I am alive.

I will not tell you who the other men were in the POW camp in Australia, for it is for them to let their families know. We all understand the shame our presence as prisoners of war will bring you, but I hope, as I know many others will, that you will be happy to see your son alive regardless of circumstances.

I once vowed to complete my mission and destroy the enemy, but I have met some of the enemy. They are called Australians. They have fed me better than my own government when they sent me to war. I have been treated well by the Australian guards, who I have grown to respect. And now I am being cared for by an Australian family. If I ever have a son, I will send him here to visit these kind people. He could live his dreams here. He would not be beaten in training to be a better soldier like I was. He could be a poet if he wished. He could be free.

I hope I will see you again soon, and then I will spend the rest of my days making you proud.

Your son,

Hiroshi

7

Mary and Hiroshi sit side by side on a dirty blanket that Joan managed to get from the church. It's been six weeks since Hiroshi found himself at Erambie. Aside from Mary's almost daily visits, the newspapers and brief visits to the lavatory where he steals a few seconds of moonlight and fresh air, it has been his Shinto faith that has sustained him and helped him believe that he will see his family again. But it is his Shinto faith that has also caused him grief.

His family's faith means they will be practising the culture and tradition of respecting and worshipping his death. Understanding this practice upsets Hiroshi even more. He knows his father will be hurt but proud that his son has died at war, died with honour in the name of the Emperor. His mother will be heartbroken and distraught that her only son died at all.

Hiroshi jumps up suddenly, startling Mary. 'We Japanese,' he puts his hand on his chest, 'believe that the spirits of the dead live forever on earth and guard their descendants. My family will think I am their guardian deity. They will be worshipping me for my effort in the war and the honour I have brought myself and them.' Hiroshi shakes his head, knowing that such worshipping is misplaced, given he is alive, but there is nothing he can do. The letter he wrote to his parents sits on the ground near where he sleeps. He has not asked Mary to post it – he knows that a Japanese address on an envelope will make someone suspicious. And what if she drops it, or worse still, gets caught carrying it? It is too risky for both of them. Writing the letter helped soothe his mind and his heart, but the words are still there, near him, and not where he wants them to be.

'What religion are the Aboriginal people, Mary?' Hiroshi asks, knowing that there would be no Shinto followers in Australia outside of his army peers.

'I am Catholic, my family are Catholic. There are only Catholics and Protestants in town. And people who don't believe in God at all. Uncle Kevin calls them atheists. My mother calls them heathens. Do you have a god, Hiroshi?'

'We don't have one god,' he says, 'we have many gods, called kami. They are sacred spirits that represent important elements like the trees and mountains, rivers and the rain.' He stops, wondering if what he is saying makes sense to the young woman in front of him. 'Our faith is Shinto, it means the way of the gods. We say prayers and make offerings to kami for health, our families, children and safety. We have a lot of respect for nature, land and the crops we harvest. We have ceremonies but we don't go to church. We go to a shrine.'

'Your Shinto faith is like our Aboriginal spirituality then, and connection to land and Mother Earth,' Mary says. 'We respect all living things. I have a totem, the goanna.' She pauses. 'Where will your family go to pray for you if they think you are –' she suddenly stops short of saying 'dead'.

'They will go to our local temple, but there is a special shrine in Tokyo they will go to also. It is called the Yasukuni Shrine.' Hiroshi can feel tears welling as he thinks of his family grieving for their lost son and brother. It is almost more than he can bear and he shakes his head as he adds, 'They will go there to worship my spirit because they do not have a body to cremate. There are no bodies buried there. And the temple is just for people who have died at war, or protecting Japan. We believe the spirits of fallen soldiers are entombed there. My family will believe my spirit is there already too.'

He takes a deep breath, looking at Mary for some understanding, some comfort, but what can this naïve young girl in front of him who understands nothing about his world possibly do? He is too emotional to explain what his supposed death means to his family. But he wants to talk – he needs to talk about what is happening back home. This friendship with Mary is not a normal experience for a Japanese man, at war or at home.

'They believe I have died for my country. I should have died.' He almost chokes on his own guilt as he says it out loud.

'No, you shouldn't have died!' Mary steps towards him. It is the closest they have ever been and it feels like there is a magnet drawing them together. It troubles them both but the desire is undeniable. Hiroshi wants to fall into her arms and cry like a child. Mary wants to hug him and let him know that no one wants him dead.

'It is important to protect your country, Mary,' he says, then adds, 'You are supposed to be prepared to die for your country. I am *expected* to die for my country.' Hiroshi believes he is a pacifist and is trying to convey that to Mary.

'Australia is made up of lots of countries,' Mary says. 'Every tribe has their own area of land, like a country. Australia is like the map of Europe – do you know the map of Europe?' Mary knows Europe and Asia and the Americas because the Smiths have a globe on Mr Smith's desk as well as an atlas where she tried to find Hiroshi's island but it was too hard. *Mr Smith likes to think he is worldly*, Mrs Smith has said more than once.

'Yes, I went to university and I spent a lot of time in the library, learning about much more than English. I was always very interested in geography.' Hiroshi motions for Mary to continue – he likes to hear her voice and see her face light up when she talks about things that are important to her.

'There are lots of Aboriginal tribes in Australia. We have different languages and foods and spiritual beliefs, so we have lots of countries in one country.' Mary hopes that makes sense to Hiroshi, because she doesn't know how else to explain it. He nods as though he understands.

'If you think about the map of Europe with Italy and Germany and Spain and all the different people and cultures, well, Australia is like that. And the white people from England, they are like a lot of noisy, angry visitors on a holiday that never really ends.' Mary giggles to herself, repeating what her Uncle Kevin has said many times. She is very fond of her Uncle Kevin. 'And this land here, it belongs to my tribe, even though the white people and the government act like it belongs to them.' Mary is now repeating what her father often says.

'But if the Aboriginal people fight for their land, then the white people won't be able to own it. Don't they fight for it, Mary?'

'My dad says there have been many wars on our land, but we always lose.'

'Why?'

Mary thinks back to a late night in a smoke-filled kitchen a while ago, when she sat at the table with her parents and her dad talked about all the massacres on Wiradjuri land. 'White people have been shooting Aboriginal people since they arrived. It's why so many Wiradjuri are gone,' she says. 'There's over a dozen massacre sites around Bathurst. That's about sixty-five miles from here. And further up north, there's a town called Mudgee, where some white man led a shooting party and killed so many people no one even knows how many there were.' Mary remembers her father saying that no one probably cared either, but she doesn't say that to Hiroshi. 'It was about a hundred years ago, I think, but back then it happened all the time. This one man called Chamberlain, well, they reckon he killed about twenty Wiradjuri people just for stealing some cattle – after the white men had come and stolen their land. That's straight out murder!'

'Did your people fight for your land, Mary?'

'Not with planes and bombs, no, but we did fight. War takes many forms, so my dad says. And there are more white people than us and we cannot fight guns with spears or fists.' Mary is repeating everything she has heard her father say over the years but they have become her feelings, her words, and her beliefs too. 'And now we are in a moral war against the government because they do not recognise us as human beings. And if they do not support us, why should we support them?'

She doesn't give Hiroshi a chance to respond to the question. 'We are not citizens, Hiroshi, we cannot vote and we can't go to war overseas either, because you have to be Australian to fight for Australia.'

'So your people do not go to the war in New Guinea or Europe either?'

'Some of our men have enlisted in the war, yes, but some also had to lie about their race, because you can't be Aboriginal and go to war. It's very confusing for us. One of our local men from here, Jim Murray, he was in World War One,' she says. 'When people talk about our soldiers, they always talk about Jim. He is a guard up the camp, but I don't see him much. Maybe you saw him?'

'I saw one guard who was the same colour as you, I think that must have been the Jim you are talking about.'

'Some Aboriginal men tried to enlist because they wanted to travel, to leave Cowra. Some also wanted to defend their land, even if the government wouldn't let them keep it. But they were rejected on the grounds of race, of being Aboriginal, but Jim reckons when Australia needed more soldiers and they couldn't use conscription, then there was some kind of order that said that half-castes could enlist in the Australian Imperial Force.'

'Half-castes?' Hiroshi asks, shaking his head, a look of confusion on his face.

'That means you had to have one white parent and one Aboriginal parent. They call you half-caste and as long as the medical officers are happy that you have one white parent, then they'll let you enlist.' Mary wishes now that she had talked to Jim whenever she saw him, because then maybe she would have a better understanding of the camp, of the war, an ounce of what Hiroshi had experienced and what Aboriginal men experience too. Sometimes, when she talks to Hiroshi, she feels incredibly knowledgeable about life and at other times she feels like she knows very little.

'So you must be white to fight for Australia?' Hiroshi asks.

'That's what it seems like,' Mary says.

'But why would Aboriginal people fight in an army for a country that doesn't really want them? I don't really understand.'

'Firstly, this is *our* country Hiroshi, *our* land, so we are still fighting for our land even if it doesn't really make sense.' In fact, it doesn't make sense to Mary as she says it out loud – Wiradjuri fighting for their land here and overseas. 'Aboriginal people are loyal to this place, it is our home. I think some of our men might want to prove that we are as good as the Europeans who have come to live here and then go to war. Our men are strong and brave and courageous like other men. Our men are warriors.' Mary's pride comes through as she speaks. 'Some Aboriginal people think that if we fight in the war then maybe the government will treat us all better when the war is over.'

Mary doesn't know how many Aboriginal men served in the First World War, only what she hears when the Elders meet at her house and talk about how men came back and were still discriminated against when it came to getting jobs and housing. Even Jim said that discrimination had got worse while he was away at war.

'My dad says that the only reason Blacks were part of the war was because the army needed more manpower, so they recruited our men into the labour corps. Or that maybe they thought they'd get more food than the rations we get here.'

There is silence as both consider her words.

'Hiroshi,' Mary says finally, in a way that makes him weak with the need to make her smile more, make her happy, 'I need to know why you broke out of the camp. Being down here must be worse than being with your friends and having three good meals and daylight and playing baseball.'

It is a genuine and fair question but Hiroshi doesn't know where to begin. He pauses to think how he might tell her that dying for the Emperor is honourable.

'It will be very hard for you to understand, Mary, because I think your people and the Australian soldiers are very different to my people. To what Japanese soldiers and people generally believe and how we are expected to behave.'

'I want to understand,' she says softly. 'I want to know why you broke out and why some of the Japanese soldiers killed themselves.' She cannot imagine what would make someone want to end their own life.

Hiroshi takes a deep breath and then speaks slowly: 'In the Japanese army there is a code, a law.' He is taking his time as he tries to find the words to simplify what is a very complex thing for someone who is not Japanese to understand. 'We have a set of morals we must live by. It is called Senjinkun.'

'Sen-gin-koon,' Mary sounds it out slowly.

'Senjinkun simply means that you must live, fight, die. That it is dishonourable to be captured by the enemy. Mary, it is dishonourable for me to be in Cowra. At the camp, and even here, do you understand that?' He shakes his head. 'I shouldn't be down here with you. This is just as shameful – hiding like this.'

Hiroshi feels tears well in his eyes and he sees Mary's eyes start watering up as well. He doesn't want to upset her but this is an important conversation they need to have.

'So it is dishonourable to be a prisoner of war like I was, like I still am. This –' he waves his hands around the space, with the tin bucket in the corner and a ratty old pillow and blanket, '– this brings shame on my family.' He moves closer to Mary. 'Please, I am grateful to be alive and that you are protecting me, but the Senjinkun is about the duty I have as a Japanese soldier to act with loyalty to the Emperor.'

Mary imagines the Emperor is like the prime minister who runs Australia.

'To show your loyalty to the Emperor and love of your country, you must die with honour rather than live with the shame of capture. I am living with shame right now.' He hangs his head as he repeats, 'Shame.'

'You are not living in shame. You are not captured, you are alive and preparing to see your family again.' Mary is angry as she says this. She doesn't understand any of what Hiroshi is saying although she is trying to. She moves closer to him but does not touch him. Her voice softens as she says, 'I understand you didn't want to be a prisoner but three meals a day, and your friends and baseball, has to be better than this daily darkness and loneliness, and better than killing other innocent men at war. And surely it has to be better than death?' She looks into his eyes, seeking an answer.

Hiroshi says nothing. He knows she doesn't understand and he can't see the point any more in trying to make her. The code is what it is. It is something the Japanese are raised with and will literally die with.

'I am *glad* you escaped. I am *glad* you are here, safe.' Mary's voice has a quiver in it.

Hiroshi hears it and his instinct is to hold the woman in front of him, but he dare not. He must show respect both to Mary and to the man who first brought him down here. He knows he owes them his life.

'I should leave,' Mary says. Her parents will be furious at the length of time she's been here.

Hiroshi has a lump in his throat and his heart is beating faster than usual, reminding him of the night he escaped. He feels anxious about wanting Mary to understand so much that he can't explain. He also wants her to know that the security and comfort and three meals a day, playing baseball

98

and being with his friends cannot be measured against the happiness and comfort that the small length of time he gets to spend with her each day brings. He doesn't think she will understand; he's not even sure he understands himself. This is not anything he could ever have imagined or planned. None of this scenario is the Japanese way.

As she heads back up the ladder, he simply says, 'Arigatō, ashita mata.'

8

8 SEPTEMBER 1944: 195 JAPANESE KILLED:
BRUTAL MURDER OF OFFICER

CANBERRA, Friday – A full, official account of the mutiny at a country prison camp in the early hours of 5 August, has been released by the federal government. Official reports state that more than 800 Japanese prisoners of war set fire to their huts and made a mass attack on their guards. Many scaled the fences and escaped. 195 Japs were killed, 108 wounded and 36 suicided . . . One Australian officer was brutally murdered by a party of Japanese.

It's the headline and story that everyone has been waiting for: answers to the many questions the Williams family and the Elders have. Mary has taken to reading the text out loud to them all as they sit with mugs of tea around the Williams' kitchen table. It is something she feels more confident doing lately, and she wants to do more.

'"The Japs completely ignored the machine-gun fire and many died of wounds from the hail of lead. Eighteen of the twenty sleeping huts in the camp, and two administration huts, were burned to the ground. The incinerated bodies of Japs were found in these huts."' She takes a breath and reads on, the others listening carefully. '"Many of the Japs who died were killed by their comrades. Only two Jap officers were among the casualties."'

There are tears in her eyes as her mother moves to stand behind her. She puts her hands on Mary's shoulders. 'You don't have to keep reading,' she says softly in Mary's ear.

Mary shakes her head, gently shrugs off her mother's hands and wipes her nose on her sleeve. She takes a long breath and continues.

'"Twenty Japs died from strangulation inflicted by themselves or other Japs. Nine suicided by stabbing themselves and two by throwing themselves under a train."' Mary puts her hand over her mouth in shock, not believing what she has just read out loud.

'Dear Lord,' Joan says, putting a hand to her heart. 'Why?'

Banjo stands and puts his arm around his wife's shoulder; they are all disturbed by what they have heard, by what is happening in their own town. Such violence, self-harm, killing of your own men is not something they have any experience of. The history of war on their land was understandable, but the suicides, the trains, that is something none of them, especially Mary, will ever understand.

Mary carries on reading, fast. She is desperate to see if there is any mention of Hiroshi, if they are still looking for him, how much danger he might still be in. She is trying not to imagine any of the hideously violent scenes that the newspaper is painting with its words. She skips what she doesn't think is necessary, reading only what she believes is relevant to the six people around the table.

'"Casualties among Australian personnel were comparatively light. Sixteen of the wounded had attempted suicide before they were captured. All but a few Japs were recaptured the same day. No complaints as to their treatment had been made by the Japs. Camp conditions were in full accordance with provisions of the International Convention."'

Kevin typically bangs his fists on the table and yells, 'No complaints! There wouldn't want to be bloody complaints.'

'Kevin!' Joan chastises.

'Sorry,' he says to Joan and Mary but not the men. He's still furious, though, and while he controls his language, he doesn't hold back on what he thinks about the Japanese. 'The conditions in that camp are better than here. And imagine if we burnt down our huts and shot white people. What do you think might happen?' He looks at them one by one. 'You all know exactly what would happen. These yellow bastards are unbelievable.'

Joan walks around to Kevin and places her loving hands on his shoulders. 'Are you okay to go on, Mary?' she asks her daughter, who is still visibly upset, with flushed cheeks and tears in her eyes.

Mary nods and continues, '"A report of the mutiny has been furnished for forwarding to the Japanese Government.

The rest have been rounded up since then."' She stops, then repeats, '"The rest have been rounded up since then."' She bursts into tears. Hiroshi is safe.

'They don't know he's missing,' Banjo says, puffing his chest out. 'We did it!'

'That also means there could be more of the bastards on the loose. Dumb whitefellas can't even count.' Kevin shakes his head. 'If the paper reported that one was missing and they couldn't find him, then that would mean we'd done it, as you say, Banjo.'

Banjo doesn't reply.

Kevin stares his brother down. 'What is it you think you've achieved, Banjo, other than putting all of us at the table at risk of trouble from John Smith for supporting the Japanese?'

'We outsmarted them, Kev. This isn't just about protecting that soldier – it's about putting one over the white institutions, the government, and the people in power who keep our people down. While we successfully hide Hiroshi, we are outsmarting them all. And *that's* what I'm happy about. We have no real power anywhere, but in some ways, hiding that soldier proves we do.'

Joan places a cup of tea in front of Mary, who is silent. She is churning with emotions: relief, happiness, hope. She wants to tell Hiroshi immediately; she wants him to know that he is safe, that they are not looking for him. That he is one step closer to getting home. Although she has no idea what the next steps will be or how they will happen, she knows Japan is a long way away and it will take money and plans. And the truth is she doesn't want him to go. She just wants him to stay forever.

'I'll take the paper to Ryan's Place so everyone else knows what's going on,' Kevin says, and before Mary has the chance to say no, her Uncle has the newspaper in his hands and is flicking through it. 'I suppose this is good news for your man.' He looks up and gestures to the other men and Joan, but his gaze lingers longest on Mary, until she looks away.

'We all agreed to do this, Kevin, we must stay united,' Banjo reminds his brother. 'Don't tell anyone. It's not safe yet.'

Mary has tears rolling down her flushed cheeks and her mother is soothing her. 'I'll take the food down tonight,' Joan says, concerned about her daughter's anguish, and now regretting they had put such responsibility onto her young shoulders.

'No!' Mary cries. 'It is *my* job, I want to finish what I started.' She no longer sees taking Hiroshi his daily food parcel as a job, it is something she is compelled to do. Something she *wants* to do. To keep him alive. To keep him sane through conversation. To fulfil her own emotional need to see him.

'I am responsible for Hiroshi,' she says, taking a sip from her tin mug. The war has stolen the lives of many men, but she will not let it steal her time with Hiroshi.

As she looks up, her mother is watching her suspiciously. She is grateful that Kevin is looking through the paper and starts to read another headline, which captures the attention of the Elders and deflects anything her mother might have been thinking.

'"POWs on Farms: More control sought by diggers."' He reads the headline out, skims the article quickly and explains simply, 'Just something about Australians being sacked and

Italian prisoners of war being paid less money. Some old fella at the Soldier Settlers' Conference wants them all shipped back to Italy.' He slams the paper down. 'I'm with him. Ship every one of the bastards back to Italy, Japan, Korea and wherever else they come from.'

'I think it's fair to say that those men want to go back to their own countries,' Sid says. 'Wouldn't you?'

'I suppose so.' Kevin is slightly calmer now there is at least agreement with his own stand. He changes the topic with no warning. 'I heard that William Cooper fella from down Victoria way lost his son in the First World War and reckons the sacrifices that Aborigines made was not worth it.' He shakes his head. 'Our mob are fighting for a White Australia, not an equal Australia.'

The women are all at Marj's for card night. She has the best table, a kettle and a wireless that they sometimes listen to. Marj is in fine form and although no one admits they like her gossiping, the ladies always look forward to hearing whatever news she brings to the game. It's not long before she starts.

'You know that experimental farm next door to the camp?'

The others nod.

'Well, there are girls there of *that age*.' Marj winks to the other women who nod back in acknowledgement. Mary isn't sure what they are referring to but listens anyway. 'Well, some of *those* girls are supposedly having flings with the Italian soldiers.'

'They are philanderers.' Ivy laughs as if she is a young girl again too.

Mary doesn't know what that word means but guesses it has something to do with women. She wants to look it up in the dictionary at the Smiths' place, even though she can't spell it.

'And as you know, I am not one to gossip, but someone told someone who told someone else who told me – and you know I don't disclose names of those who share with me – and well, the bootmaker is really angry at the Italians because *apparently* they are really good at repairing shoes.' Marj raises an eyebrow as if she's not convinced.

'Really?' Joan asks, thinking about all the holey shoes and boots in her own family that need repairing but she has no money to pay a bootmaker. She wonders if it would be possible to get the Italians to fix them. 'So what do they do that's different?' she asks, hoping the answer is they work for free.

Marj keeps her eye on her cards as she speaks. '*Apparently*, and it's all hearsay you understand, the regimental bootmaker glues the soles of shoes, but, and here's the twist, the Italians glue the soles *and* sew them.' Another raise of the eyebrow.

Joan knows exactly what that means. 'The stitching helps the shoes last longer!'

'Apparently. So they are better than our own at doing the same job. It's not just the shoes, though,' she says, looking at her cards intently, 'they are also good at lots of things.'

Ivy giggles. 'So we've heard.' She winks at the ladies, who burst out laughing.

'You are wicked,' Joan says.

'I meant trades, Ivy, *trades*,' Marj says, putting her cards on the table. '*Apparently*, they are good plumbers, painters and carpenters too, and *apparently* they are good woodworkers.'

'The Smiths have photos in wooden picture frames that the Italians made,' Mary says, 'and Mr Smith has a chess set but he says no one around here is smart enough to play, so it's just for show.'

'A chess set, that is fancy woodwork, your Banjo better watch out, Joan, or he'll be like the bootmaker,' Marj warns.

'My Banjo is beyond compare,' Joan says adamantly, angry at the suggestion that anyone, let alone an Italian prisoner of war, is going to be a better carpenter than her husband. 'No one is better than he is. Your hut was built by my husband, Marj, you might do well to remember that.' And she uncharacteristically throws her cards on the table.

'No, I didn't mean anything by it, Joan. You know I know how good Banjo is.'

Joan can already hear the gossip mill working overtime tomorrow when Marj is retelling the story to others, but she doesn't care, because Joan knows what she knows.

'Our men have a history of building here. Banjo's father cut timber too. The Welfare Board may have provided the nails and roofing iron, but our men provided the skills to build their homes.'

'I've often said to Sid how fortunate we are to have Banjo do so much work around here for all of us,' Ivy says.

'Who's that?' Marj says, getting up quickly and changing the subject. 'Someone's out there, again. Fred! *Fred!*' she squeals. 'Oh, where is that useless man?'

Joan and Mary are on their feet with Marj at the window, hoping it's not Hiroshi.

'You do go on, Marj, always seeing things and hearing things,' Joan says, trying to move Marj away from the window.

'It's Claude!' Mary exclaims. 'He's smoking! He does it every night, hiding, I've seen him but didn't want to dob on him.'

'Well, I guess he's old enough,' Ivy says. 'All the other men do it.'

'I'm sure his mother wouldn't approve.' Marj sits back down and picks up her cards. 'And I'm sure she'll be hearing about it soon enough.'

Joan and Mary look at each other, hearts beating fast.

9

Hiroshi was at university when Japanese troops entered Peking in 1937, invading China in an attempt to dominate Southeast Asia. His father spoke passionately about how Japan should be the world leader, that even though they were a small cluster of islands, Japan was strong. His father fully supported Japan taking over other countries to increase its power and Hiroshi was sad when he realised his father wasn't concerned about his only son going to war.

At university, Hiroshi and his friends talked about Japan signing the Tripartite Pact and asked each other why Japan joined the Axis alliance with Germany and Italy – questions that were never really answered.

When a former general of the army, Hideki Tojo, became prime minister, his followers included Hiroshi's father, and Hiroshi became more nervous about the war. When Japan attacked the US Navy at Pearl Harbor, his father was more than pleased that the strike sank many ships. Hiroshi's mother cried, though, because she knew her son would go to war. Hiroshi's father was proud to see his son off to die in a war that would, he believed, see Japan become a world leader. He flexed his muscles just like Japan flexed its military muscle, and he laughed at news reports about the destruction of Pearl Harbor.

In the shelter behind Mary's hut, Hiroshi sees his father's pride in one frame and in the next he sees other men from Shikoku Island. They are all on a ship on their way to the war. He is at war. He is in New Guinea and he is fighting for food, the food his government has not sent to sustain them as soldiers. He sees men bloodied and dying, dropping from gunshots. He is tired, aching from crawling in and out of trenches, from carrying his own body as well as those of injured Japanese soldiers. He is so tired when the Allies attack, he can't move. He can't fight. He looks around at his countrymen, all too injured or sick to save themselves from capture. Save themselves from the enemy. Some are begging to be killed. Some are biting their tongues off. Hiroshi's ears are filled with the sounds of grown men screaming in pain, yelling in anger, crying with shame and fear.

Hiroshi wakes with a startle and throws up. He is drenched in sweat and riddled with anxiety as he tries to shake off the nightmare. It's the same violent dream he has had over and over again.

As Hiroshi sits in the dark, he sobs like a child. The fear of war and the weight of witnessing so much death falls heavily on his entire being. His body feels drained of life although he is still breathing. For the first time – without thoughts of Mary

112

to soothe him – he wishes he had died in New Guinea or, better still, he wishes he could turn back the clock to before the war was declared, before Japan had become involved. Back to where the dread of the unknown did not destroy his sense of peace or his sanity.

'I hope my sons never have to go to war,' Hiroshi says as he and Mary sit with their feet almost touching. He is wearing new pants and a clean shirt Mary delivered the day before, courtesy of Father Patrick. Joan had told the priest there was a visitor in need of trousers and a shirt. It wasn't really a lie, she told herself, as Hiroshi *was* a visitor and *was* in need of clothes. She did, however, set herself some penance that night, saying ten Hail Marys, an Our Father and a Glory Be to the Father, for good measure.

'I was taught honour before shame. I had to say it out loud all the time,' Hiroshi says, as if such a statement is like a friendly greeting. He is not sad, he is not maudlin, he is simply thinking about the future life of the sons he hopes to have one day.

Even though she has heard Hiroshi talk about honour and shame before, Mary still listens to his words because she believes he is wise, that he will do whatever he sets his mind to and that his sons will have a hero for a father. She is in awe of the man in front of her. He appears to be emotion-ally strong, like her father and Uncles, like the Elders she has gained much of her knowledge and history from. And he is gentle and wise like her mother.

'It is difficult in my country to have ideas that are different from the majority.' He is talking to Mary, but he is also saying out loud for the first time things he has thought for many years, opinions he could never share back home. Words that are so incredibly private to him – he is surprising himself with being so open, so honest with a young female foreigner. 'Japanese people are forced to think and act the same. Wa wo motte totoshi to nasu,' he says, then translates: 'Acting with harmony is of the utmost importance.

'We should all agree in public, not be against each other. A person, a man, may have had a dream when he was young but it was beaten out of him.' Hiroshi is talking about himself, about his own dream, about wanting to be a poet, to use his university education to be creative, but knowing that the national conscience and expectations meant otherwise.

Mary looks at the man she is falling in love with. She wonders how the world can be so cruel. How governments can send innocent men to fight wars that never really have a winner. How can one country lock up another country's citizens as prisoners in compounds like the one in Cowra? Her Uncle Kevin said the Japanese were doing brutal things to the Australian soldiers. How could that be true when Hiroshi is so gentle? Mary doesn't want to believe it. None are better than the other, regardless of what her Uncle has said, but she could never say that out loud to the Elders.

She doesn't allow herself to think long about what the Nazis have done to the Jews, but she knows enough to realise it has been horrific. She has overheard enough conversations in the Manager's house to know that the war in Europe is ugly. She knows that war is ripping lives apart, and there are men just like Hiroshi from many different countries feeling the same grief and trauma. She is grateful only for one thing that war has achieved: it has brought Hiroshi to her.

Hiroshi looks at Mary. She looks away, trying to think of something to say, something that isn't too gloomy.

'Is it the same here, Mary, can *you* have dreams? Can *you* be different?' Hiroshi is hoping that at least outside of his homeland people have the freedom to dream, to live autonomously.

'This is such a big question, Hiroshi. Of course you can dream in Australia, and we mightn't have to go to war training camps, but it is still hard to make your dreams come true, especially if you are Aboriginal.'

'What kinds of dreams do you have?' Hiroshi wants to escape into the dreams of someone else just for a little while and experience a world removed from his own.

'I dream about being able to live and work wherever I want to and not have to do as Mr Smith says. And I want to go back and finish school.' Mary has thought about all this before and is grateful for the opportunity to express herself without sounding unhappy with her lot, or ungrateful, because she knows her parents have given her the best life they can within their power. She doesn't want her parents to think she is not thankful for all they have done to keep their family together, but she does dream about the future and what might be possible for her as she gets older.

'I dream about marrying the man I fall in love with without the Manager or the government telling me I can't.' She blushes, because she knows she is young, she knows that no one will ever understand that she has feelings for a Japanese soldier. She knows that he might not even love her back, but right now she can't imagine that she will ever feel like this again about another human being. She wonders if this is how her parents felt when they first met.

Hiroshi's eyes twinkle at her words about marriage, and his glance sends a rush through her body, which makes her blush again. She swallows and composes herself, and turns serious, hoping he has not noticed any change in her. 'I dream about having the same rights as white people, so I can live a full life.'

Hiroshi wishes that the woman he is closest to right now could have all her dreams come true. She is the woman who has brought light into his daily darkness. The woman who has saved his sanity and his soul and, most importantly, his life. She has given him flickering moments of joy simply with her smile. He wants to be able to bring some happiness to Mary's life and wonders how it is possible with the regime she and her family live under, and the fact he remains a soldier on the run.

'Is this dream possible, Mary?'

'My Uncle Kevin says if we want to have what white people have, all the rights they have to go places and do things, get married, live where they want, or even to have just a little of what they have, then we must assimilate. There is a government policy to try to make us be like white people.'

116

Hiroshi looks confused.

'It means we must *act* like white people. We must be more like them, even though we look like this.' She runs her hands over the dark skin of her cheeks. 'But we will always be treated like we are Black, even if we try to pretend to be white.'

Hiroshi frowns.

'I don't want to be *like* a white person, I want to be *me* but treated in the same way as white people are. But to get the same things we must not *act* Aboriginal any more. Whatever that means,' she says.

'But I don't understand.' He still can't fathom what Mary is talking about, what she is going through, what kind of life the people walking around above him are living, having only spent minutes above ground when he first arrived, and a few moments each night when he empties his bucket in the lavatory.

'Twenty years ago, the Manager actually expelled people from Erambie because he said they were too white to be treated as Aborigines under the Act. That means they weren't dark enough to be treated badly.'

'What is the Act?' Hiroshi asks. Even with his good English, he is finding it hard to follow the complexity of Mary's words, while Mary is finding it difficult to explain what it means to live under the Act of Protection. Nevertheless, she continues with the same fire in her belly that she knows both her parents have, and most people at Erambie have too.

'Where we are, this place Cowra, it is in the state of New South Wales,' she says, 'and there is some government policy just for Aborigines who live in this state and it is called the

Aborigines Protection Act. If we want the rights of white people we can apply to be non-Aborigines and get something called an Exemption Certificate.' Mary motions to form a square.

Hiroshi nods then asks, 'What does this certificate do?'

'If you get the certificate, it means you do not have to live under the Act or the rules that most Aboriginal people live by.' Mary is not completely sure she understands the policy herself and she certainly doesn't know why it exists. She is trying to remember all the details her father and her Uncle Kevin and the other Uncles have shared around the kitchen table when they have their meetings, or when they are just there yarning and drinking tea.

'What can you do that's different if you have this certificate?'

'With the certificate you can vote, you can drink alcohol legally and you can go wherever you like. You can talk and socialise with other people.'

'You can't do that now?' Hiroshi can't imagine any people not being free to live in Australia as they choose.

'No, most of us here can't do that as freely as we'd like to. Some of the old people say we are like prisoners in our own home. We have a lot of people here now, we are strong and can be united against the Manager, but at the end of the day, he still has control over our lives.'

'But the certificate sounds good then?'

'No,' Mary says, 'it also means you cannot see your family, you have to leave the mission and if you get caught socialising with other Aboriginal people who don't have the certificate, you can go to jail.'

'Is that true? The laws say that?' Hiroshi's eyes are wide.

'One woman from here got the certificate and went to Sydney to work and when she wanted to come home for a funeral she had to get written permission from the Manager to do so. But this is her home, Hiroshi, and all her family live here, and she needed permission to come home. This is just wrong, wrong.' Mary stands as if she is about to leave. Hiroshi stands too.

'I don't understand how a piece of paper can make you be something else? How can it change your life so much?'

Mary begins to pace, explaining to Hiroshi the reality of her own existence, of the existence of all the people in her world that has made her agitated. 'If you get the certificate you can get a pension, and an allowance when you are pregnant. Black people don't get these things. We should get the same things as the other people in town.'

Hiroshi shakes his head in disbelief. 'This can't be true! I believe you, of course, but how is this true?'

'It's true,' she says. 'There's even separate toilets at the theatre.' She stops short of telling him that the goonans are only segregated until they hit the main pipe and then they integrate into the sewerage system. She wonders what the white people might think about their poo mixing with the Black people's poo, but she doesn't really think that much about it, and she certainly doesn't want to share that thought with Hiroshi.

'This is crazy,' he says, confused that a country that treated him so well at the camp could treat its own people so badly. 'This paper changes all that? Changes the way people treat you, and how you can behave? But you are still Aboriginal. A piece of paper can't change that.'

Mary sighs. 'We still look the same, think the same, know the same and understand the same history that has led us to where we are today. And that is what makes us *still* Aboriginal.' She takes a deep breath, exhausted by what feels like schooling. None of the talking will change anything about her lot, other than the man she has feelings for coming to a better understanding of who she is and the life she leads.

'This certificate system is ridiculous then,' Hiroshi says.

'Yes, it is. But if you get the paper, it means that you are free of some discrimination. And that's why some Aboriginal people get it. It makes life easier for them.'

'Will you get this paper?' Hiroshi wants his food angel to have an easier life than she appears to have with the Smiths.

'No! My parents will *never* let us have dog tags,' she says sharply, then sees the confusion on Hiroshi's face. 'Most Blacks call the certificate "dog tags", which is not a very nice phrase; some people call them "dog licences", because having the certificate is like being a pet who must be registered. But my parents say you can never trade your identity for anything. And my dad says if it means you have to cut ties with your family and forget who you are, then he will never get it. That if we have to give up who we are as Aboriginal people to get jobs then we will just not work. I want to go back to school and learn more, and I want to work, Hiroshi, but not if getting the certificate to do so means I have to say I am not Aboriginal.'

Banjo is at work but it's just him and Fat Bobbo alone, early in the morning. The sun is high and Banjo is swinging his hammer, dripping with sweat. Fat Bobbo is nursing a hangover and hasn't picked up a tool yet.

'The Japs are crazy, they'll do anything,' Fat Bobbo begins, launching into a rant. 'Kill the enemy, kill each other and kill themselves.'

Banjo can't help but look up and ask, 'What the hell are you on about?' He just wants to work today, finish the job, get paid and get away from the laziest man he's ever known.

'When the Allies invaded Saipan, the Japs reckon thousands threw themselves off high cliffs. They call it a mass suicide. That's just crazy, they're all crazy, we can't have that kind of crazy yellow peril here.'

Banjo hopes the conversation is over because it's taking his concentration and he has to finish the barn by the end of the day or he won't get paid. But before he gets to even plane down a piece of wood, Fat Bobbo is off again.

'You know they ate some of our soldiers too.'

'Don't be ridiculous,' Banjo says, thinking back to what Kevin had said the day they found Hiroshi, or the day he found them.

Fat Bobbo is adamant. 'It's the truth. Everyone knows the Japs ate the dead Australian soldiers at Kokoda, and then they started eating their own.'

Banjo shakes his head. 'I don't believe it! I never saw it in the paper – where'd you hear it?'

'Listen. Their government never sent them food, they were fighting the war *and* for food and when they killed our men they ate them cos they were hungry! We can't have Jap cannibals here in Australia. *We're* not cannibals.' Fat Bobbo has broken a sweat and is red-faced.

'The fact is, Japs, Chinks, Gooks, they're all the same. Asiatics, that's what they call them. Doesn't matter, they're all a threat and we must fight against them. The yellow peril is real.'

'I've got work to do, even if *you* don't.' Banjo ends the conversation but he feels trapped, thinking about Kevin's comments again and how everyone had dismissed him.

'Joan, did you hear?' Marj is at the door as Joan is scrubbing the floors.

'Hear what?' she says, standing up and holding onto her aching back.

'June was hanging out the washing and her youngest gootha was crying and crying and making a hell of a racket, but June, you know, she just wanted to get the linen on the line quickly. And then all of a sudden the littl'un stopped and when she went to have a look, well, Lord, strike me dead if I tell a lie, she said a Jap was rocking the pram.'

Joan immediately wonders if he is the fella they are looking after. But surely not? She thinks fast, trying not to show any reaction, but camouflaging her emotions has never been a strength of hers. 'So, what happened then?'

'Well, all the screaming drew attention – I don't know how you didn't hear it, Joan.' Marj looks at her with squinty eyes.

'I was working,' she says. 'Go on.'

'People were running from left and right, then King Billie appeared, of course, and that was it. The Jap was tackled to the ground and they took him back to the camp.'

Joan's heart is racing. It had to be Hiroshi. There's been no other Japanese soldier around. She feels bile rise in her throat.

'Was he in a uniform?' she asks. The last clothes Joan sent down to Hiroshi were brown pants and a white shirt turned grey over time. He wasn't dressed like a soldier.

'I don't know. Why?' Marj looks at her suspiciously.

'No reason, just wondered.'

'You're acting very strange, Joan Williams. If I didn't know better, I'd think you were up to something.'

'Mary!' Joan exclaims as her daughter walks through the door. 'Don't be silly,' Joan says to Marj as she puts her arm around her daughter's waist. 'You're always looking for some news, aren't you?'

'Mary, did you hear about the Japanese soldier here at Erambie?'

'No, Aunt,' Mary says, worry in her eyes as she looks at her mother. 'But maybe Uncle Fred knows something.' She points in the direction of her Uncle, walking into his own hut.

'Yes, and if he doesn't know, I better tell him,' Marj says, turning and walking as fast as her stocky legs will take her.

'I was so worried,' Mary says. 'I thought the soldier they were talking about *had* to be you. It sounds like there's another one on the run. Or was – they took him back to camp.'

Mary doesn't notice Hiroshi's distress, too busy with her own relief. But he is reminded of his friends, his fellow soldiers still in the compound and possibly still on the run. The captured soldier may have been Masao. He stands there motionless, eyes glazed over, looking at Mary but transported back to the night of the breakout in his mind. He wonders who the other soldier might have been, momentarily pleased that another had managed to remain on the run for so long.

10

29 September 1944

> *Cherry blossom smile,*
> *Benika I miss you so . . .*

'No, no.' Hiroshi is framing poetry out loud. Walking out the Haiku beat – five, seven, five – Benika on his mind and his lips. *But is she in my heart?* he asks himself. *What about Mary? Mary my food angel.* Hiroshi has taken to answering his own questions, desperate for conversation and the sound of something other than silence.

> *Mother please forgive*
> *A soldier's heart so homesick*
> *For his family*

Hiroshi's thoughts are chaotic but all lead to his life back home. He collapses to the ground. *I want to go home. I want to go home.*

He sits and breathes in the musty scent of the rotting wooden beams keeping the dirt walls and the roof in place. The smell of his waste lingers constantly in his nostrils, even though he empties his bucket every night. With the lantern off to save kerosene, he has nothing but his senses of smell and sound to focus on. He sniffs his armpits and is disgusted. At least at the camp he was clean. His clothes are ratty, dirty, worn, and the soles of his feet are rough. He can taste the dirt under his fingernails as he bites each one, trying to make them short again. He spits dirt from his mouth but the taste of filth remains.

'Benika,' he says out loud. 'Where are you? Would you love me again, would you love me like this?' He puts his head in his hands and weeps. *Love*, he thinks to himself. What love did he feel when his father sent him to war? What love can his mother feel for a man who is so cold?

He stands up again. Pacing, he stretches one leg at a time behind his body to relieve the stiffness. He is not in control and wants to climb the ladder up to freedom. But he is not free. He is a prisoner and the only way he can feel free, can escape the torment of shame, is to make the decision of when to die. But it's a decision that nowhere in his mind can he find the means of making.

'Mary, Mary!' he hears a child's voice above calling. He wants to call for her too; for some company, some friendship, some conversation. He feels guilty about his growing interest in a girl so much younger than himself. A girl and a family who have treated him with nothing but respect and dignity, even within the confines of being underground. His gratitude is beyond the food that Mary brings each day, for it is her presence and her humanity that has nourished him more than any meal possibly could. He is indebted to the people of Erambie, although he has only met two. He is grateful for the family that has no doubt lied to others to keep his secret, to protect him.

His guilt over his feelings for Mary and the goodwill he has been shown is compounded when his thoughts shift to the death and tragedy of the war that caused him to be here in the first place. He is overcome with grief when he is reminded that many of those he fought and was captured with are no longer alive.

'*The Jungle Book* is showing at the Cowra Theatre,' Mrs Smith tells Mary as the children jostle around them both. 'The children have read the book many times,' she adds, handing Mary a copy. 'Rudyard Kipling is also one of my favourite poets, a poet of the Empire. I want the children to see this movie.'

'I want to see the Old McDonald and Donald Duck cartoons,' Carmichael whines.

Mary doesn't want to see the cartoons or the film. She doesn't want to go to the theatre at all. It's hard because she's dark and is supposed to sit up the front while the Smith kids can sit anywhere they want. As always, she chooses seats as close to the middle as possible and the kids don't know any different. The Donald Duck cartoons come on first, and then the film. It's about a boy who grows up in the jungle, with animals for friends. Mary thinks the Indian actor who plays the boy hero, Mowgli, is very handsome.

But it's difficult for Mary to focus on the movie. She's thinking about Hiroshi the whole time, trying to understand the spell she is under. *Is this love?* she wonders, *because if it is, then it feels wonderful.* Mary wants to know if love is also supposed to be full of anxiety and fear. And if the butterflies in her stomach will ever go away.

Mary isn't even aware if she is looking at the screen when there is some disruption next to her and Catherine pokes her in the side.

'Shh, what is it?' she asks. 'I thought you wanted to see this.'

Catherine whispers, 'Carmichael just said that abos belong in the jungle.'

Mary is disgusted but there is little she can do. She has never liked the Smith children because, compared to the Williams kids, they are over-indulged, have more than they need and are ungrateful for their privileges as white people. However, she also knows that the children just follow what their parents say, and Mr Smith is no doubt to blame, and has probably referred to the local Blacks in derogatory ways more than once. So she does nothing, because there is nothing she can do.

But when they walk home she refuses to hold Carmichael's hand in her own private protest.

There is a strong stench in Hiroshi's bunker. Hiroshi has become immune to it, and Mary tries to ignore it. She hands him a hard-boiled egg, some damper and the newspaper. He starts eating straight away. The occasional egg is protein but his muscles are weak; even though he's been doing push-ups and trying to exercise, there is little muscle tone left in his arms. The damper is something his taste buds have grown accustomed to, and his stomach appreciates it, but he never feels full.

'I can't stay,' Mary says with disappointment, 'the Smiths are going into town for a meeting and I have to sit with Catherine and Carmichael.'

Hiroshi doesn't look up. He is grateful but preoccupied – he wants to see what's in the newspaper, if there's any more news about the other escapees. Any word about when they might go home.

'I'll try to come back later.'

'Arigatō,' he says, already scanning the front page of the paper.

As he always does, he turns each page quickly, searching for any war news before starting at the beginning and reading through the paper line by line.

He stops when he sees a photo. He reads the headline: US Marines Blast Japanese'. There is no story, just the photo of a plane being shot down. The caption says: *US Marine howitzer hurls shells into enemy positions on Guam Island, strategic base in the central Pacific, which was recaptured by American troops.*

The image is harrowing, and he wonders how many men have died. How many families have been ruined? How many Japanese felt proud to die with honour for the Emperor?

He grabs his stomach, feeling like he has been kicked in the guts by a size 14 army boot. He slumps against the mud wall before hitting the ground. The war is still happening and rather than being there fighting, or even in a camp with other Japanese soldiers, he is hiding like a coward. Self-loathing settles in. He grieves for his own shame and that of his family.

A few hours later he hears the iron sheet move and panics. Mary has already visited once tonight, but she is here again.

'Mary, what are you doing here? What is wrong?'

'I just wanted to check you were okay.' She pauses. 'You seemed different today.'

'I am good, thank you. Thank you,' he says, grateful for the girl caring so much, but not wanting to talk any more, emotionally drained from the endless uncertainty. 'But I do not want you getting into trouble.'

'I must go, but I am glad to see you are good.' She departs as swiftly as she arrived.

Mary walks quickly back up to the hut where both her parents are standing in the kitchen with hands on hips.

'What do you think you are doing?' Joan says, straining to keep her voice low. 'Going down twice in one night is just a silly and irresponsible thing to do. We can't risk you getting caught. What were you thinking?'

'He's not well,' Mary says.

'Sick? What kind of sickness?' Banjo panics. 'The last thing we need is for him to get sick. It's not like we can look after him down there if he's sick.'

'Not sick like that, Dad, sick like sad sick. His face is sunken and his eyes . . . Do you know what I mean?' She looks at both her parents. 'He is sad sick.'

'My girl, there is nothing you can do about that. It is something that will come from being at war, from being locked up and from being away from family.' Joan is hugging Mary. 'But all we can do is keep him fed and safe right now, I don't want you getting too close to him.'

Mary says nothing.

'Do I make myself clear?' Joan is straining not to raise her voice.

Mary nods.

'"13 October 1944: He'll sink their ships . . . While you provide the means . . ."' Mary reads the heading of an advertisement for Victory Loans to her parents, and her Uncles Sid and Fred. Her Uncle Kevin is back from droving but it's his birthday and the men reckon that women and dancing will be on the cards. 'He'll find another heart to break too,' Banjo had said earlier, sarcastically.

Mary continues, '"Between him and Tokyo stands a Jap armada – but he and his mates are out to sink every Nip in the Pacific and Indian Oceans. We've a thousand times as many hearts of oak as Drake had. And we've got the ships for them to man. But we want more and still more ships. We want myriad torpedoes to blast every Jap from the ocean. But every torpedo fired costs 3,230 pounds. So lend, lend every pound you can muster to speed Victory. Invest in the Second Victory Loan."'

'I really hate those advertisements,' Joan says. 'Do you think anyone in Cowra actually supports them?'

'Fat Bobbo!' Banjo, Sid and Fred all say simultaneously, then laugh. It is the only moment there has been humour for some time when talking about the war. Although the war is no laughing matter, and they all know it.

Mary doesn't take the paper to Hiroshi; she knows that this kind of thing will only cause him grief. His mental stability is already questionable. She knows he feels guilt and regret and longs to be with his family, if not on the warfront. She wants to take his mind away from the misery that causes the grief, even if momentarily.

'What are you doing?' Mrs Smith asks Mary as she catches her flicking through a book from the shelves she should be dusting. Mary has to think quickly because she doesn't want to get into trouble and be summoned to the Manager.

'I would like to read some poetry,' she says cautiously. 'Since I left school I have nothing to read, just the newspaper, and that's nearly always depressing.' Which isn't a lie. 'You mentioned you loved the man who wrote *The Jungle Book*,' she says, thinking on her feet.

'Yes, dear, but this is also a very, very good collection you could read.' Mrs Smith takes the volume from Mary, and runs her fingers over the title, *The Man From Snowy River and other verses*. 'A. B. Paterson has written the finest poems you are likely to read, right here.' She waves the book in front of the girl.

Mary listens, grateful for not being caught red-handed in the throes of theft. But she is also interested in knowing more about the poet so she can share it with Hiroshi.

'Do you have a favourite poem?' Mary asks, impressed with her newfound ability to think and lie on the spot, 'or is there a popular poem that I should focus on?'

'There are two very famous poems,' Mrs Smith says, flicking through the volume, looking for them. 'Mr Smith occasionally recites them after dinner. One is obviously "The Man from Snowy River" and the other is called "Clancy of the Overflow".'

Mary makes a mental note to read those poems a few times over before sneaking the book to Hiroshi. 'What does the A. B. stand for?'

'Andrew Barton, but everyone calls him Banjo,' Mrs Smith says as if she knows him personally. 'His nickname as a child was Barty, but apparently when he started publishing his work it was under the name "The Banjo", which everyone knows was adopted from one of his favourite horses. Can you imagine that, Mary, naming yourself after a horse? I haven't heard anything more ridiculous in my life. But I do like his poetry.'

'My dad's nickname is Banjo too,' Mary says excitedly. 'He taught himself to play the banjo, that's why, and he is the best player in all of Wiradjuri country.' Mary speaks proudly, but Mrs Smith ignores her comment, almost as if she wants to ignore the fact that Mary and her family are Black, and continues to look through her prized volume. Mary is a little nervous now, but to her surprise the woman hands the Paterson book back to her and takes another book from the shelf.

'You *must* read Henry Lawson as well, because, like Banjo Paterson, he is one of the best poets in Australia. It's one of the first things I learned when I came here. They are not like our British poets Keats and Blake, but they are very good nonetheless.' Mrs Smith's eyes almost light up when she talks about *her* British poets, and Mary thinks that there is possibly something about her boss she doesn't know. 'I can't imagine anyone ever writing more beautifully than these men about this country that is now my home.'

'Do you mean I can borrow this?' Mary asks, trying to hide her excitement but wanting to be absolutely clear about what Mrs Smith is offering.

'Yes, I think it is very important for your education, Mary. There is history to be learned, my girl. You see, Henry Lawson's mother, Louisa, helped get women the right to vote in Australia. She was what we call a suffragette. We owe her a lot.'

Mary doesn't point out that her own mother doesn't have

the right to vote yet – and neither does her father, for that matter – so she doesn't owe Louisa Lawson anything. She just keeps her mouth shut; she wants the books and right now that's all that matters. She feels an overwhelming sense of relief and gratitude because she didn't have to 'borrow' the books and that makes her feel even better.

'*In the Days When the World was Wide and Other Verses*,' Mrs Smith reads the title and hands the volume to Mary. 'Lawson was born in Grenfell, which is not far from here, Mary, so that's something to remember too. His inspiration may have come from these very parts.'

Mary thinks it's strange that Mrs Smith is so loyal to Cowra and wonders how she can forget about her own land in England so easily. Mary could never imagine doing that – she'll always just love Cowra.

She nods, takes the books with genuine gratitude and says, 'These are wonderful, Mrs Smith. Thank you. I will read them over and over again.' It's not a lie; she will read them over and over before giving them to Hiroshi, so if Mrs Smith quizzes her she'll have the answers.

For the last few days when Mary has visited Hiroshi, he has been sad. He appreciates all the meagre offerings of food she has brought with her, but he barely tastes anything any more. It's like his senses are failing him as he spirals into an emotional darkness that matches his surrounds.

In some ways, he's glad to be in a physically dark space so he can hide, withdraw into his even darker emotions and memories. Mary's smile each visit offers only momentary flashes of brightness to his day, and he is struggling to remain sane with so much solitude, only his thoughts as company.

When she descends the ladder, he notices something bulky under her dress that seems too big to be food. And he doesn't even know if he could eat much more – while he is hungry, he is also nauseous, and wondering if there is any purpose in eating to stay alive.

'Hello,' Hiroshi says softly, standing, as he always does, out of respect, but with shoulders sagging.

'Konichiwa!' Mary responds, so full of life and energy Hiroshi is taken aback. He has not seen her this bright ever.

He is grateful to hear his own language again, even the simple greeting that he had taught her weeks ago that she now feels comfortable saying. He immediately wonders what has happened to make Mary so cheerful – perhaps the war is over?

'I have something for you. A surprise,' she says, handing him some rabbit stew and a jar of water, before working the surprise out from under her dress in as ladylike a fashion as possible.

Hiroshi takes the food and water and doesn't have much interest and even less imagination at that moment to begin to wonder what his surprise might be; news that the war is over, or word of his friends from the camp is what he would like. He sets the food down beside him and looks at Mary like a lost child.

'Two books of poetry,' she says, 'the best poets from Australia, apparently. They are from around this area. I thought you would like to read something.'

Hiroshi can see that Mary is excited about the gift, but as hard as he tries, he just cannot muster a reaction to match her mood. He can see the disappointment in her face when he can only manage to nod his thanks. He takes the books, appreciative of the gesture, knowing that they must have come from someone else, but not knowing from whom or where; unaware that the girl in front of him was willing to commit a crime, get herself into a lot of trouble, to make the gift possible. Hiroshi wants to be grateful but poetry will not fix anything. Nothing.

The moment is awkward. There is so much expectation and emotion: one wants to see a smile; the other wants to see the world again. Both want the space between them to be different.

'I better go,' Mary says, embarrassed that her gift has not been received as it was intended. She wonders if she has overstepped the mark, if she has misinterpreted their friendship. If Hiroshi really doesn't care about anything other than getting out, then the books of poetry are a stupid offering.

Seeing the disappointment in her face, Hiroshi steps towards her. She does not hide her feelings well, and that makes Hiroshi feel uncomfortable. 'Arigatō,' is all he can say. He moves to touch her arm, but knows that is not the right thing to do. It is not respectful. But he says, 'Thank you,' once more and smiles sincerely.

Mary's heart fills with relief that he is grateful and that they are friends.

IT RAINED RED MUD: DUST STORM ENVELOPES COWRA

No one at Erambie needs the newspaper to tell them about the dust storm that has beset Cowra over the last two days. The reddish brown dust from the dry western plains turned the rain into globules of red mud falling from the sky. The kids all loved it. They got as red and dirty and muddy as they could. But Joan found it a nightmare to get the bed linen clean. It felt like she was wearing her own path from the kitchen where she had to boil the water in copper pots before carrying it to the tub outside. Washing in a galvanised tub was also hard on the back.

Everyone is keeping windows and doors shut tight to keep as much dust out as possible. With rising temperatures taking the mercury to 93 degrees Farenheit with high humidity, no one is comfortable. Mary and her family sit in the kitchen but the walls are thin and the heat penetrates from early in the day. Although locals complain about the humidity, everyone is grateful that the drought looks like it will be broken by the downpour of rain, regardless of the dust storm. Joan is trying not to complain too much about the extra work in the laundry when rain is so needed.

All of the kids and most of the adults just want to swim in the Lachlan River, which is usually fed by the summer rain rather than the unexpected downpours of recent days. No one cares if the water is cold or not, the wet relief is all that matters. And the heat doesn't seem to bother the kids as much as the adults. They are out for hours on end picking blackberries along the river and making plenty of noise, because snakes like blackberries too. And according to the stories that Uncle Kevin tells, snakes also like little kids. The stories he tells make little James never want to leave Mary's side, but she doesn't mind. She likes having James and the other kids around and she teaches the younger ones to only pick large, plump, deeply coloured berries because, she says, 'They are the ripest and taste the best.'

For Mary, the dust storm also means extra cleaning at the Smiths' as a thin veil of reddish dust has settled throughout their home too. As she dusts the bookshelves she looks carefully at what else she might take to Hiroshi. Even though his reaction to her previous gift wasn't as she had hoped, she didn't think she should stop trying to keep his mind occupied, and there is little else she can offer to do. She looks for the poets Blake and Keats that Mrs Smith mentioned and finds them after some searching, but she guesses that they are prized possessions so will most definitely be missed, and decides not to 'borrow' them.

As she dusts the sideboard at the Smiths' she sees a pile of letters that have Red Cross stamps on them. They are addressed to people in Italy. She picks them up to read the names.

'Thank you, Mary,' Mrs Smith says, taking them from her. 'They are letters from the Italian soldiers, probably to their families, their girlfriends.'

Mary frowns.

'We have a letter exchange program,' Mrs Smith explains. 'The men write letters home. We post them, and quite often, they get letters in return.'

'All the prisoners do this?' Mary asks cautiously to conceal her excitement.

'No, just the Italians,' Mrs Smith says. 'Oh, we did have one Japanese soldier, but mostly they don't write home.'

When she arrives at the air raid shelter late that night, Mary can't wait to tell Hiroshi she has found a way to post his letter. But before she can share her news, Hiroshi gently takes his sleeve and wipes Mary's right cheek, an uncharacteristic gesture. It is the first time they have touched and while Mary is shocked, she doesn't show it, nor does she move.

'What is this?' he asks as he wipes her left cheek and looks at the dirty material, forgetting for the moment that back home he would never be so forward with a woman.

Mary explains what a dust storm is as best she can, trying to describe the debilitating heat and how it was talked about on the wireless at the Smiths' place.

Hiroshi has experienced the Cowra heat at the compound, and even though some of the dust has made it under the corrugated iron sheet and down to where he is hiding, he cannot imagine what the actual dust storm looked like above.

Mary can see that he is frowning with confusion. 'Do you have red dust and dust storms in Japan?' she asks.

'My home is near the sea, we have short, mild winters and long, hot summers, but we don't have the dust like you. We have a lot of rain in summer, and many typhoons.'

'Typhoons?'

'Yes, where my family live is the most dangerous place in all of Japan because of the typhoons. They are big storms that come from the ocean with very strong winds and torrential rain.'

'That's probably why we don't have typhoons in Cowra – there is no sea for hundreds of miles.'

'It rains mainly in the middle of the year when it is warm, but in spring and winter we have very little rain.'

'When is the best time of year?' Mary asks. 'When is it the prettiest?'

'Autumn is beautiful.' Hiroshi's mind wanders back to his home. 'We have very colourful leaves, we call them koyo.'

'Koyo, sounds like yoyo,' Mary says.

'Yes, and the koyo in autumn are like the cherry blossoms in the spring. And it has been a tradition for a long time for people to view the koyo.'

'Where do people go, is there a special place?'

'Oh, Mary, there are many special places all over Japan, each region has its own time in autumn when the leaves are at their most red or yellow or orange. Hiroshima, Fukushima, Nagana, Tokyo and Kyoto – they all have mountains and gardens people visit to enjoy the beauty of koyo.' Hiroshi closes his eyes for a few seconds.

'Are you okay?'

Without opening his eyes, he says, 'I miss my country when I think about the landscape. It is very different to here.'

'The mornings are darker later here and the days get cooler in autumn, and the leaves change colour in Cowra but we don't have a name for it,' Mary tells Hiroshi, who opens his eyes. Before she can think of anything else to say, he speaks.

'My favourite season is spring; I love the cherry blossoms. Near my home is a park, Kagamino Park, it has hundreds of cherry trees. Every weekend in spring my parents would take us there.' Hiroshi savours the memory. 'We would have picnics under the cherry blossoms. Special Hanami picnics where we looked at the cherry blossoms. I was a young boy who loved flowers. It must have been funny for my parents seeing me so happy with flowers.' But his happy memories cause sadness that overwhelms him again. He slumps down. 'I miss home. I miss my family.'

He buries his face in his hands and Mary doesn't know what to do. She sits next to him for a few minutes but she knows that her time is up. She must get back to the hut. She puts her hand on his shoulder as she stands and says, 'We are your family, too.'

As she gets to the ladder, she turns. 'I can't believe I almost forgot. I can post your letter, safely – it will go through the Red Cross.'

'Really?' Hiroshi feels renewed hope that there may be a chance he can contact his parents.

'Yes, quickly, here.' From her apron pocket she pulls an envelope that she has 'borrowed' from the sideboard at the Smiths'. She hands it to him. 'Can you write your address on here?'

Hiroshi rummages around in the dim light for the pencil he wrote his letter with. His hands are unsteady as he writes on the envelope. When he finishes, he slips his letter inside and hands it to Mary.

'I'll take care of it,' she says, and leaves.

11

2 November 1944

The Williams children run into the hut, breathless and scared but excited at the same time. James is squealing and as soon as Mary lets him off her hip, he heads straight for his mother, nestling between her legs as usual although he's shot up in height in recent months and he's almost too tall to fit. He clings to her thigh and the grasp is so uncomfortable that Joan has to pry her son from her body. She wonders if being the baby of the family and the only boy means he will always be this clingy.

'What's going on?' she asks Mary, who looks overwhelmed by all the noise.

'I don't know, I was just coming back from the Smiths' place and all the goothas were screaming and running in all directions and the mirris were howling and chasing their tails and I can't work out what happened.' Mary rubs her temples. 'It's giving me a headache.'

'I'll tell you what happened,' Betty says. 'Dottie, Jessie and I were all helping the littler kids play drop the hanky.'

'I got the hanky,' James pipes up, grinning widely as if he was the fastest in a race. Joan pats him on the head and nods for Betty to continue, but Dottie butts in.

'Then,' she says, 'a small man came and joined the game. He seemed friendly, he just wanted to play too, but –'

Before she can finish, Jessie jumps in. 'We all remember what Uncle Kevin told us about the birricks, and we got scared.'

'Uncle Kevin said the birricks move around the mission at night, remember? He told us to make sure we had all the wood we needed and everything inside before dark. Before the birricks start moving around the mission.'

Joan knows the story only too well. Like others, she believes there are spirits moving around outside of a night. 'That's it, no more playing outside after dark.'

'Oh, Mum,' comes the collective cry from Betty, Dottie and Jessie, and when James finally catches on, he says in a whiney voice, 'Oh, *Mum*,' and starts jumping up and down in protest.

'Don't make me get your father to talk to you about this. From now on, as soon as the big lights come on, I want you inside.' Joan is not going to argue with the children about it, and is glad that at least there is a little electricity at Erambie to give some light during the night.

'But, Mum, you know that playing outside when it's warm is what we do, there's nothing to do in here,' Jessie says grumpily.

Banjo walks in with Kevin just as Joan turns to wash some potatoes. 'What's all the racket? I can hear you lot outside. A man doesn't want everyone knowing his business.' He walks over and plants a dusty kiss on his wife's cheek.

The kids hope their mum doesn't tell their dad what's going on. Their father doesn't get cranky often, but they've seen him get wild when they misbehave and, as Jessie says, 'it's not good'.

'Maybe your Uncle Kevin can tell the story about the bunyip again,' Joan says, hoping her brother-in-law hears. She thinks it's a good time to remind the young ones of the stories the Wiradjuri live by and the beliefs that have been passed down from generation to generation that keep them all safe.

Kevin pulls up a stool, sits down and rolls a cigarette. 'The bunyip is half man and half beast.' He opens his eyes up wide and looks at each child one at a time to suck them into his story. The kids' eyes and mouths open wide too. They love it when their Uncle tells stories and it doesn't matter how many times they hear the same one over and over again, or how scared they might get, and they often do.

'The bunyip only comes out at night.' Kevin looks at his watch. 'So he's out there now!' The girls squeal, James cuddles into his mother and Joan smiles, grateful for the story. 'If you go near the river, and you know you are not supposed to, then the bunyip will drag you under and . . .'

The children all wait in anticipation as Kevin leans in.

'He will EAT you!'

With that, the girls all scream and run into their bedroom and James starts to cry.

'Come on, big fella, don't bung on the waterworks.' Kevin picks James up and mouths 'cry baby' to Joan as he carries the child into the bedroom, where the girls are cuddled up in the bed together.

'What was all that about?' Banjo asks.

'It's all under control,' Joan says and winks. 'I'll tell you later.' She doesn't want to stop her kids having fun, but the stories of the birricks, bunyips and gooligahs, the long held Wiradjuri stories are the same stories she heard as a child and they are real. She's not going to take any risks.

'Come,' Mary says the minute her feet touch the ground. 'Come.' She motions to the ladder.

'What are you doing?'

'It is a clear sky and a full moon, I want to see the rabbit. I want to see the rabbit with you.' Mary knows it's a risk. She knows it goes against everything her parents would allow. It's against everything her Uncles Sid and Fred had agreed to. But she wants to see the rabbit in the moon. 'Come,' she says again.

Hiroshi does as he is told, following Mary up the ladder and into the night air. It is hot and dry but the air is clean and the sky is a blanket of stars. Mary leads Hiroshi quietly behind the lavatory, where they sit on the grass and look at the moon high in the sky.

Hiroshi clears his throat then says, 'And he sees the vision splendid of the sunlit plains extended, And at night the wond'rous glory of the everlasting stars.'

'You remember the words from "Clancy"!' Mary says, astonished at how beautifully he recites poetry.

'Yes, I have read them many times, and usually they make me feel sad that I cannot see this.' He waves his hands in the air as if to run his palms across the starlit sky. 'Being trapped without this beauty, it is one of the hardest things, Mary.'

There are a few moments of silence.

'I heard alarms today Mary, I was worried.'

'It is November the eleventh, Armistice Day,' she explains. 'Everyone in the town stops at eleven am to remember those who have died in war.' She pauses. 'I was at the Smiths' today and I slipped your letter into a pile of Red Cross letters written by Italian soldiers. I think it will be on its way to Japan now, Hiroshi.'

Hiroshi closes his eyes and imagines his parents reading the letter but his thoughts are broken when Mary asks, 'Can you see the rabbit?' She is so enthusiastic he can't help but smile. 'Is it there?'

Hiroshi stares up to the moon and Mary stares at him, waiting to see recognition in his eyes. When he breaks into a smile, she knows he has seen it and she too looks to the sky.

The pair sit for a few minutes. There is silence, other than a barking mirri somewhere across the other side of the mission. Hiroshi is conscious of the female next him. He is only human.

He is present in the moment, enjoying the fresh air on his face. His thoughts shift to a vision of cherry blossoms – the warmth of the light pink flowers, the pure whites and the soft yellows – that always calmed his mind, that often inspired his own poetry, the blooms that carried him home whenever he was lonely. The blossoms he knew as a child were in a world that is so far removed from the life he is living now that he wonders if he ever really had a childhood or if he just dreamed it.

Life is like the cherry blossom, he reminds himself; short, but exquisite. He thinks of the last time he was in Ueno Park when he was at university and how he sat beneath a tree waiting for a cherry blossom to fall on his head for luck – the myth that most students half-believed in, just in case their study didn't pay off. Back then he had Benika, also a uni student. They were in love. He momentarily forgets that Mary is there and remembers the feel of Benika's flesh against his and wonders if he will ever feel a woman's breath on his skin again. Will he ever know the joy of love again? Will he ever have children? A son that he might one day may be forced to send to war? His head is aching with the same thoughts he has had over and over and over again.

He thinks of Benika naked, her soft flesh against his own, of their lovemaking in a hotel room they rented for a few hours before he left. It is a treasured memory that kept him warm and hopeful in the brutal landscape of New Guinea.

Then Mary gasps, startling him from his thoughts.

'I see it! I see it, Hiroshi.' Tears form in her eyes – her belief that they could be brought together by sharing the sky was correct. Sharing the rabbit in the moon has helped them connect like she knew they would. She feels close to Hiroshi, and he lightly touches her hand.

148

'What's that?' he asks, breaking the spell Mary is under. 'There.' He points.

Mary sees the red glow of a lit cigarette in the distance and imagines it's Claude still trying to hide the fact he smokes. She strains to see the figure more clearly and realises it's her Uncle Kevin. The cigarette is moving in their direction.

'We better go,' she says, getting up quickly and running around to the opening of the bunker. 'Quick,' she urges Hiroshi. 'Get back down there. I'll see you tomorrow.'

Hiroshi moves like a fox, just as he did the night he arrived here, and Mary catches her breath as she walks back to the hut, arriving there at the same time as Kevin.

'What are you up to, Mary?' he asks.

'Nothing, Unc, just using the lav.'

'I think you should get to bed,' he says, looking towards the bunker.

Mary goes inside, hoping her Uncle didn't see anything, doesn't go down to see Hiroshi and doesn't mention anything to her parents.

A week later, while Mary is dusting the bookcase at the Smiths', she's surprised to find a book of poetry by a woman, and wonders why Mrs Smith hadn't given her this one to read. The poet's name is Mary Gilmore. She reads the title of the volume to herself, *Under the Wilgas*. She assumes it means the wilga tree. Then she opens the book gently as if it is a precious gift, and it will be, a gift for Hiroshi. She turns the pages slowly, reading the names of the poems until she stops at the words 'The Waradgery Tribe'. It sounds a lot like her tribe, even though her family spell it differently. *This is a book about Aborigines*, she thinks. *This is a poetry book about* us. She puts it in the band of her undergarments under her calico dress. *I'm just borrowing it*, she tells herself. *I am not a thief.*

There's a knock at the door and Mary panics. The book is secure, but it looks a little bulky.

The grocery delivery boy Raymond is standing at the door when she opens it. 'Hello, Mary,' he says, grinning from ear to ear. 'You look a little flushed, are you okay?' He walks in with the box of food.

'Yes, I'm fine thanks, just about to leave for the day, so I'll unpack these before I go,' she says, gesturing for him to get out of the kitchen. 'I'll tell Mrs Smith you were here, of course.'

'Has Mrs Smith been baking, Mary? She usually gives me a biscuit.' Raymond looks hopefully around the kitchen.

'No, not this week,' she says abruptly.

'Oh, I really like her biscuits, Mary. That's one of the reasons I like dropping off the Smiths' groceries.'

'Okay, well, you better get going, Raymond. I'm sure you've got other deliveries.'

Raymond doesn't move. 'No, this is my last delivery for the day. I can stay and talk if you like.'

'I need to get Catherine and Carmichael from school,' Mary says, walking to the front door. 'Thank you for the groceries, see you next week.'

'Oh, okay, I'll see you next week,' Raymond says.

Mary thinks he's got a weird look on his face, but she's just relieved the book hasn't fallen to the floor while he was standing there.

After their stolen moment sharing the moon, Mary feels even more brave about taking Hiroshi out late at night, even though she's still not sure whether her Uncle Kevin saw them or not. She wants Hiroshi to have more to his hidden days and nights than her brief visits. He can be protected, but he also needs to experience some of the land here, the country she loves so much.

'Come,' she says again.

'Okay,' Hiroshi says, without hesitation this time. 'The moon?'

'No, the river,' she says. 'Would you like to swim?'

'Yes!'

They climb out quietly and run, hunched over, to the river, Mary leading the way along the well-worn path the kids use every day. It takes only a few minutes before they hit the riverbank.

'We're here,' she whispers. 'This is the Lachlan River.'

Hiroshi doesn't hesitate to take his shirt and pants off. 'This will be the first bath in years,' he says, while Mary stares at the ground, blushing. She hears a splash and looks up to see her love in the water. He is laughing.

'Shh,' she says. 'Don't make too much noise, the mirris will come down.'

'Oh,' Hiroshi replies softly.

As he swims around and washes his body with only his hands and the fresh water, Mary sits on the bank, looking around to make sure no one sees them.

'Are you coming in?' he asks.

'No, it's safer if I stay here.' Mary knows that if she bumps into her Uncle again, being outside at night will be a lot easier to explain if she is not dripping wet. She is happy that Hiroshi is experiencing the river and the life just being in it could bring.

'It's time to go,' she says ten minutes later. 'We should get back.'

Hiroshi is on the bank and dressed quickly, revitalised by such a simple yet risky act.

'Do you feel better?' Mary asks.

'I feel like I have just been born again,' he says. 'Thank you!'

Mrs Smith tells Mary she can finish as soon as the laundry is done because the family is going to Bathurst to do some Christmas shopping. Mrs Smith says she'd rather live in Bathurst because it is nearly twice the size of Cowra and has more things to do – and obviously better shopping. Mary wishes the Smiths lived in Bathurst too, but today she's just grateful they are there for the afternoon. She has already decided she will spend some time with Hiroshi. Seeing him more often and not telling her parents has become normal for her; she doesn't see it as deceit, rather, she tells herself she is saving them from worrying.

As she descends the ladder, Hiroshi is surprised by the early visit but stands immediately, holding a piece of paper with both hands. He presents it to her as if it is an official document.

Mary is consumed by emotion before she has even read the words, then she whispers to herself:

> *Mary my angel*
> *Nourishes my heart and soul*
> *Gives me hope to live*

As she pores over the Haiku she is overwhelmed, flooded with warmth and love for the man in front of her. She starts to cry. Hiroshi moves slowly closer to her and holds out his right hand. She takes it, holding the paper in the other. It's the first time they have been so intimate. Their eyes lock, the powerful emotion of the moment so new and exciting for both of them.

Mary is not sure what to do. She does not know how to behave with a man when she has feelings like she's never experienced before. She has never kissed a man.

Hiroshi doesn't know this but guesses she is pure. Either way, she is an angel to him. The angel who gives him hope for the future.

The silence seems like an eternity, but neither can find the appropriate words to fit the moment they are caught in. They move towards each other. Hiroshi is only a little taller than Mary, and he places the softest kiss on her forehead, his heart beating like a taiko drum, though not for war. *She smells like spring*, he thinks, like the flowers he misses seeing and whose scent he misses breathing in. He places his arms around her, feeling how frail and thin she is; a waif hidden under the clothes that conceal his food each day.

Mary falls comfortably into his embrace. 'You're safe,' she whispers in his ear. But she means she is safe too. There is a comfort in being held so close to another person who is not a family member, a different comfort that brings a new dimension to her life. She pulls back and looks slightly up into his eyes, and a single, dignified tear falls down the left side of her face.

Their first kiss is full of everything the war lacks: love, compassion, respect. It lasts only seconds but will linger with them both for a long time after.

The December sun is scorching. It's stifling hot in Cowra, days are hitting one hundred degrees and everyone wants to spend the time lying around like the mirris, who find any shade under any tree or hut where they can collapse. Mrs Smith is too hot to do anything with her children so Mary is charged with taking them to the pictures or to the river to swim.

There are dances at Jubilee and Lyric Halls and Mary wonders what it might be like to go one day. When the war is over and Hiroshi is one of the community and they can live there together, will they both be able to go to the dances? She knows it's a daydream, even if she dreams it in the night time. Mary now devotes the time she used to spend plaiting her younger sisters hair on herself instead; brushing her own hair one hundred times a night and wearing it out when she visits Hiroshi, removing the band from it as she walks down the yard.

Most nights now, Mary is happy to be in bed as early as possible after her visits. She pretends to be asleep and spends hours thinking about the kiss and about a future with Hiroshi. She desperately wants the war to be over so he can live above the ground like a human being and not some caged animal.

12

Over the next few days, Joan notices something is differ-ent about her daughter aside from Mary's increased attention to her appearance. She is not as attentive at meal times, and eats barely anything of the meagre helpings she receives. She's caught daydreaming and is forgetful about doing small chores: boiling water to bathe James; brushing Jessie's hair; making sure the bedroom floor is swept spotless in case the Manager happens to come and check. Joan knows something is going on but says nothing until Mary drops an egg.

'You silly girl,' she says, bending down to tidy up the mess from the floor she had already scrubbed clean that morning.

'I'm so sorry,' Mary says sincerely, getting on her knees to help, picking up fine pieces of eggshell as her mother mops up the egg yolk with a rag.

'Sorry is not good enough.' Joan raises her voice. She can't remember the last time she was this angry with her daughter, with anyone. 'We don't have food to waste because you're daydreaming, Mary. What's going on?'

'Nothing's going on. Accidents happen, Mum,' Mary says. She has never answered her mother back before.

'Don't take a tone with me; I know it's that man you're spending time with. You've changed, and I don't like it.'

'It's not Hiroshi!' Mary cries. 'He hasn't changed me. He's very nice and smart and never raises his voice, and when the war is over and he can live up here and get to know everyone, you will see he is just like Dad and Uncle Kevin.' Mary stops suddenly, knowing she has said too much.

'Like Kevin! Dear Lord,' Joan says, looking towards the heavens. Not only does she not want her daughter to be romantically interested in a Japanese soldier but she also doesn't want Mary to fall for a womaniser like Kevin. 'Mary, when the war is over, Hiroshi will go back to Japan. You know that, don't you?' She clutches her daughter by both arms. 'He's only here until it's safe for him to leave. He won't be staying here forever.'

Mary breaks free from her mother's grip and runs out the door.

'You're not thinking clearly,' Joan yells after her, distressed about their argument, concerned about her daughter's welfare, and wondering how far her meetings with Hiroshi have gone.

When Mary returns, Joan has the food and a jar of water packaged up as usual. 'Go into the bedroom, kids,' she says grumpily. 'Get out from under my legs, James, and go with your sisters.' She pulls him away from her. 'Now!'

'What's going on?' Mary asks, glancing at her father.

Banjo looks up at his first born, his most trusted daughter, and feels pain at the knowledge she is growing up, but also that something untoward might have happened with Hiroshi.

Joan wishes both she and Banjo had gone down to Hiroshi earlier, but they hadn't wanted to risk a trail of different people back forth; keeping it simple, one routine, one person, was the safest thing to do. Perhaps they have been too trusting of their daughter. And obviously had been too trusting of the man. Joan is angrier with herself and Banjo than with Mary. All the negatives about the Japanese are floating around in her mind and she feels sick at the thought that maybe the man they are protecting is as bad as Kevin had said. There is no proof of anything, only Joan's hunch that something has happened between Mary and Hiroshi, but she is certain that her daughter has feelings, however naïve, for the man they are hiding. What had she and Banjo been thinking?

'Mum?' Mary asks. 'What's going on?'

'I'll take the food down to him tonight. I want to meet him and see why you've become so silly lately. All you were ever supposed to do was deliver the food. Keep him alive. We were just doing what good Christians would do. And now look.'

Mary looks at her father. 'Dad?'

'Do as your mother says, Mary, we've been waiting for you to come home so you can sit with the kids while I watch your mother. Now go into the children and keep them in there until she comes back.'

Joan is nervous as she walks out the back door. She hasn't really thought about what she's doing, of what Mary has done for months.

'Be careful,' Banjo whispers behind her.

Joan knows that she is supposed to be pretending to go to the lav, is supposed to look slyly at both sides of the backyard to see if anyone is watching. She is most concerned about Marj, who poses the biggest threat. It's a hot night and there are flies around. Joan's not as confident as she thought she'd be but she is determined to get to know the man she believes Mary is besotted with.

She slides the corrugated iron sheet across. It is still warm from the heat of the day. She's noisier than she wants to be, and fears the sound will draw attention, but she can hear music in the distance and hopes that will drown it out. She climbs down the ladder carefully. When she reaches the last rung and has both feet firmly on the ground she can't see anything and panics.

'Oh no,' is all she can say as she fumbles for the lantern.

Hiroshi sees it is not his angel and he panics too. Joan lights the lantern and they stand still, just looking at one another.

'I am Joan,' she says, struggling to be calm. 'Mary's mother.' Joan is stern, she is angry with herself for even allowing her daughter to be alone with a man she doesn't know.

Hiroshi just looks at her, confused.

'Here's your food, some damper and water. It is all we have tonight.'

Hiroshi takes the food and bows his head with respect. 'Arigatō, thank you,' he says gently. 'Thank you for everything.'

Joan stares at him. She watches him attempt to straighten his dirty clothes. He is unshaven and crumpled. She knows he has only been able to change clothes when she has given them to Mary and she is looking at him the same way Mary has been. She feels sorry for the man in front of her.

'My mother will be very grateful that you have saved my life. I don't know how I can ever repay you, but in my heart I am so thankful.' Hiroshi is sincere, his words the most genuine of any stranger Joan has ever heard. She thinks of Hiroshi's mother, and tries to imagine what she is going through, not only having sent a son to war but probably believing he is dead. She thinks of little James who never leaves her side, and as clingy as he is, and as sooky as many believe him to be, she hopes he never has to endure a war like that happening in the world today. It is the first time she has thought about Hiroshi and what they have been doing for him from the position of a mother.

Joan feels relaxed with Hiroshi and can see almost instantly how easy it would be for her daughter to be comfortable around him. And although she doesn't want Mary to have an emotional attachment to him, she can understand the sympathy and caring her daughter must feel. 'I must go,' she says, making her way back up the ladder. She struggles to put the sheet across again and walks at speed up the yard. When she gets to the hut, Marj is there.

'You're out late,' her neighbour says.

Joan fumbles and stammers, 'Ah, so, so . . . are you.'

'I saw you take off down the yard,' Marj states with an official tone, 'but it took me a few minutes to get out of my housedress and get my boots on. Everything okay?'

Joan's heart is racing, she's not good at lying, and what could she possibly be doing in the dark outside for such a length of time?

'I'm on my rags,' she says, which is all she can think of. 'Very heavy,' she adds, hoping Marj doesn't want to talk about it anymore.

Marj peers at her, distrusting. 'Hmmmm, at least it means there's not another one on the way, James never leaves your side as it is.'

'Yes,' Joan sighs.

'Well, I hope you get a good night sleep, Joan.'

'Yes, I am so tired, a big day at the convent and another one tomorrow, so I need to get to bed early. Good night.' Before Marj has the chance to say anything else Joan is inside with the door shut, her heart beating frantically, and Banjo waiting anxiously.

'What happened with Marj? I saw her out there but couldn't do anything.' Banjo puts a cup of tea in front of Joan as she sits down, exhausted from the stress of it all.

'Marj is fine, I fixed that. But that man, he is not fine. I feel sorry for him.'

'So you can understand why Mary is so concerned then?'

'Oh no, Banjo, I am concerned like a mother,' Joan says.

'And Mary is concerned like a sister then,' he says, seeking confirmation.

'Perhaps she is, but I know that dreamy look, Banjo, and it's not one a girl has for a man she thinks of as a brother.'

13

'The goothas are talking about Santa coming, so we'll have to do something for Christmas,' Joan says to Banjo who is counting the endowment, knowing the three younger girls and James should have something from Santa. It's two days before Christmas and times are tough. Gifts are rare and food is still rationed but he and Joan will do what they can. Banjo wants to provide for his family and has been lucky with the work he has had building barns for some new farms near town. He's only half listening as his wife continues. 'Father Patrick has promised me a chook to roast,' she says, her mouth watering with anticipation. Christmas is the only time of the year they have chicken and it's a treat for everyone. 'There are some benefits for working at St Raphael's, Banjo,' she says matter-of-factly. Banjo doesn't respond but she keeps talking, and as much as he loves his wife, he'd be happy for silence. 'They have given me a lot of old clothes that I can mend and keep as well. You'll have some new trousers next week, and there's some for you know who,' she says with a nod towards the back of the house. Banjo finally looks up and nods back, knowing she means Hiroshi.

Banjo looks as his wife warmly for a few seconds. He wishes he could give her a better life. He wishes he could give her some money to go into town and buy some perfume or stockings or a nice pair of shoes. He wishes she could have some of the things the white women in town enjoy. A wireless to listen to like Marj has. He feels so much love for her as she pours his tea from the billy can that he wishes she would talk more now. He does love the sound of her voice, and hates himself for thinking otherwise only minutes ago. As he drinks his tea he has an idea about something for her for Christmas Day as well. It won't be fancy, but he knows she will like it, if he can just get that last job done. 'I have to go out for a while,' he says and leaves the hut.

Banjo walks into the kitchen with Kevin in tow. 'It's all goothas and mirris out there,' he says. They sit down at the table. It's already hot at nine am and Banjo is covered in sweat. 'It's good the church donated a few toys – I distributed them last night and it looks like most of them have something to play with.' He and Kevin have passed little dark girls sitting in circles and giggling, playing with fair dolls with blonde hair, not even caring how different the plastic girls in their hands are to themselves. One had a tea party set and was pretending to pour cuppas for the others, who were enjoying acting like grownups. Boys of all ages were throwing around not one but three footballs that had made their way to Erambie on Christmas morning. Banjo wishes he didn't have a bad leg so he could kick a ball around too. He's a bit envious that Kevin has always been able to be more active than he is.

Banjo disappears during breakfast, leaving Kevin at the table reading the paper. After the children finish their porridge they wash their faces and hands under the tap out the front of the hut and put on their best outfits. The girls have new calico dresses that Joan has sewn for them from material the nuns at the convent gave her; Joan worked late into the night to make sure her children had something special to wear. The clothes are a dull cream shade but each girl has a beautiful ribbon to put in her hair for colour. James has a new pair of shorts but they are a bit big and are being held up by the piece of rope. He loves them and smothers his mother in hugs and kisses.

'Uncle Kevin, Mary gave us a penny to buy you a present, and we got you this,' young Jessie says and hands over a box of matches.

'This is the best present anyone has ever given me.' Kevin hugs Jessie, then winks at Joan and says sternly, 'But you know little kids shouldn't play with matches, don't you?' And the four children all nod a wide-eyed yes. The girls look more than pleased with their efforts and the gratitude their Uncle has shown.

'You know what we can do with this newspaper?' Kevin asks the children, waving it around in the air. 'We can make it fly.'

The children all moan, not believing a word their Uncle says.

'Don't be silly, newspapers can't fly,' James says, hitting himself on the forehead.

'What? You haven't seen a kite before?' And the kids all laugh.

For the next little while Kevin is busy making a kite from the newspaper, using twigs he sent the kids out to find. When it's finished Kevin is very proud of himself and the kids are excited. 'Well, come on then, a kite is meant to be in the sky, not inside!'

James is the first one outside, bouncing up and down and clapping his hands with excitement. Before long other kids from the mission are standing close by as Kevin tries to woo the low, hot breeze to lift his newspaper kite into the sky. When he finally gets it up there are cheers and roars of laughter. 'Give me a turn,' James squeals and his Uncle helps tie the string around the little boy's hand so the kite doesn't get lost to the atmosphere.

Banjo returns to the hut looking very pleased with himself as they all sit around drinking glasses of water with cordial. A treat for Christmas Day. He approaches Joan and hands her a brown box.

'What's that?' the four youngest children say in unison and Banjo grins from ear to ear.

'It's for your mother,' he says, a look of pride on his face. Joan and Banjo haven't given each other gifts since before the kids were born; everything has always gone into the children's health and wellbeing, and something extra like a toy at Christmas, if they can manage it.

There is confusion and surprise on Joan's face. James is at her apron within seconds, tugging and jumping and wanting to know what's in there. 'Is it for me too?' he asks.

When Joan opens the present she beams and hugs Banjo hard. Then she pulls an iron kettle from the box.

'So you like it then?' He puts his arms around his wife. The children are excited about their new iron kettle too, fighting over who's going to take it outside and fill it up.

'This is so fancy,' Joan says. 'I'm the luckiest mum on the mission today.' She's happy because even Marj's kettle is an old one. 'But how? There was no extra money,' she whispers in his ear.

'I built a table for old man Jones yesterday and he paid me enough to buy this, but said not to tell anyone. So don't tell anyone,' he replies, slapping her on the backside. Joan squeals and James and the three younger girls all giggle.

At lunchtime they sit down to roast chicken and potatoes with gravy and there's extra watermelon for dessert. Everyone is happily munching away, savouring every delicious mouthful, though Banjo notices Mary is quiet and not eating much. But he doesn't say anything, simply happy to have all his family around him.

As they relax after eating, James starts combing Jessie's hair and yanks out a big knot that stays in the comb. Jessie squeals and pushes her brother away. He's fascinated with the hair he's caught, struggling to pull it off the comb before throwing it on the ground.

'Ouch,' he says, in a delayed reaction to the shove and immediately starts sooking, looking at his mother.

'You don't want to leave that lying there,' Kevin says to his nephew, who stops his fake crying and looks adoringly at his Uncle.

'Why?' he asks as he climbs onto Kevin's lap and starts combing the hair on the man's arm.

'You should never leave hair in your comb or just lying around. You should burn it, or throw it in the fire.' Kevin looks at the stove. 'Not you, James, you aren't allowed to play with fire, but adults should put hair in the fire.'

'But *why*?' James whines.

'Because if the clever man gets hold of the hair he can use it against you.'

'But *why*?'

Banjo sits back and rolls a cigarette, listening to his brother tell an old story he's heard many times.

'Don't you know the story about the person who was really sick and the clever man went to see him and rubbed the sick man's belly, and he rubbed and he rubbed, and when the clever man walked out of the room he carried a bowl full of hair! Do you want to end up with a bowl of hair in your belly?' Kevin asks seriously, frightening the boy.

'NO! Mummy, I don't want to have hair in my belly,' James cries as he runs to his mother.

Kevin stands up and says bluntly, 'Well, don't leave the hair lying around then, okay?'

Joan shakes her head at Kevin, who shrugs his shoulders as if to say *What?* and walks out of the room.

168

On Christmas night, Mary takes some chicken down to Hiroshi. She ate as little as she could so there would be something special left for him, something different in case he hadn't had roast chicken before. She has struggled all day knowing he has been alone on such an important day; a day for family and celebration – and for some people, gifts.

'Chicken,' she says as she hands the meat over. 'We really only have it on Christmas Day.' Mary wonders what Hiroshi must think about them being so poor. What his own life was like back home and if they ate chicken often. 'Merry Christmas,' she says. 'Do you like chicken? My mum roasted it.'

'I like chicken,' he says, taking the small piece of white meat from her. 'Yakitori,' he says, hungry. 'Our chicken is called yakitori, we cook it under the heat,' he adds, gesturing to show how they serve chicken back home.

There is very little meat and it disappears quickly. But there is watermelon too, which he puts aside to eat later. Mary stands, waiting for the opportunity to hand over his gift.

'What?' Hiroshi asks because she is beaming. It's contagious and he smiles back. 'Why are you so happy?'

Mary hands him the book of poetry, pleased with herself for the find, and also feeling like an accomplished 'borrower' from the Smiths' house.

'Under the u-i-ru-ga-su,' Hiroshi sounds it out the way a Japanese person reads English characters and looks to Mary for approval.

'Willll-gaaahss,' she says. 'It's a tree. A wilga is a tree. And my Uncle Kevin told me wilga means orange tree.'

Hiroshi nods and to Mary he looks happier than he has since arriving. 'Merry Christmas, Mary, I am sorry I have nothing for you.'

'Oh no, I don't need gifts,' she says, stopping short of telling him that *he* is her gift. That his sharing, his friendship and what he has given to her heart is her gift.

14

EVEN DEAD JAPS

Mary reads out the headline on the front page of the *Guardian*, and then puts her hand over her mouth. She reads to herself the rest of the story that suggests the bad smell in the town's water can be blamed on rumours of dead horses, cattle and 'even dead Japs' found at Lithgow water supply. She summarises the claim for her parents and then adds, 'It's okay because it's been emphatically denied by Lithgow Council.'

The three of them screw up their faces anyway at the thought of dead anything in the water supply and wonder what is actually coming through the one and only tap at the front of their hut.

'Cuppa anyone?' Joan asks, trying to break the moment with some humour. 'The water's boiled so most of the germs will be gone anyway.' Neither Mary nor Banjo accept the offer, both thinking about what they had possibly already consumed.

Thankfully it's not long before the sweet, sugary juice of watermelon is dripping down everyone's chins – Kevin and a few of the other men have swum across the Lachlan to the Chinese gardens and pinched a few of the region's best fruit. Joan has struggled to cut the massive fruit into pieces the kids can manage with the only half-decent knife she has, but once done, the slices are shared and enjoyed.

'Where did you get this, Uncle Kevin?' James asks innocently. Everyone knows stealing is bad, but eating watermelon this way has been part of life at Erambie for a long time; all the locals indulge in the treat but no one thinks of it as really stealing. And it's always shared around, so the guilt is shared around too, until there is none left.

'I found it,' Kevin says, rubbing the young boy's head. 'I found it on the other side of the river, and I thought I heard it calling out to me to go get it and bring it here.'

James starts giggling. 'Don't be silly, watermelons can't talk,' he says, lightly slapping his sticky hand on his Uncle's arm. James looks at his mother. 'Why don't we grow watermelon in our garden?'

Joan gives her son the biggest smile he's ever seen. 'There's not enough room out there, and potatoes are a bit more filling, don't you think?'

James nods enthusiastically.

'This is better than the speck fruit the fruito gives us,' Jessie says, referring to the local fruit grower who sometimes gives away apples with spots on them.

'Yeah, it's not damaged. This is the most perfect watermelon ever,' Dottie says with a big slurp before giving her Uncle a hug. 'Thank you.'

Everyone jumps when there's a thumping on the door.

'Banjo, it's John Smith, open up.'

'Dear Lord,' Joan says, looking at the watermelon. 'There's no time,' she says to Kevin and Banjo.

'It's fine,' Kevin says. 'Leave it to me.'

John Smith walks in looking hot and bothered, his few strands of hair straggly and damp, and his shirt half hanging out and covered in sweat patches.

'Where'd you get that watermelon from?' he asks, knowing there's been thefts reported.

'I got it given to me for some droving work,' Kevin says.

'Would you like some, Mr Smith? It's very sweet,' Joan asks.

'I haven't got time.'

'Here, you can take a piece with you.' She hands him the largest piece she'd cut. 'And that's a nice shirt.'

Smith is taken aback by the compliment but tucks his shirt in and smoothes his hair over. 'Mrs Smith does like me to look good at work.'

'Of course she does,' Joan says.

'Was there something you wanted, John?' Banjo asks. 'I'm sure you didn't come for the watermelon.'

'No, that's right. There's been some sightings of a stranger around the station. Especially late at night. You know what's going on everywhere, Banjo, I want you to come to me if you hear or see anything. You got that?' With that, Smith walks out, slurping on his watermelon.

FUTURE OF ABORIGINE MISSION

A story Mary is reading in the *Guardian* causes her great concern: there's a proposal to either rebuild or relocate Erambie Aboriginal Station. She informs Banjo, Fred and Sid that two members of the Aborigines Board have already visited Cowra; one was a part-Aborigine named Mr W. Ferguson, who was a railway worker in Cowra from 1915 to 1916 and then a shearer at a number of district shearing sheds. '"Mr Ferguson admitted that the present camp was a disgrace and that the homes were little better than humpies."' She looks at her parents, knowing how proud they are about their home.

'Well, I don't like people saying Erambie is a disgrace,' Joan says. 'We all keep our homes as clean as any of the white people in town and we don't have any fancy cleaning tools or anything.'

Mary knows that her mother and Aunties Marj and Ivy and the other women are very proud of their efforts in maintaining their homes, even though the conditions they live in are generally well below the standards of the white people in Cowra.

Banjo stands and puts his arm around his wife. He's growing angrier by the minute but trying to remain calm for the benefit of maintaining peace. 'What else does it say, Mary?'

'"Mr Sawtell said that the policy of the Aborigine Board was to gradually assimilate the Aborigine into the white race.

The number of full Aborigines was growing smaller each year."' She stops reading, wondering if it is true.

'They think we are dying out,' Fred says, 'that eventually there'll be none of us left.'

'That's what they want, then we won't be a problem to them anymore,' Sid adds.

Banjo takes a deep breath.

Kevin walks in with a paper of his own and sits down. Mary keeps reading to herself while the others discuss their future and the proposed relocation. She thinks about the article she had read a few days before, about the evacuation of Tokyo. One million civilians have left the city. Mary has no idea what that means for the Japanese at war, for the Japanese in Cowra – for Hiroshi. She wonders if Hiroshi's family has been evacuated too, not really knowing how far his home is from the city. Mary decided not to show Hiroshi that day's newspaper, not wanting to upset him unnecessarily and make him worry. Her concern for him has been heightened since they kissed; Mary is consumed by her feelings for Hiroshi. She wonders if this is what her parents felt when they met. Did they think about each other constantly? Did the well-being of one become the main concern of the other? She wishes she could talk to her mother about this but she knows that's impossible.

When there's a gap in the conversation she finishes summarising the article to them. 'Mr Sawtell says he is doing interviews in town also and apparently there is considerable local opposition to the station remaining where it is as it covered a large part of an area that would be a future residential area of Cowra.'

Kevin lights a cigarette and it's stuck to his bottom lip as he says bluntly, 'It's all about land. They took the land that was ours. Then they moved us onto this land, and now they want to take *this* land from us too.'

Joan looks her brother-in-law square in the eyes and says with conviction, 'It will never happen, Kevin. Most of the people here will never want to leave. They'll have to physically remove us.'

Easter doesn't really mean much to most of the people at Erambie, except for Joan. She gets up early on Good Friday and says her Rosary with an extra Hail Mary for the community and one for Hiroshi. For everyone else, Good Friday is just another day but without school and work, for those who are lucky enough to have work. While Mary is at the Smiths' preparing breakfast for the family, most of the kids are playing rounders and kicking footballs while the men are smoking and yarning. Joan and the other women are busy doing their usual chores and preparing what food they have for later in the day.

When Mary gets home, Jessie walks in behind her. 'Mum, the Aunts want to know what time they can eat meat today?' On Good Friday the women on the mission check in with Joan because she works at the church and everyone reckons she'll know what the proper rules are around Easter time – even if they're not really Catholic, people still try to do what they think is the right thing.

'Tell them after twelve o'clock they can eat all the meat they want,' she says. 'And,' she adds as Jessie gets to the door, 'let them know cards are at Aunty Marj's again tonight.' The girl skips off cheerily.

When it's dark and everyone has been fed, Mary heads to her Aunty Marj's house where the ladies have started playing cards. She sits with the children as she always does. Mary is maternal and has always thought about the family she will have one day. In recent times when she gets carried away with her daydreams, she has wondered what a life and family with Hiroshi might be like. She can't imagine moving away from the mission, because Erambie is all she has ever known, but the thoughts of cherry blossoms and Japanese mochi rice cakes and rabbits in the moon are very exotic to her, and something she is convinced she would like to try, just for a little while. Meeting Hiroshi has opened her up to a whole new world and way of thinking. She has never travelled away from Cowra before and she has only really thought about as far away as Sydney, because some other girls her age had gone there to work. But now she is dreaming about a life in Japan with its Shinto religion and four main islands, and lots of fish to eat. What a different life she could have if she married Hiroshi. No more cooking and cleaning for the Smiths. No more rations. No more wearing calico dresses.

Mary is smiling to herself when she sees her mother looking in her direction. Joan is aware that Mary has done the food drop off, and links her daughter's beaming face to the man they're hiding. Joan would like to do the drop offs

177

herself but she knows, they all know, that there is more suspicion to be raised by an adult walking back and forth around the place than a young person. The young people are always out and about.

'Where's your father?' she asks Mary.

'Sitting on our verandah smoking with the other men,' Mary answers calmly, not wanting to give away the fact that her heart is still beating too fast for the rest of her body to catch up.

'Okay, let's play,' Marj says authoritively, bringing everyone's attention to the game and dealing the cards.

As usual, it's more of a gossip session than anything else, and before the first game is over, Marj begins in her standard way: 'You know I'm not one to gossip.' She says it so seriously she almost convinces the others it's true. Marj looks at her hand, then at Ivy and Joan. She lowers her voice and leans into the table, almost whispering, as though someone outside might hear her. 'But I heard on the grapevine that there's a woman in town who is pregnant to an Italian soldier.' Marj shakes her head in disapproval. '*Apparently* he did her gardens and taught her how to make spaghetti for her rabbit stew.'

'Sounds like he did more than her gardens.' Ivy chokes with laughter as she speaks. Joan chuckles but Marj isn't impressed.

'What's spaghetti?' Mary asks. No one really knows as they've not tasted it before.

'Obviously they're not married but *apparently* they're in love.' Marj shakes her head in disapproval again. 'Silly girl.

Why would you bother falling in love with a soldier from another country, *and* who's a prisoner of war?'

That last line makes Mary's ears prick up. She starts to worry, and wonders if Aunty Marj knows about Hiroshi; after all, she seems to know everything about everyone else, on and off the mission. She tries not to react in any way and pretends to be focused on entertaining the smaller girls, who are playing with dolls. But she keeps one ear on the conversation to see how the other women, especially her mum, react.

Ivy wears a cheeky grin that she is trying to force into a serious face so as not to annoy Marj, who is scowling. 'Yes, I did hear the same thing,' Ivy says, 'but to my mind, the Italians seem like very happy men, and that would be an attraction for any woman.'

'They are philanderers!' Marj states aggressively, as if she is the judge, jury and executioner. 'Sid doesn't like them either. He says they are doing the farming out at Mulyan and the vegies from there go to Edgell's, so they are taking jobs from locals. *And* he says they are too smarmy.' No one believes what Marj says about Sid, because he's the nicest fella, but they are careful about contradicting her. Not many people argue with Marj.

'I don't know,' Joan says, not wanting confrontation, but also knowing that the general feeling around town is that the Italians are trustworthy. 'Most people say the Italians can be trusted, they don't even have any supervision most of the time.'

'That's right! No supervision, then girls get pregnant.' Marj tut-tuts and places a card on the table aggressively.

'And what about that one fella who got back to the camp too late and the gates were locked and he was knocking to get back in,' Ivy pipes up, laughing as she talks. 'Have you ever heard of anyone trying to break *in* to a prison camp? Never in my life.' She slaps her thigh.

'They sound like a funny lot.' Joan is chuckling with Ivy but Marj isn't buying into the humour of the situation. 'And I'm told they can sing too.'

'So can *our* men. Isn't that right, Mary?' Marj says, attempting to garner support away from the table.

Mary smiles. Everyone knows the Williams men can play guitars and banjos and sing up a storm.

Joan jumps in: 'No one can compare to our fellas, but I have seen some of the Italians in church. They sing beautifully and they are also okay on the eye.'

'Mum!' Mary says, thinking it's wrong for her mother to even joke about looking at other men.

'What? My girl, I'm at church when I see these God-fearing men – at least they're Catholic. Did you know they have their own chaplain in the camp? They get to go to church more than I can.'

Mary knows now that her fears about Hiroshi being Japanese, a soldier and not Catholic are well founded. Her smile has disappeared as she thinks about how many obstacles they will face when the war is over and they want to be together. All of a sudden it seems nearly impossible.

Mary's thoughts are interrupted when Marj continues, 'Someone else told someone else who told *me* that rumour has it that the Japanese had threatened to castrate the Italians if they didn't participate in the breakout.'

Joan looks at Marj and nods in Mary's direction, wondering if her daughter knows what castrate means, and hoping she doesn't have to explain it.

Ivy is chuckling again. 'Well, that would've been a tragedy for the Italians, wouldn't it? I mean, if they are philanderers and all.' She laughs harder and Joan manages a giggle too.

'I thought we were playing cards,' Marj says in a serious voice, cutting off the conversation.

The Williams family are sitting down to breakfast on Easter Sunday, eating quietly as Joan is saying the Rosary. She won't go to Mass today because only white people go to church on Easter Sunday and Christmas Day.

Mary waits till dark, when the women are playing cards again, to take the food to Hiroshi. She's tells her mother she's going to bed early to read, but Joan knows what that means. Although it's not a full moon, Mary still searches for the rabbit he has told her about. She tells herself she can see it, because she so desperately wants to. To see the rabbit once more would connect her to Hiroshi via the sky again. She wants to experience his culture. She wants to experience the rabbit in the moon again, but the only rabbit close right now is the stew she carries with a potato for him. There is a little more than usual so she feels like it's a hearty Easter celebration, even though he doesn't celebrate Easter. She wonders if he will kiss her again. She hopes so. There is a feeling that the kiss creates that nothing else does and she wants to feel that again. But there hasn't been the chance till now. Mary has been paranoid not to draw attention to her infatuated self, but tonight, she is filled with anticipation.

'Hello!' she says when she reaches the bottom of the ladder. 'Happy Easter!' Mary cheerfully hands over the food, trying to get the official side of her visit out of the way so they can really talk.

'Arigatō,' he says, taking the parcel from her hands, holding his glance a little longer than is usual, and making Mary blush. 'Mary,' he says softly. 'Sometimes I sit here at night, counting the hours down until you will come back, and it is hard to believe that in the middle of this war, so far away from my family, hiding down here . . .' He pauses. 'I can't believe . . .' He stops. 'You make me smell cherry blossoms when there are none here,' he continues eventually. 'When there is only dirt and dampness.' He pauses again, takes a breath and says, 'Arigat̄o. Thank you for the food, but for so much more.'

Mary likes that Hiroshi looks at her with a new warmth and hopefulness in his eyes. But she blushes at his words and tries to camouflage the awkwardness with talk. 'I know you're not Christian but does anyone in Japan celebrate Easter? Do you know what it is?'

'My family does not celebrate Easter, but those who do call it fukkatsu-sai.'

'Fukkatsu-sai,' Mary repeats.

'It was a long day waiting for you,' Hiroshi says softly. 'I mean, longer than usual.'

Mary understands but doesn't know what to do next or

what to say, and is there any point? *Why couldn't Hiroshi be Italian?* she thinks suddenly.

'I really can't stay,' she says nervously, more conscious than ever before of how it will look to the outside world if she is found walking around when she told the women she was going to bed. She has become worried about everything: the neighbours finding out about Hiroshi; her parents finding out about their kiss and her feelings; her dreams about marrying Hiroshi not coming true. Heat rushes up her neck and over her face. 'I must go.'

Hiroshi takes her hand gently and says, 'If I cannot be in Japan, then this is where I want to be.'

Mary cannot think of anything to say. Could it be true that a man would rather be under the ground at Erambie with her if he had the chance to be somewhere else? No one has ever said such things to her before, but she believes him and her heart sings because of his words. She leaves, feeling a level of contentment she has never known before.

'Mum, Mum, Mum!' James flies into the room and straight to his mother's side. 'There's the biggest spider in the world in Cowra and it's eating chickens.' He's talking so fast and is so scared he nearly loses his breath. 'It's a lady spider and Uncle Kevin said it could eat little children too.'

Kevin strolls in as if on cue as Joan tries to calm James down. 'Don't go scaring the goothas with silly stories, Kev.'

Joan isn't happy that her brother-in-law has frightened her son to the verge of tears. 'You know there's enough of our own stories to keep them in line without chicken-eating spiders too.' She shakes her head, never surprised at the lengths he will go to entertain, scare or educate the local kids.

'It's no story, Joan,' he says, handing over the paper he picked up at Ryan's Place, where he'd stopped for a yarn. 'Look,' he says, pointing to the headline, CHICKEN-KILLING SPIDER IDENTIFIED AS A GIANT FEMALE TRAPDOOR. He raises an eyebrow and runs his fingers over James's head, pretending to be a spider. The child jumps right back up onto his mother's hip and almost out of his skin.

'Stop it!' Joan yells. 'It's not funny to scare kids like that. I'll have him awake with nightmares because of you.'

Chastised, Kevin leans over and takes the lad from his mother, swinging him up on his shoulders. 'He's all right, aren't you, little man?'

'Look, Mum, I'm taller than everyone!'

Joan reaches her hand out to touch her son's cheek and goes back to reading how a spider had mauled two chickens on a Cowra farm, leaving her with worry on her mind. The only reason she is happy about this story is that it's taken her mind off the war.

April the twenty-fifth is Mary's birthday, but it hasn't been a big deal since she was a little girl. It's also Anzac Day, and that *is* a big deal in Cowra. Many of the Erambie families walk into town to watch the march to show respect for those who served in the First World War. There are dawn vigils, memorial services and two-up games. Joan says an extra prayer and lights a candle when she goes up to the church on Anzac Day.

Mary is at the Smiths' when the march is on because it's also Carmichael's birthday and she is helping Mrs Smith bake a cake and some Anzac biscuits. Mrs Smith doesn't know it's Mary's birthday too. Mary isn't concerned about whether anyone knows, or even about a cake for herself, but she would really like to take a biscuit to Hiroshi if she can. And she'd rather not have to steal it.

'It's my birthday today too,' Mary says as she mixes the ingredients just as Mrs Smith has shown her many times.

The woman looks surprised, almost suspicious. 'How old are you?'

'I'm eighteen,' Mary says with pride. 'I'm nearly an adult.'

'Actually, you won't be an adult until you turn twenty-one, Mary, and that's a few years off but I think you are a very mature young lady,' Mrs Smith says as she places the tray in the oven.

Mary is grateful for Mrs Smith's words. She thinks she's a mature young lady too and is ready to make decisions about her own life, especially about Hiroshi.

There's a knock on the door and Mary moves swiftly to open it, flour still on her hands and a little on her face. 'Hello,' she says to Raymond, who is standing there with a grin. He starts to chuckle.

'What?' Mary asks.

'You have flour on your nose.' He rubs his own nose.

'Oh, we're making Anzac biscuits.'

'I thought you might be and I'll bet they're delicious. I reckon you'd be a great cook,' he says walking in. 'Hi, Mrs Smith,' he says. 'Dad says hello.' He breathes deeply. 'Gee, Mary's biscuits smell good.'

'I'll have some for you next week when you come with the delivery, all right?' Mrs Smith says, turning him back towards the door.

'Gee, thanks, Mrs Smith, I'll be off then. See you next week, Mary.' Raymond lingers a few seconds then sees himself out.

As Mary prepares to leave later that day, after the Smiths have had their dinner and Carmichael has had his cake, Mrs Smith gives Mary three biscuits in some cloth. 'Bring the cloth back,' is all she says gently. Mary knows that if Mrs Smith weren't married to John Smith she'd probably be a really nice woman.

Mary walks so fast towards the shelter she almost trips. She's being less cautious than usual about checking if anyone is watching. She slides the corrugated iron sheet across as she has done dozens of times before and rushes to get in and down the ladder. Hiroshi is her pot of gold waiting at the end of the rainbow.

She hands him some damper as a smile grows on her face, then she hands him the three biscuits. She hasn't eaten any herself.

'I helped make them,' she says proudly. 'Sometimes I bake with Mrs Smith.' She urges him to take a bite of the sweet biscuit. 'We made them for Carmichael's birthday, and Mrs Smith gave them to me because –' She hesitates, not wanting to make a big deal of it, because birthdays have never been a big deal for her family because they are so poor. 'It's my birthday too.'

'Tanjoubi omedetou,' Hiroshi says, handing the biscuits back. 'Happy birthday, but these are for you.'

Mary sits down, and Hiroshi follows. 'Let's eat them together,' she says with a level of excitement and birthday joy she has never experienced before. It was a romantic suggestion too, but she doesn't consider the forwardness of it as they indulge in the treat. The kerosene lamp fades and it is just the two of them in the dark, hearts beating so fast and loud they can hear the other's.

Hiroshi does not want to break the bond of trust he knows has been placed on him by those who send Mary down each evening, but what he feels in his heart and his body cannot be ignored. His mouth is dry from nerves and the biscuit, but nothing would be sweeter than her lips and he fumbles in the dark to find her face to kiss her. She has crumbs around her mouth.

Mary is thrilled, her heart racing and her body heating up. And her mouth, her mouth is glued to Hiroshi's and she never wants it to come unstuck.

15

'Happy birthday to you, happy birthday to you ...'
James is singing the loudest even though it's his own
birthday.

Mary is happy to see her baby brother enjoying his
birthday. He is too young to understand that his is the only
one that is ever celebrated this much. He's the baby of the
family and all his sisters spoil him with hugs and kisses.
Joan has given the girls some coloured pencils from the
church and a sheet of paper and they have made a pretty
card with a picture of a little boy that's supposed to be James
on the front.

'Sticky men, sticky men,' James squeals as his father hands
him two carved figures made from wooden rods. The sticky
men are traditional toys at Erambie. 'Sticky men, sticky men
go to war,' he says again as he makes the toy men fight each
other. It's clear to Banjo and Joan that their son has not

missed what has been going on around him, or that all little boys seem to like to fight like men.

Kevin has been away droving cattle to market, and he comes home laden up with meat from the trip. This time he has sausages too, which are a treat especially for James, who doesn't remember eating sausages before. Because Kevin has been working a lot and has some extra money, he takes the kids into town and buys them an ice block each. It's a real treat that only happens once or twice a year and only when their Uncle has been away working.

'You spoil the goothas,' Joan whispers to Kevin when they are all back later in the day.

Kevin looks at his nieces and nephew sitting in the shade of the kurrajong tree in the middle of the mission and feels a pang of loneliness. 'They're like my own,' he says. 'I love them like my own.'

Mary has missed the celebrations as she's been at the Smiths', but she walks over to the little children playing under the tree, picks up James and gives him a big kiss. She gives him a biscuit that she's made that day and that Mrs Smith let her take.

'It's my birthday,' he says, taking the biscuit and looking at it critically. 'I want to put this under my pillow and keep it for tomorrow,' he says, trying to wriggle down. 'I'm taking it home.'

'You should share it, James,' Mary urges.

'But it is too small to share with the other kids. They'll just get a crumb each,' he replies, racing back to their hut.

As she heads home slowly behind her brother, Mary's mind is preoccupied with her future. She has become increasingly edgy about what will happen when the war is over. Her head is filled with questions, with ideas and plans that may never work out, but she doesn't stop dreaming – the dreams keep her happy. The dreams give her hope. She keeps the dreams to herself, however, for she is not sure that Hiroshi is dreaming as well.

Churchill to Broadcast Tonight

Mary begins shaking when she reads the front page of the *Guardian*. Today the Williams' hut is full with her Uncles, Aunties, friends and as many goothas that can fit under the kitchen table and on the laps of the older people.

"'Winston Churchill will broadcast the official announcement that the war is over in Europe at eleven pm tonight, Sydney time. The King will broadcast at five am tomorrow, Sydney time. The delay in announcing the news after the signing of the peace terms is due to the disorganisation of German facilities. Time had to be allowed for all German troops to be contacted and ordered to lay down their arms. German commanders are making every effort to get the order to troops to cease fire.'"

The room erupts with cheers before Mary has the chance to finish the article. The war in Europe coming to an end is worth cheering for.

Mary scans the paper for anything that mentions the Japanese, but she finds nothing. She doesn't know if this is a good thing or a bad thing, but she hopes it means the end of the war in the Pacific too, and the beginning of her and Hiroshi being together.

Joan takes the paper from her daughter and starts to read quickly. 'There's a church service tomorrow at St Raphael's. I'm going to go to that.' She passes the paper to Ivy.

'I'll come,' Ivy says.

'Me too,' Marj adds.

'There's flags and streamers in the shops in town and on some houses,' Kevin says. 'Apparently there's going to be a Red Cross ball as well, do you think maybe one day we can go to those kinds of things?' He sits down, and James climbs onto his lap.

'There's no more war, Uncle Kevin,' James says.

'Ah, well.' Kevin looks at the adults. 'The war in Europe is over, but our fellas are still in the Pacific, so we need to wait for that to end too!'

'Come to our place, early in the morning,' Marj says, 'we can listen to the King's speech there.'

Marj ushers her neighbours into the hut through the back door; Joan and the kids are all half asleep but no one wants to miss out. They like listening to the wireless whenever they can but hearing the King speak, and about the war, well, that's something very important, and they know it. Fred is sitting and Marj makes tea as everyone takes a seat where they can. James sits uncomfortably on Joan's lap. Banjo arrives just as the broadcast begins. He doesn't want to listen to an Englishman who is supposed to be *his* King, but he needs to know what's going on with the war, and this is the best way to find out. He stands near the doorway, just close enough to hear.

'Shh,' Marj orders as the broadcaster introduces King George VI. Then the King begins to speak:

'Today we give thanks to Almighty God for a great deliverance. Speaking from our Empire's oldest capital city, war-battered but never for one moment daunted or dismayed – speaking from London, I ask you to join with me in that act of thanksgiving.

'Germany, the enemy who drove all Europe into war, has been finally overcome. In the Far East we have yet to deal with the Japanese, a determined and cruel foe. To this we shall turn with the utmost resolve and with all our resources.'

Mary is struck by the words 'determined and cruel foe'. And she thinks that is no way to describe Hiroshi: he is warm and kind and thoughtful and a man who misses his family. Cruel people aren't like that. They don't care about anyone but themselves. Mary doesn't like the King at all and wonders why she bothered to get out of bed to listen to his lies. She looks around the table to see the reactions of the older people. No one is looking at her, they are all straining towards the wireless to hear the broadcast through the crackling.

'Let us remember those who will not come back: their constancy and courage in battle, their sacrifice and

endurance in the face of a merciless enemy; let us remember
the men in all the services, and the women in all the services,
who have laid down their lives. We have come to the end
of our tribulation and they are not with us at the moment of
our rejoicing.'

Joan makes the sign of the cross in memory of Bibby
and Dooley Newton, at least one lost in the war, but she is
thinking of all the local men who sacrificed themselves to
fight for their Australia too.

'Armed or unarmed, men and women, you have fought
and striven and endured to your utmost. No one knows that
better than I do, and as your King, I thank with a full heart
those who bore arms so valiantly on land and sea, or in the
air, and all civilians who, shouldering their many burdens,
have carried them unflinchingly without complaint.'

Banjo hears the words 'and as your King' and can feel
his blood boil. King George VI is not his king. An English
monarch will never be his leader. Banjo's leaders were his
ancestors, his own father and Uncles and those who stayed on
Wiradjuri country and fought invasion.

'With those memories in our minds, let us think what it
was that has upheld us through nearly six years of suffering
and peril. The knowledge that everything was at stake: our
freedom, our independence, our very existence as a people;
but the knowledge also that in defending ourselves we were
defending the liberties of the whole world; that our cause
was the cause not of this nation only, not of this Empire and
Commonwealth only, but of every land where freedom is
cherished and law and liberty go hand in hand.'

Banjo is furious when the King talks about freedom and independence and liberty, none of which his own people have, none of which the Australian government will give his people, even if they went to war for them. He wants to scream so loudly that the King will hear him all the way over the oceans in Britain: *Freedom is only cherished by those who have it.*

Kevin has joined them, looking a little worse for wear, but nobody takes much notice. He stands in the doorway squashed next to Banjo with his arms folded, a cigarette stuck to his bottom lip.

'This comes upon us at a time when we have all given of our best. For five long years and more, heart and brain, nerve and muscle have been directed upon the overthrow of Nazi tyranny. Now we turn, fortified by success, to deal with our last remaining foe. The Queen and I know the ordeals which you have endured throughout the Commonwealth and Empire. We are proud to have shared some of these ordeals with you and we know also that we together shall all face the future with stern resolve and prove that our reserves of will-power and vitality are inexhaustible.'

'What the fuck would they know about anyone's ordeals?' Kevin says into the silence, expressing what Banjo had been thinking but would never have said out loud, especially in front of his wife and children.

'Kevin!' Joan is disgusted. The kids are scared by the violent outburst but also a little entertained, as they often are by their Uncle's unconventional language and behaviour.

'Are you drunk?' Banjo asks.

'Shh,' Marj orders with a glare that pierces right through Kevin's body. If looks could kill, Kevin was dead and buried three times over.

'There is great comfort in the thought that the years of darkness and danger in which the children of our country have grown up are over and, please God, forever.

'We shall have failed and the blood of our dearest will have flowed in vain if the victory which they died to win does not lead to a lasting peace, founded on justice and goodwill.'

Kevin is not game to say another word for fear of not only being thrown out of the hut but of being ostracised by Joan forever. But when he hears the words 'justice and goodwill' he huffs and shakes his head.

'To that, then, let us turn our thoughts to this day of just triumph and proud sorrow, and then take up our work again, resolved as a people to do nothing unworthy of those who died for us, and to make the world such a world as they would have desired for their children and for ours.

'This is the task to which honour now binds us. In the hour of danger we humbly committed our cause into the hand of God and he has been our strength and shield.

'Let us thank him for his mercies and in this hour of victory commit ourselves and our new task to the guidance of that same strong hand.'

Joan makes the sign of the cross again as people get up to leave the hut. Banjo ushers his girls through the door, Kevin steps out of the way, and for the moment they all think about going back to bed.

'The war in Europe is over,' Mary says.

Hiroshi is not sure if that means all of the war is over or not, but he assumes that he is closer to being a free man, to going home, to seeing his family. This is the reason he wanted to stay alive, to see out the end of the war.

'This is very good news,' she says.

Hiroshi moves towards Mary and puts his hands gently on her waist. 'Yes, it is good news . . .' He looks in her eyes under the dim light of the kerosene lamp and says, 'Watashi wa, anata wo aishiteimasu, Mary.' After ten months of almost daily visits, conversations, sharing of food, stories, cultures, fears and hopes, Hiroshi declares what he has felt for some time now. 'I love you.'

Mary throws her arms around his neck like James does to their mother – urgent and affectionate. 'I love you too, Hiroshi,' she whispers into his ear with tears welling in her eyes as he holds her close. 'Please don't leave.'

Hiroshi doesn't answer. He loves her but he loves his family too and he wants to go home. He wants to see them again. Mary is in his heart now, but his family is in his veins. Hiroshi will go home, and if he can, he will take her with him. He knows it will be difficult given what he understands about her life here, and knowing what the Japanese are like too. No one in his family has ever married someone who is not Japanese. He knows that he will be expected to marry someone with the same social standing as he has – he should marry an equal. He knows his father will be critical of him for not following the traditional protocol for choosing the right wife, and that it will reflect on his whole family. First he did not die as soldier in war and now he wants to marry outside Japanese tradition. This will be double shame for him.

It would not be enough to tell his parents that he loves Mary. They would expect their son to follow the normal way of getting married – the kind of arranged marriage that had brought his own parents together. But Hiroshi wonders if such arrangements are why his own parents are so different to him. That maybe if they'd gotten to know each other before marriage, they may not have chosen each other. His parents do not have a love marriage; his father is traditional even if his mother isn't, and Hiroshi knows the expectation for him to conform is strong. Social responsibility is more important to his father than love and affection. The more he has thought about it over time, the more he remembers the lack of physical contact between his parents, between Japanese people in general. This is not the kind of man he wants to be, though. He wants to hold Mary, all the time.

These are the thoughts Hiroshi has had over the long days and nights and weeks when he has had to do nothing but think – about his feelings, about his future, about how he will re-enter his life in Japan. These are the thoughts he has not shared with Mary for fear that she does not feel the same. For fear that she will not understand his thoughts and feelings. And for fear that a future together may not be possible. Mary doesn't know that late at night, early in the morning, and through the long hours of daylight that he never gets to see, Hiroshi has been thinking about marrying her. He has thought about her being his bride and how she will look in a traditional white shiro-kakeshita kimono, tied with a white obi. He imagines her in the white tsunokakushi – the white silk veil with a topknot that would gently cover her dark brown hair, which he has not even touched.

He has pictured in his mind what their traditional Shinto ceremony will be like with him in a formal kimono-hakama-haori ensemble. He wants to share these imaginings with Mary but, like her, he is cautious, not only concerned about rejection but also about the reality that dreams can turn to nightmares through no fault of their own.

Their hearts beat fast as they hold each other for long minutes. It isn't enough, but they know instinctively when they must break their embrace and Mary must leave. There have been no other words spoken. You need time to absorb a declaration of love, to reflect upon it, to enjoy it.

'Hello, Mary,' Marj says.

Mary is startled out of her dream-like state, having just had the most heart-stopping moment of her life.

'Aunty Marj! Um, hello.'

Marj is looking past Mary, seeing if there is anyone behind her. 'It's a bit late to be out, isn't it?'

'I-I-I was at the lavatory,' Mary stumbles, panicking, not knowing what her Aunt has seen.

'I don't think you were, Mary. I don't think you were at all. I've seen you walk down here a lot at night. And sometimes you don't go to the lavatory, do you, my girl?'

'Mary?' Joan sings out from the back door, and Mary has never been more grateful.

'Coming, Mum.' Mary moves to pass Marj.

'I know you're up to something, young lady, and I will find out. You know people always tell me things.'

That night, Mary can't sleep. Memories of her embrace with Hiroshi and confrontation with Aunty Marj have her emotions swinging. She feels nauseous, lovesick – yet hopeful. There has still been no mention in the newspaper of the Japanese prisoners of war in Cowra. At the Smiths' earlier that day, Mary read with interest a story about a conference in Bathurst where diggers argued that all the Italians should be sent back to Italy after the war. She wonders what Aunty Marj will make of that. And the woman in town who is pregnant. She wonders if all this talk about sending soldiers home and the war being over is because the war is, in fact, nearly over. The end of the war is what Mary prays for each night when she goes to bed. It's the time of day when she closes her eyes, waiting for the sounds of the mission to settle, for her family to all go to sleep, before she allows herself to think and dream.

Mary has only been to one wedding at Erambie. It was a cousin who was also very young. She didn't take much notice at the time but as she strains to recall the day, she remembers it was romantic. Mary wants a wedding too, with family and friends and flowers – and Hiroshi. There has never been a wedding on the mission that's not between two Aboriginal people and she knows that Hiroshi being Japanese is an issue. Mary starts asking herself questions, considering possibilities and hypotheticals: *What if no one will want us to get married? Maybe the locals will not allow it. Maybe Mr Smith won't allow it. I was baptised at St Raphael's, we all were, so maybe Father Patrick will marry us up there. Mum is a hard worker. Father Patrick likes her. He often sends extra food home to our family, and old clothes that Mum mends, so he must like our family too. He will most definitely like Hiroshi. He has to, because God loves everybody. It's his job. Maybe I should start going to church. Maybe I should go in and say a prayer and light a candle when I go to get Catherine and Carmichael from school. Maybe if Father Patrick sees me there he will think I am good. He will be happy to marry us. But what about Hiroshi? Is Shinto marrying Catholic like white marrying Black? Does Hiroshi even want to marry me?*

Mary's thoughts and feelings are a rollercoaster, one minute she is positive and hopeful, the next she is depressed and resigned to the fact that they will never be together. Her sleep is fraught with anxiety and yet she can't wait for the next morning so she can count the hours and minutes to seeing Hiroshi again.

'Joan! Joan! Open the door!' Marj bangs her chunky fists on the thin door to the Williams' hut. 'Open it, Joan, we need to talk.'

Mary has left for the day and Joan is trying to sort the kids out before she heads up to the church to start work. She opens the door.

'I know about him!' Marj declares.

'Who?'

'The Jap. *I know.*'

Joan grabs Marj's arm and pulls her inside. 'Shh, someone will hear you.'

Marj pulls free from Joan's clutch. Her face is blood red with anger. 'Don't shh me, Joan Williams, and don't you ever grab me like that again.'

'I'm sorry.' Joan rubs Marj's arm, panicking.

Marj stares at Joan and presses her lips together in an unforgiving way.

'You know your mouth looks like a cat's bum when you do that, Marj.'

Marj's mouth softens, taking the harshness out of her eyes and face. They both know it's not the first time she's been told that.

'Why can't I ever stay angry with you, Joanie?' Marj sits down at the kitchen table and Joan is relieved. 'But I *will* stay angry with Fred, that's for sure. He didn't tell me about the Jap you've been hiding and I don't know why. He only cracked under pressure last night after I saw Mary and knew something was up.'

Joan wonders who else has seen Mary out at night and who else Marj has told.

'I mean, I can keep a secret as good as the next person,' Marj says, so believably that she almost fools herself as well

202

as Joan. 'I think he only told me last night because the war is over. Pretty much, anyway.' Marj is looking around the small hut. 'So, where is this fella? Is he, you know . . .' Marj stops momentarily, tilting her head to the left and nodding.

Joan has no idea what Marj is referring to. 'Is he what?'

'You know,' Marj says, then lowers her voice, 'yellow?'

'Oh, for goodness' sake.' His skin colour is not anything she even took notice of when she met him for the first time. 'If *you* know, then who else knows?'

'Well . . .' Marj pauses, 'I haven't really told anyone.'

'Good!' Joan says but she isn't convinced.

'I may have mentioned it in passing to Ivy, in fact, I think I heard her and Sid having a few words on my way here too.'

Before Joan has a chance to respond there's a knock on the door and both Ivy and Sid walk in, closely followed by Banjo and Fred. As they enter, Marj starts up again, making a racket, asking who had the right to do what, without telling her or anyone else, and that people will be gossiping and she hates gossip. No one is surprised that Marj is talking about herself.

Then Kevin arrives with a swagger that says he's got it all under control. 'Calm down, Marj, you're making more noise than the spruikers at the sale yards,' he says while he rolls a cigarette.

'I'm telling the police, there's probably a reward,' Marj says, having found her anger again now that the men have arrived. 'This is not something that we should be doing. You are harbouring a criminal. And Lord knows why!'

As Marj moves to leave the hut, Joan sees Mary walk in through the back door and head into the front of the house with some mending from the Smiths for her mother to do. As she gets to the front room Mary sees her father blocking the doorway so Marj can't leave through the front. The air is thick with tension. Fred and Banjo have never come to blows but Fred knows he needs to stand up for his woman. It's what any decent man would do, and any man who valued his life would most definitely do.

'Banjo, don't,' Fred says, trying to defuse a situation that has quickly deteriorated and thrown the hut into chaos with Ivy, Sid, Joan, Mary, Banjo, Fred and Marj all huddled around the doorway and talking over each other.

Banjo is a talk man, but Marj isn't afraid of him and moves right up to his face. Fred panics because he fears he may have to finish what Marj starts and he is not a fighter.

'Step back, Marj, we've got this under control. We know what we're doing, we're saving lives – lives like yours and mine, lives that matter.' Banjo doesn't like having stern words with a woman, but they haven't come this far to have everything ruined because Marj can't keep her mouth shut.

Marj doesn't move. 'Get out of my way, Banjo Williams, there might be a reward for this yellow man.'

Banjo stays where he is and so does Marj. It's a Wiradjuri stand-off as the two eyeball each other. Mary is getting teary. Then Kevin speaks.

'There's only one way to solve this,' he says. 'Like we always do. Up at the railway gates.' Everyone at Erambie knows that a quick round of boxing away from the mission near the railway tracks where the police can't touch them is the best way to resolve local disputes.

'Kevin!' Joan exclaims, mortified. 'We are not boxing over this. Banjo Williams, you are not fighting.' Before the brothers can argue about their proposed fight, Claude is at the door.

'Come quickly,' he says, trying to see past Banjo. 'There's a fight up at the railway tracks. There's supposed to be a Jap here on the mission and they're fighting over who should hand him in. They reckon there's a reward.'

Everyone turns to face Marj, knowing she's the one who let the secret out.

'Looks like someone's beaten us to it,' Kevin says.

Joan is relieved that neither of the Williams brothers will have to fight and holds her own children back from the older people heading towards the makeshift boxing ring.

When they arrive, there is a big circle drawn in the dirt with dozens of people around the edges. On one side are those who don't want to hide the Japanese soldier, and on the other side are those who do. It's the type of fight that could've happened back when Hiroshi first arrived. Fights up at the railway tracks mark the end of a dispute, and everyone adheres to the outcome, as hard as that may be for some families. Today's fight is no different.

Both men have their shirts off and fists are raised high. Only a few punches are thrown before one fella is knocked to the ground for the count. The crowd count in unison: 3, 2, 1. And then there are cheers about the win rather than the issue which not everyone has become aware of.

The winner is a Murray, who has boxing blood in his veins. He helps the other fella get off the ground and when his opponent is standing upright again, shakes hands with him and then walks over to Banjo.

'So, I won,' he puffs. 'No one will put him or your family in. But I need you to tell me why. I only fought against it cos I don't really have much time for that fella. I don't really have a proper reason.'

'His government has been fighting our government,' Banjo answers quickly. 'Our government doesn't even recognise our people even when they go to war to fight for them. I am at war with this government too. That makes us on the same side as the Japanese.' Banjo still believes in his words with the same passion he felt the first time he said them to Sid, Fred and Kevin the morning they found Hiroshi.

'Right, it's good that I won then,' the Murray fella says and he turns around and announces to everyone who has been listening to the whole conversation, 'No one is to say anything to anyone about the Jap until Banjo says so. I won and you all know the rules up here.' The crowd nods but doesn't move just yet. All eyes are on Marj who is agitated.

'No one,' the winner repeats in her direction. 'We will stick together on this. You know the whites love it when we argue, let's not give them that. Let's wait till it's safe for this fella to come out and we can give him a proper welcome and send off back home.'

16

In early June, Mary reads to her parents from the paper about the issue of immigration. '"Immigration will be a big thing after the war, and at present federal ministers are almost unanimous that only white immigrants will be invited within Australia's gates to settle and raise families of future Australians."'

She panics, knowing that Australians think of the Japanese as yellow and that will mean that even when Hiroshi is free, he won't be able to stay.

'I heard some fellas talking about it at the cannery,' Fred says. 'It's called the White Australia Policy and they reckon it started with the Chinese diggers near Lambing Flat – that's not far from here, you know.' They all nod. 'It was a long time ago, but you know, people round these parts have long memories. Apparently, the miners don't want people who aren't white taking their jobs, and that must mean us as well.

Not that they'd give us the jobs anyway. Or they'd expect us to work for less and then when we do, the whitefellas hate us even more.'

'There's a test people have to do as well,' he continues, shaking his head. 'You have to write in English and if you don't pass, well, you can't come in. As far as I can tell, most whitefellas like this policy.'

'Well, when you've got the prime minister saying that Australia will remain forever an outpost of the British race, what hope have we got?' Banjo asks.

'I reckon some of those Italians will stay here, marry the women and take the jobs too,' Kevin says. 'We can't have that. It's bad enough they've been here, bludging off our government, waiting until the war is over, but they really must go home now that it is. Surely.' He looks at the others for acknowledgement and agreement.

'I can't see many, if any, of them marrying, can you?' Joan says. 'Surely they want to go home to their families.'

Mary is trying not to think about the White Australia Policy and what anyone thinks about soldiers staying and getting married. She is not prepared for Hiroshi to leave. She would marry him in an instant if he asked, and happily keep him here with her. And if they won't let them stay in Cowra then she'll run away with him to Japan.

The idea of living in Japan both excites and scares Mary. She loves the idea of cherry blossom picnics and eating udon noodles, but she knows a lot of Japan has been destroyed by the war. And what about her family? She's never slept a night away from them. How would she cope? She says a prayer.

'Dear Lord, please make sure that after the war, Hiroshi and I can stay together here in Cowra. He is a good man. And please bless Mum, Dad, Betty, Dottie, Jessie and James. Even bless Aunty Marj and help her not to gossip so much. Amen.'

8 June 1945: Japan Expecting Invasion: Preparing Home Guard

Mary reads the headline and her palms start to sweat. Her stomach is churning and she feels nauseous. She almost doesn't want to read any more, knowing that the end is closer every day.

'Are you all right?' Joan asks. The colour has drained from her daughter's face.

Mary passes the paper to her mother and Joan starts to read the article out loud.

'"An emergency call has gone out from the Japanese Army Headquarters to every man, woman and child in Japan to make a suicide stand in defence of the Empire."' Joan sits down and makes the sign of the cross, feeling the same nausea that Mary experienced only minutes before.

Mary takes back the paper and continues to read: '"Japan is expecting an invasion, and booklets issued by army heads tell those in the Peoples' Volunteer Corps that their training must include preparation for 'death-defying charges and bodily attacks against tanks'. The people, it says, must cooperate with the army in suicide attacks to kill and wound the invading enemy. Food and medicinal supplies in Japan are reported to be short."'

Everyone is silent.

'What does all this mean?' Mary asks, thinking first and foremost about Hiroshi. 'I don't understand.'

No one really understands the methods of the Japanese but from the article, Banjo has made a decision.

'Sounds like the Japanese have pretty much said the war is over.'

Mary wants to change the subject quickly and flicks through the paper, anxiously looking for something to alter the mood as well.

'Wow!' she exclaims with real enthusiasm.

'What is it?' Joan asks.

Mary reads the headline: 'ABO. BOBBY-SOXERS SAID "WOO WOO": COWRA CROONER IN THE NEWS'.

There's immediately excitement in the Williams' hut as a relation has made it as a singer in the city. Although the headline about Japan has made everyone feel uncomfortable, no one is talking about it because the story of Burrah Williams is too good to let anything ruin the moment. Mary is once again reading the paper to the family, including Uncle Kevin, who has been back for a few days and is enjoying catching up on all the news.

'"Former Erambie Mission resident Merv Burrah Williams is making a name for himself in Sydney. That's what Hugh Dash, sporting editor, wrote of the Cowra crooner in Friday's *Daily Telegraph*,"' Mary reads, and everyone in the hut is already impressed.

'"All Blacks footballer Merv Williams is something more than just an even-time winger. He's the Bing Crosby of Sydney's Aborigines, with a bobby-sox brigade all of his own."'

'Oh, please, the Black Bing Crosby, I don't think so.' Only a few sentences in and Kevin is already commentating. Kevin has always fancied himself as the Black Bing Crosby, and has said so more than once, but the title never got picked up by anyone else. And now to hear about Burrah being called Bing Crosby, he's feeling left out of the musical limelight that he has always felt should've been his.

Mary waits for her Uncle to finish then continues. '"The dusky teenage belles, who black-track him from dance to dance, never swoon. When he croons they stamp their feet and chorus, 'Woo woo'."'

Kevin rolls his eyes and groans with disgust. He mightn't be known as the Bing Crosby of the region but he's certainly adored by the ladies, and he knows it.

'Stop it, Kev,' Joan orders and then gestures for her daughter to read on.

'"Merv is known as the double-breasted blue-bird. He's as black as a Pelaco shirt advertisement, with a Ronald Colman moustache and a pair of natty sideburns."'

'He does too,' Joan says, having seen a couple of movies at the Cowra Theatre that had the English actor in them. 'That moustache *is* just like that Colman fella's. I remember Dawnie saying it used to tickle when Burrah kissed her.'

That makes Kevin even angrier. Dawnie was another beautiful local woman Kevin just couldn't snag years ago, and now it is too late. She married a fella and moved off the mission.

There always seemed to be other men who got to marry the women Kevin couldn't win.

'"He's also a number one pin-up boy at La Perouse –"' And before Mary can read any further, Kevin is up and walking to the door.

'Pin-up boy? I can't listen to this any more. I'm going for a walk down to Ryan's Place.'

'Stop it, Kevin, don't be so jealous of other people all the time. It's good one of our own has done well. He works hard and he's talented at what he does. Come back and sit down.' Joan is standing behind the chair, waiting for him to return. Banjo sits back and watches his brother do as he is told. Only Joan can make the two Williams brothers behave well. 'Mary?' she prompts.

'"Merv is a fugitive from a gumleaf band in Cowra. He played the alto leaf, and found that by corrugating the leaf with the sharp point of a woomera he could achieve a double-stopping effect. That was the finish. His fellow musicians pointed the bone at him and asked for his resignation."'

'What does pointing the bone mean, Mum?' Dottie asks, and the other kids look to their mother for an explanation too.

'It's something that Aboriginal people do when they want to get even with someone else. If someone does something bad, then they can be punished.' She stops short of saying someone can die because she doesn't want to go into it in front of little James.

Meanwhile, Kevin can't believe that the newspaper has written the phrase or that Burrah would even suggest that. 'That's just crazy! As if anyone would point the bone because of music. I can't believe he told the newspaper that. From what I hear, he was only asked to leave the band.'

'You can't believe everything that's in the paper,' Banjo says. 'He mightn't have even said that.'

Kevin's not listening to reason. 'How long is this article anyway, Mary, is it ever going to end?'

Mary holds the paper up to show the two lengthy columns of text. 'It's quite long, Uncle Kevin.' Mary looks at her mother. 'At least this is a positive article about Aboriginal people. You're always saying what they write about us is bad, Mum.'

Kevin shakes his head. 'What more could they possibly be saying about him?'

Mary scans the paper. 'Well,' she says slowly, 'it says he's sung at dances and on the radio and somewhere called the Tivoli and he has a new band. And that he played with the All Blacks against the La Perouse Warriors last Sunday in Redfern.'

'Good to see he's keeping the football up too,' Joan says, trying to deflect the music side of things.

Mary starts to chuckle.

'What?' Kevin asks, as if the whole article is an attempt to annoy him personally.

'The paper says that Uncle Burrah thinks Frank Sinatra's singing is just organised asthma.'

'That does it!' Kevin pushes his chair back in a rage and storms out of the hut. Joan and Banjo look at each other and roll their eyes.

'Mum, Dad!' Mary is breathless when she runs into the hut, distressed, and with tears running down her cheeks. She almost collapses at the table as she throws the newspaper down and starts to cough. Her mother passes her a glass of water, and her father stands protectively over her.

Mary wipes her nose, coughs again, sips the water and takes a deep breath. It's 7 August 1945 and the headline on the front page of the newspaper has rocked her.

FIRST ATOMIC BOMB DROPPED ON JAPAN.
2000 TIMES BLAST OF TEN-TON BOMB

The article has been written in Washington, which Mrs Smith told Mary is in America. Mary doesn't know what an atomic bomb is but she knows it's severe if it's two thousand times stronger than a normal bomb. She knows that this bomb will have caused enormous damage and it has been dropped in Japan. Although she doesn't know how far the bomb site is from Hiroshi's hometown, she knows the news will devastate him.

Her mother picks the newspaper up. 'Oh dear,' she says, making the sign of the cross. 'Banjo, you better get the others here.'

Banjo is out the door and back in the time it has taken her to boil the kettle and make six mugs of tea. Mary has composed herself and wants to read the article when they are all seated and silent.

'"The US dropped the first atomic bomb, the most devastating weapon the world has ever known, on the Japanese city of

Hiroshima today.'" Tears start to form and Mary doesn't know if she can get through the entire story, but she knows she must try, it's her duty and a sign of her commitment to Hiroshi.

"'This bomb has two thousand times the blast of the largest bomb previously used, the RAF ten-ton bomb. Experts say that three atomic bombs could cause as much damage as all the bombs dropped on Japan in the past six weeks.'" Mary is shocked because she hasn't read about the other bombs, they must have been reported on days she didn't get the paper from the Smiths'. But it also means that Hiroshi doesn't know about the other bombs either. All she can think about is whether his family are safe.

"'Since the bomb was dropped, Hiroshima, a port and arms centre, has been completely cloaked in an impenetrable cloud of smoke and dust. President Truman warns the Japanese, 'We are now prepared to completely obliterate every productive enterprise Japan has above the ground in any city, and sea and land forces will follow up this attack in such numbers and power as the Japanese have never seen.'" Mary gasps, putting her hand over her mouth. She is torn about showing Hiroshi the paper. She wants him to know what's going on, and she wants to understand why, if the war in Europe is over, the US and Japan are still at war. Maybe Hiroshi will be able to explain it to her.

Sid has given Joan some leftover potatoes for Mary to take to Hiroshi and as she hands them over with some damper and a jar of water, Hiroshi can see that Mary is shaken. He holds her briefly and she pulls back and hands him the article.

'There's been a bomb. An atomic bomb. Lots of . . .' She starts to cry and steps back while Hiroshi reads the article.

He is only a few lines into the story before he closes his eyes, shoulders sagging. 'My family,' he says. 'They are not close but if there is one bomb, there will be more.' He sighs. 'There will be many deaths. My beautiful country, the land-scape . . . gone.' He tries to imagine that his own country has survived some of that devastation, but knows in his heart it won't have. How could it? The Americans have atomic bombs. How can anyone fight that?

Hiroshi becomes lost in his own misery at the thought of the destruction of Japan by the United States and Mary stands there watching the man she loves, lost in the deep hate he feels for those who have dropped the atomic bomb.

17

31 August 1945

A Burning Hatred For Japs

It's hard for Mary not to take the headline in the *Guardian* personally. The Australians are with the Allies, but they too have caused enormous death and damage. Why weren't atomic bombs dropped on the Germans, if they were the enemy as well? She wonders if the Japanese talk about the 'American Peril'. Mary feels betrayed by Australians, although she knows her judgement is clouded because of what she feels in her heart. But at the end of the day, no one is better than the other in the war.

Mary has taken to reading the paper just to herself and leaving it for her parents to read on their own. She has lost her interest in the shared experience, only wanting to be with Hiroshi. As well as Hiroshima, the US has dropped an atomic bomb on Nagasaki, and Japan has surrendered at last. There was a parade down Kendal Street, celebrating the end of the hostilities. The war has come to an end and Mary knows countries will sign documents and make agreements and war reparations will be agreed upon, but she doesn't know what will happen to the Japanese soldiers still in Cowra. She's confused about everything going on around her; about her feelings, about what she should say and should not say to Hiroshi. She doesn't think he needs to know that American troops are pouring into and occupying Tokyo. He doesn't need to know that miles of Tokyo have been burned to the ground, leaving citizens living in huts on the fringes of the city. She knows the shame that surrendering must bring on Hiroshi's home country, even though she is glad that the surrender has ended the war altogether. What Mary thinks Hiroshi needs to know is that he is not alone. But he also needs to know the truth about the surrender, even if she doesn't tell him they are going 'splendidly'!

As she walks to the bunker that night, Mary is trying to decide what she will say, even as she concedes there is no easy way.

'The war with Japan is over,' she says to Hiroshi, but she does not smile.

Hiroshi is grinning though, and rubbing his hands together. 'We won?' he asks, eyes sparkling with the hope that this will be something his father will be happy about.

'Not really,' Mary answers cautiously.

'What does that mean, Mary? "Not really." The war is over, yes?' He nods at her for agreement, to check he heard correctly in the first instance.

'Yes, the war is over, Hiroshi, but . . .' She takes a breath. 'But the Japanese, they – they surrendered.'

'Oh, no, no.' He shakes his head, ashamed for his nation, for every soldier who went to war, for the soldiers who died in the war, and the Emperor. 'No, no, no.'

'Hiroshi,' Mary says softly, 'are you okay?'

He nods but says nothing. The shame of surrender has overshadowed any relief either of them may have felt that the war is finally over.

Two weeks after Japan's surrender, there is a dance at Erambie. Music is blaring out freely as John Smith is too busy with official business in town with his friend the mayor. Some of the Blacks who are married to white people and have moved off the mission have arrived at the party as well. Everyone is happy, kids are running wild and there's damper and rabbit stew aplenty. Kevin is chatting to all the pretty women who aren't spoken for.

No one has noticed that Mary is not there, and thankfully no one sees her walking down the yard and into the shelter. Even though people are aware Banjo's family are hiding Hiroshi, Mary is conscious of what people will think about her spending so much time with him. She knows the Cowra rumour mill and she doesn't want to be the main focus of gossip. It's not the first time she has dared to see Hiroshi in daylight, but she doesn't want to startle him. Life is about to change and she is desperate.

As she moves the sheet of corrugated iron across roughly, almost carelessly, Hiroshi panics, not knowing what to expect. As soon as Mary descends, however, he is holding her. He is as scared as she is – hearing all the noise above but not knowing what's going on.

'The troops will be coming home soon. They are celebrating here and in the town,' she says breathlessly. 'What's going to happen to us?' She breaks down in tears and sobs into his chest.

Hiroshi holds her close but doesn't have the answers. He is not in a position to make any promises to the woman he loves, as much as he wants to. He is not in a position to ask for anything more, given all that he has already received. He cannot do anything but wait to see what fate holds for him.

18 SEPTEMBER 1945: COWRA BOYS RELEASED: REG WENHAM FLYING BACK

The town is celebrating again as newspapers report that Sergeant Reg Wenham, son of Mr and Mrs Wenham of Cowra, will be among the thirty-four released Australian prisoners soon to arrive at Rose Bay in Sydney. Mrs C R Bayliss of Liverpool Street has received a wire to say her husband, Lieutenant Clive Bayliss, who was captured in Borneo early in the war, is alive and well and returning to Cowra.

'I wonder if we will hear the truth about what happened to Australian POWs,' Banjo says. 'And if any of our men had the same experience as Hiroshi, being protected.'

'I don't know, Banjo, but the war is over, people are coming home, we need to make a decision,' Joan says, conscious every day that there is a person trapped in their yard. Since meeting Hiroshi, she has felt even more uncomfortable about the long days, weeks, months he has been forced to hide, even though they have all done their best to keep him nourished and comfortable.

'Not yet,' Banjo warns. 'Let's be sure we know what's going to happen to him, and what's going to happen to *us*.' No one has talked about the consequences of them hiding Hiroshi. 'You know we're going to be punished for this, don't you?'

Banjo looks at Joan, worried. 'It's not like life isn't punishment enough here, but I still think we did the right thing. You know that I thought that if the fella was trying to escape the camp, then he didn't want to be there. That he wanted to be out.'

'I know, love, and yes, we did the right thing, but you understand that Mary is in love, don't you? This is not going to end well for our girl.' Joan is at her husband's side and gestures for him to get out of his seat before locking her arms around his neck. 'You were right,' she says, looking into his eyes. 'You did the right thing. We all did the right thing. We just need to work out how this is going to end for him, and for us.' She doesn't say *And for Mary*, but she is a mother and has been watching her daughter's moods and knows that when

Hiroshi leaves there will be a hole in her daughter's heart that will take a long time to fill.

RETENTION OF POW CAMP: CHAMBER OF COMMERCE TO SUPPORT LOCAL COUNCIL

Discussion is hot in the Williams' hut on 25 September with the news that the Cowra Chamber of Commerce is talking about the post-war possibilities for the prisoner of war camp on the outskirts of the town. Mary has taken to reading the paper out loud again as she needs to be part of the yarns concerning Hiroshi's future – and her own. Her mother is keeping a watchful eye on her, as she is showing true signs of being lovesick: she is eating less and is much more distracted.

'"At last week's meeting of the Chamber it was decided to support the Municipal Council in any plans it had for the retention of the camp area. Mr Donaldson said that the people of Cowra should consider a proposal whereby the camp buildings could be retained for peacetime activities. An up-to-date hospital has been erected in the area, and the whole property was serviced with electric light, water and sewerage. It would make an ideal camp for convalescent soldiers or the training of youth for farm work, he concluded."'

'I wouldn't mind living up there,' Sid says. 'Seems more ideal than this place.'

'Electricity, water and sewerage,' Banjo says, 'wouldn't that be a nice change to our lives too?'

Kevin is not so calm though, and slams his fist on the table. 'How many times do *I* have to remind people that those prisoners lived better than *we* do? *They* had a bloody hospital service! A hospital! We can barely get treated in the public one in town.' He storms out.

Banjo gets up and watches his brother walk over to the railway gates. He hopes there's not a boxing match on, because Kevin is ripe for a fight.

'Let's go for a walk,' he says to the other men, and they follow him out the door.

There's mirris and goothas and lots of noise as the three men walk and roll cigarettes.

'We need to tell King Billie about Hiroshi. We're in a good position to do that now,' Banjo says, then takes a long drag on his cigarette.

'We can't,' Sid says. 'We don't have any say in this place, King Billie won't take any mercy on us.' He starts to panic when he sees they are walking in the direction of the Smiths' house.

Sid is not the only one panicking: Fred has been getting an earful from Marj for weeks now. And for his part in the 'town secret' he has had to tell her every single secret he has ever had, just to keep her happy and to stop her telling King Billie or anyone off the mission about Hiroshi. In exchange, Marj has demonstrated incredible restraint in her gossiping, which has surprised both herself and her husband – and everyone else, for that matter.

'We're going to tell King Billie that we found Hiroshi hiding,' Banjo says matter-of-factly. 'We'll tell him we found him this morning and kept him a prisoner.' Banjo has thought about how to approach the problem a lot but this is the first time he's said anything. 'We don't have to tell him that he's been here all that time. I *know* that will make him wild. I'm not stupid!'

'Why do we have to tell him at all? Why don't we just let the man walk back into town and get on with going back?' Fred asks.

'Yes, yes, that's a much better idea,' Sid says enthusiastically. 'It takes any responsibility from us at all. Let's just let him out and point him in the direction of town and make him promise he won't say anything at all.'

Banjo screws his face up at how simple the others think the situation will be to end. 'Because we want him to stay here until they send him home. We've fed and sheltered him for over a year, he is one of our community even if no one knows him. Anyway, where's he going to stay if we send him off? Back with all the other soldiers, who already think he is dead? If he wanted to be back there he would've left of his own accord before, don't you think?'

'Banjo's right,' Fred says. 'He's stayed put because he wanted to be here. We can't just chuck him out now. We've looked after him this long, we can look after him a little while more.'

The three men turn left and keep walking with five mirris trailing behind them, sniffing each other, and rolling in the dust.

'But since when can we tell white people what they should do? We can't tell King Billie not to put us in and he isn't going to be happy about this.' Sid is shaking his head. 'Nup, I reckon he'll get the cops straight away.'

'Sid's right, Banjo,' Fred says, 'we're lucky if our own mob listen to us. And you know what happens if we disagree: straight up to the railway gates.' Fred points in the direction of the homemade boxing arena. 'You think King Billie will wanna fight this one out? He's white, don't forget, Banjo, and he's the boss of us.'

Sid stops in his tracks and three mirris sit at his feet and start scratching. He gently moves them away with his foot. '*He* makes the rules, Banjo. *He* tells *us* what to do, not the other way around. The *Manager* tells us what to do to make sure everyone lives by the rules. He's going to be furious that we've harboured a POW as it is, let alone asking him to then protect *us* from punishment.'

The three men have walked around their huts a few times, smoking cigarettes and making it look like they are just having some exercise. Banjo's bad leg is starting to ache.

'I don't know why we just can't wait a little while longer,' Sid says.

'Because that fella needs to go home. He's been sad and lonely down there. I think we owe it to him to get him out as soon as we can. And now's the time.' Banjo is certain. 'Follow me,' he orders and turns towards his own hut. 'We need to plan what we're going to say. It needs to be foolproof.'

18

Banjo knocks on the door. Sid and Fred wait behind him, ready to follow his lead. Banjo hopes that being calm and rational will save them and Hiroshi from any more drama and, importantly, from ending up in the lockup. He knows, however, that everyday pleasantries go nowhere with King Billie.

John Smith opens the door in his long johns.

'Oh dear,' Sid mutters, thinking they've got here too early and that's going to make him even grumpier.

'What d'ya want, Banjo?' King Billie asks bluntly, then nods to Fred and Sid. 'Men,' he offers.

'We need to talk to you about something,' Banjo says, trying to keep the conversation as low key as possible. *The less drama the better.*

'Who's done what now?' King Billie asks, always assuming the worst has happened or is in the process of happening.

Banjo laughs nervously. 'No one's done anything,' he says, 'but we've found something that might interest you. We found something that could make you a bit famous.'

Smith's ego takes over and his disposition shifts to one of hospitality. 'Right, well I guess you should come in then,' he says, inviting the men into his home for the first time.

Mary is in the Smiths' kitchen washing dishes and going about her normal morning duties. She has no idea what her father has planned, or even that he is there. The men are hoping that whatever it is, it doesn't end them all up in jailhouse.

'Well? What have you found and what's this idea you have?' King Billie pushes the few strands of hair he has over his balding head from left to right. He knows that if he can be famous he can also get out of Erambie. 'What's going to make me famous?'

Banjo starts confidently. 'You know that breakout from the camp last year, with all the Japanese soldiers climbing over the fences? You know how some of them ran for miles and miles in all directions and there were stories of some of the escapees being seen at the hospital and around on farms? And of course there was Mrs Weir and the scones, we all heard about that, you would've heard about that too, Mr Smith?'

Smith nods and squints with suspicion.

'And you know all the reports said that two hundred and thirty-one soldiers died, and the others were captured over the next days. And of course they burnt down the huts and they had to then sleep in tents.' Banjo keeps talking to lessen the chance of Smith butting in, but half of his brain is now thinking about Joan. He's worried about spending time in the jailhouse and Joan being alone with the kids. And all of a sudden he has a vision of Kevin moving in and taking care of his family. He breaks into a sweat. He's gone from calm to almost desperate within minutes and he can see that Smith is getting agitated because he's taking so long.

The other men are looking at Banjo with a mix of confusion and disbelief, and because Banjo is panicking, Sid strays from the plan and declares, 'There's a Jap here!'

John Smith stands up, clearly angry. 'What? Where? Here at Erambie?' And he starts looking for his rifle, which everyone at Erambie knows about but thankfully has never seen. 'Where is the yellow bastard?' He's so loud that Mary hears him and moves to the kitchen door where she listens but can't see anything.

'Yes, here.' Sid points to ground. 'He's a soldier. He must've escaped that night, or after, we don't know, but he's here.' Sid is relieved he's said it and repeats, 'He's here. We found him.'

King Billie's face looks ready to explode so Banjo acts quickly. 'Actually, John, he found *us*.' Banjo is back on plan and he nods to Fred and Sid. 'He must've run here, while the others ran in other directions, and . . .' Banjo pauses, taking a deep breath for dramatic effect.

'And what?' Smith asks.

'And it looks like he's been hiding here all this time. Found him in our outhouse this morning. Looks the worse for wear, of course. But he's alive, so that's a good thing.'

'Why is it a good thing, are you mad?' Smith says. 'A living Jap is *not* a good thing.'

The three Black men are shocked by Smith's response and they're worried he'll find that shotgun and kill Hiroshi himself. Mary starts to shake.

'Well, it's good he's alive because if you, as the Manager of Erambie, say you found him, and you were going to lead the way in the after-war effort, well I think the *Guardian* might be interested in doing a story on you.'

John Smith sits down again. 'Go on.'

'Well, it's meant to be peacetime now. What if you showed the way in terms of peace in this town, a kind of way forward for everyone?' Banjo can see the harshness in King Billie's face softening and knows that his strategy is working. 'You could make a statement about how we have a duty now to return the Japanese prisoners – who are not really prisoners any more because the war is over – and return him in good condition, unharmed. Not like what we know they did to our POWs over there. This will just prove that we *are* better than the Japanese! Because we all know the Allies are better.' Sid and Fred nod.

Smith is squinting with suspicion at Banjo, not sure that his idea will work, but he doesn't tell Banjo to stop talking.

'A statement about how peace must start today, and you could use this one prisoner as an example of how to do it. You would be like the leader, a true leader.'

Mary has her ear pressed against the door and she doesn't like the way her father is talking about using Hiroshi, as though he is not a human being with feelings, a man who has already endured the trauma of fighting in New Guinea, before being imprisoned in a military camp and then hidden under-ground in the dark and damp for over a year. She wants to say something but she can't. She stands silently, hoping Mrs Smith doesn't come home early from her Red Cross meeting.

Banjo looks to Sid and Fred with a frown.

'I reckon that Sydney paper, *The Telegraph*, would love to write about you,' Fred says, picking up on Banjo's request for backup. 'And they'd probably take some photos.'

'Maybe.' Smith shrugs and becomes less angry as the minutes tick by. His own mind is working as fast as Banjo's as he thinks about how this could work well for him. 'What else were you thinking, just in case I choose not to take this straight to the police, because that's what I should do, you know that, don't you? I am, after all, a law-abiding citizen and I am a good friend of the Mayor, as you would also know. And many of the councillors.' He pauses. 'But, Banjo, I tell you, it feels like something doesn't sound right here. And if I find out you're lying to me, well, there's no telling what the Welfare Board will do to you.'

Banjo has small beads of sweat on his brow and is starting to feel a little nauseous. While they have all been part of the plot, he's never told so many lies straight-faced or straight to someone's face before.

'What if . . .' Sid butts in. 'What if we have a shindig for the one who got away? I mean, a shindig for the one who you found!' he says excitedly, pointing at the Manager.

'I'm the good guy, then?' Smith asks, and the men can see his mind ticking over. 'I can see the headline now: JOHN SMITH GIVES A HOME TO A JAP.' He shakes his head. 'No, that won't work, I can't be seen as a Jap lover, that won't win me any friends. I hate the Japs. Most people in town hate the Japs.'

'Or,' Sid says, 'maybe something like, JOHN SMITH GIVES A HOME TO SOMEONE WHO USED TO BE THE ENEMY.'

Smith screws his face up, but Fred has a better idea, 'Or what about MISSION MANAGER TO START PEACE PROCESS HIMSELF?'

'Oh, I like that, that's a good one,' Smith says.

Fred smiles because he knows they all need to make King Billie happy about what they have done. But the truth is the three men feel sick at the lengths they're going to so that they aren't thrown into the lockup and Hiroshi isn't just thrown back into the thick of the military camp. Although none of them know him, they understand that the choice they made to take him in originally means they have a responsibility for his welfare until the end.

'Mary!' Smith calls out.

Mary's stuck where she stands behind the kitchen door, frozen with the reality that Hiroshi is about to be made public and returned to Japan. Everything is suddenly out of her control. Emotions overwhelm her and she feels dizzy.

'Mary!' Smith calls again. 'Your daughter needs more discipline,' he says to Banjo, who has completely forgotten, in the midst of everything, that his daughter is here somewhere, working.

'Mary!' he calls one more time, and the girl appears. 'I need my best shirt and suit cleaned and pressed for photos.'

'Yes, sir,' she says without looking at her father or the other men. Her head is spinning, her heart is hurting, tears are welling, and she feels flushed and sick.

Banjo doesn't like the way Smith speaks to Mary, but he is exhausted from the charade and can't summon the words to deal with the Manager any more. And what would he say anyway? Sid is right, the Blacks never tell the whites what to do.

Smith stands up. 'Where is the Jap now, then? Is he chained up? I should meet the yellow bastard, I guess. You need to get his name, and does he speak English?'

'We've got him locked up in the air raid shelter down the back of my lot,' Banjo says. 'We got his name out of him. And he said thank you when we gave him some damper.'

'Right, leave him there.' Smith paces as he thinks. 'That's a good place to keep a prisoner. But we probably can't have him looking sick for the cameras. I am a generous man, you know, I need to have him looking half-decent, because we aren't cruel like the Japs. I don't want him here, but I'll get the wife to make some food and send it over with your girl. When she's finished here, of course.'

There are so many things wrong with Smith wanting to feed Hiroshi but no one comments. As far as all the men are concerned, they've saved their tails, made life a little easier for Hiroshi and got King Billie on side for the time being. They all know he could turn at any minute, but they will cross that bridge if and when they come to it.

When the children are in bed and most locals are inside, Banjo, Joan and Mary welcome Hiroshi back into the world with little ceremony. Mary goes to the shelter to fetch him.

'We're letting you out!' Mary says. There's fear in her voice.

'What do you mean? Hiroshi asks.

'Tonight, we're letting you out. My dad told the Manager about you. It's time for you to come up and . . .' She bursts into tears and rushes to his embrace. 'I don't want you leave. I don't want you down here, but I don't want you to g away.' Her heart is beating so fast and hard Hiroshi can feel it.

Hiroshi has spent months waiting for the moment of release and now it is upon him, he shakes with nervousness. He is not ready for what he will face in the coming days and weeks. All he can think about is the impact freedom will have on his senses. He wants to hear the unfiltered sounds of cockatoos and kookaburras like he did back at the camp, when he sat outside in the mornings. The barking owl that the men would all complain about because it sounded like a screaming woman will now be music to his ears. Having lived with only the muffled sounds of life above ground, and the regular sound of his breathing and Mary's voice for so long has challenged him mentally, taking him almost to the brink of insanity.

Mary wipes tears from her face. 'Come,' she says, taking his hand to walk to the ladder.

Hiroshi takes each rung cautiously and nervously. He knows as he climbs this time it will be the last.

Mary emerges from the dark of the bunker, followed by Hiroshi. He climbs out slowly, seeing the stars in the night sky, and he knows the day ahead will be clear; there will be sunshine and a blue sky that has been missing from his sight for too long. He wants to see the sun rise and set and to feel the breeze on his skin. He doesn't care that the air will be hot, it will be fresh and not filled with his own odour, which he has had to endure for months in the bunker.

In the dark of night, Hiroshi can't see the lush green of the grass that has grown with recent rainfall, but he can smell it.

And he can smell the sweetness of spring. He breathes deeply, and he inhales his new freedom. Freedom is seeing the stars, smelling the land, hearing the wildlife and touching the woman he loves. And she is there, anxious, conscious of her behaviour in front of her parents. Aware that as much as she wants to throw her arms around Hiroshi, she can't.

It is an awkward moment for all of them. No one knows how to behave; Hiroshi doesn't know how to react. He wonders if the same awkwardness will greet him when he gets home.

'Clean clothes for you,' Joan says as if she's a nurse speaking to a patient. She hands Hiroshi some folded clothes: fresh shirt and pants, shoes and socks. 'You can wash over there.' She points to the tub the family wash in, which Banjo has strung a hessian sheet around for privacy. 'We live up there,' she adds, 'and you can come and have something to eat with us when you are ready.'

It seems like an eternity before he is standing at their door. He knocks gently and waits for someone to answer. The children are asleep and Mary leads him into the kitchen. They all sit drinking tea for a while and eat damper and treacle. Hiroshi and Mary strain not to look at each other; he feeling guilty for falling in love with the daughter of the family who rescued him, she feeling scared of what her parents will do.

'Well, it's time for bed, Mary,' Banjo says. He has not told Fred and Sid or their wives what he is doing tonight for fear of overwhelming Hiroshi, and because they'd all agreed to keep him locked up. 'Big day tomorrow, with Hiroshi being interviewed for the paper. I need to talk to him about that, so he knows what to say.'

Mary takes some time before she nods; she doesn't want to leave. Hiroshi looks up and meets her eye. A grin takes over her face.

Joan sees the spark between the two and knows this is not going to end well for her daughter. She gets up with Mary.

As the women leave the room, Mary turns back once more and throws a tiny wave, her heart racing but glad at the thought that her love will be sleeping in the front room tonight, while she squeezes in with James and her sisters.

Hiroshi listens to Banjo talk about Mr Smith, the story the men concocted, and what the newspaper will probably ask him.

'Keep your answers short,' Banjo advises, 'do you understand?'

Hiroshi nods. 'Yes, I understand.'

'Your English is very good.'

'I went to university. I studied English. And Mary has helped me practise a lot.'

When Mary wakes she is out of bed before her eyes open, excited about the day ahead, about the planned celebration and about the newspaper coming to interview Hiroshi. She hopes everyone will try to be kind, even though she knows that most people think like her Uncle Kevin and hate the Japanese. But she's not prepared for what she sees when she emerges onto the verandah: her father and the man she loves drinking tea and smoking cigarettes. She didn't know Hiroshi smoked and she doesn't care, because it is something that has connected him with her father. This is a good thing, she thinks as she gets ready for work.

Banjo and Hiroshi sit near the spot where Banjo first found him in the cold of an August morning, sniffed out by the red cattle dog. KB sits by Banjo again this morning, only slightly suspicious of the new character.

One by one, the Williams children come out and introduce themselves to Hiroshi. He stands and bows to them. The girls bow back, giggle, and return to Joan in the kitchen. James climbs onto his father's lap and within minutes has managed to shift onto Hiroshi's, just as he would've if his Uncle Kevin had been there. The young fella notices only one thing: that there is another man in the house, which is often overrun with women.

Nervously, Mary walks to the door of the verandah to leave. 'Good morning, I have to go to the Smiths' now,' she says to her father, only half looking at Hiroshi. 'I'll see you afterwards.' She is worried that she is behaving unusually and her father will notice – or worse, that Hiroshi will think she is strange now that he is out in the daylight. But she is already late and hasn't got time to waste wondering about things like that. She stumbles as she leaves their hut, embarrassed and blushing as she makes her way to the Smiths'.

John Smith is in an unusually good mood today. He doesn't even yell at Mary for being late, but he doesn't speak to her either. She goes straight to the kitchen and prepares breakfast for Catherine and Carmichael and listens to Mr Smith whistling all the way into the lounge room.

'I'm going to be in the paper, probably the front page,' he yells out to the children. 'I'm going to be known as a human-itarian,' he says walking back to the kitchen. 'Do you know what that is?'

Neither of the children responds, they are not used to their father being in such a good mood, or talking to them over breakfast.

'It means I do good deeds.' He nods. 'And I do! I could've just handed the Jap over to the military but, no, I didn't. I've fed him up and given him clothes and we're giving him a farewell. Because I'm a good human being.' Smith uncharac-teristically cuddles his wife. 'And the good press might get us out of this place. I know you'd love to live somewhere bigger, somewhere like Bathurst.'

'King Billie's in his element, isn't he?' Banjo says to Fred and Sid.

Fred is frowning as he looks at Smith, who has his arm over Hiroshi's shoulder. 'If he really does hate all Japs, then he's hiding it well – they look like best mates over there.'

'Hiroshi looks like he's trying to get out from King Billie's grip, but he's playing the part. He's a bit of an actor,' Sid says. 'And the newspaper loves it.'

Smith is talking non-stop about how peace begins in Cowra and he is happy to feed Hiroshi back to good health. 'Of course, we had no idea he was here until a couple of days ago, he hid in a bunker, of all places.'

'Genius idea, Banjo, just genius!' Fred says to his friend.

Banjo takes the moment in and draws on his cigarette. 'We actually beat them again,' he says proudly.

Mary walks from the Smiths' and stands next to her father, saying nothing.

All the mission kids have gathered around, noticing how different Hiroshi looks. Someone calls out, 'Samurai!'

'Wait!' Hiroshi says and walks away from John Smith. Everyone follows him with their eyes and the kids start to follow with their feet.

'What are you looking for, mister?' one asks.

'A stick, so I can make a sword,' he says.

Soon every kid and most of the teenagers are picking up sticks and branches and showing them to Hiroshi, hoping theirs is the one he will want. He finds a small branch and starts to make a mock sword by pulling all the twigs and leaves from it until it is almost completely smooth. He sits on the ground and the kids sit around him. The newspaper journalist has walked over and so has John Smith, not happy that the spotlight has been taken away from him.

'In ancient times,' Hiroshi says, and everyone is surprised at how good his English is, 'Japanese warriors were chosen for being good leaders.' Someone hands Hiroshi some long reeds and Hiroshi uses them to tie a short stick to the long one for a small handle. 'And if you were chosen you received a sword from the Emperor.' There is not a word spoken as the locals become mesmerised by the skill of the stranger as well as the story. 'The modern soldier also wears a sword as a symbol of justice and peace.' Hiroshi stands up and hands the sword to John Smith. 'I give this to you as a sign of peace.'

The Manager is basking in the glow of his own ego. Everyone knows it, but no one cares. As long as he is happy they can have their day of fun, including music by the Williams men, who have started playing already.

'Harry is really talented too,' Joan says, looking proudly at Kevin's cousin who's also a musician.

'The whole family is talented, and I reckon they got it from their Uncle Major Murray,' Marj says, proud to have married into the Murray family.

Banjo brings his own banjo out to play.

'Can I?' Hiroshi asks, and Banjo hands it over.

'How can a Japanese soldier play the banjo?' Marj asks. 'Surely it doesn't come from Japan!'

Hiroshi tries to pluck the six-stringed instrument and all other noises dissipate. He attempts a traditional Japanese song, which is difficult with more strings than he is used to, but Mary is impressed. The kids all gather around and look more interested in banjo playing than ever before. One little kid tries to dance to the song and the old people cheer.

'How?' Mary asks, proud of the man she is in love with.

'At home, I play something similar, it is called a shamisen but it only has three strings. I think this one might be easier to play.' As people approach slowly to introduce themselves, Hiroshi shakes hands and bows. Each time he does, some of the kids mimic him and the adults tell them to stop. Everyone laughs, though – it's a day of happiness.

Hiroshi can feel the rays of the sun penetrating his skin. He had almost forgotten what it was like to feel natural warmth. His lips are stretched to their limit with a smile that spans his face. Mary's heart is singing as she stands back and watches from a distance, nodding to herself in a reassuring kind of way. She is overjoyed to see Hiroshi in the open, no longer a secret or conspiracy, no longer one of the enemy. Her mind is working overtime now that she can see that he fits in, that people like him. If people like him then it will be easier to convince them that he should stay. That they can be together.

'Here, mister, here,' one of the young fellas sings out, holding a boomerang. 'Come.'

Hiroshi walks to the paddock behind the mission. The boys show him how to throw a boomerang, with varying degrees of success. When he finally throws it and it comes flying back close to them all, there is a huge cheer.

'He's a natural,' Banjo says to Mary, putting his arm around his daughter. 'I think he is a good man.'

'He is, Dad, he is.'

19

The day has come for Hiroshi to leave. He will travel in an Australian Army truck to Sydney, where he will go by sea to Japan with the few remaining soldiers from the Cowra Camp. John Smith claims to have kept his end of the bargain, promising that he would pressure the authorities to let Hiroshi stay in town longer; more time meant more potential press. But no matter how many names he dropped or how friendly he was with the Mayor, the army said they weren't going to let a former POW stay anywhere other than under their watch. There was going to be an investigation into how Hiroshi had been missed in the head counts and someone was going to wear the blame for embarrassing the Australian military that way. Banjo hopes that nothing about Hiroshi's time at Erambie is ever traced back to him and the others.

Banjo and Joan would not let Mary stay with Hiroshi in the front room on his final night at Erambie, but they agreed they could sit on the verandah as long as they liked. Mary and Hiroshi don't speak much, knowing there is little left to say. The thought of running away together plays in each of their minds, but where would they run? Mary lives under the Aborigines Protection Act and the White Australia Policy will prevent Hiroshi from any real life in Australia. Besides, after being a soldier at war, a prisoner and finally an escapee in hiding, Hiroshi doesn't want to run any more; he wants to be at home, he wants to be the son, the brother and the poet he has always dreamed of being. If Mary can't be with him now, he will work to make it happen as soon as possible – as soon as his family understands why he is alive and how he came to fall in love with an Aboriginal girl and her family in Australia.

The sun is rising too fast and neither has slept. Mary wants it to be dark for longer, because the moment the sun is completely up, the end will arrive. Her heart is already heavy with sadness. They hear movement in the kitchen – Banjo has lit the fire to make a cuppa.

Banjo coughs loudly to let them know he is nearby, though he knows there will be nothing sexual going on, his Mary is a good girl. A good Catholic girl, like her mother at the same age. Banjo doesn't want his little girl to grow up. He doesn't want her to be in love with anyone, let alone a former Japanese POW who is going back to his own country today and who will tear his daughter's heart apart. No one knows how difficult today is going to be for Banjo when his baby girl gets her heart broken for the first time.

Mary and Hiroshi sit to attention as they hear Banjo approaching, letting go of the embrace they had found themselves in.

Thankfully the morning glory vines had provided protection from the rest of the community while they enjoyed their final moments together.

'Cuppa?' Banjo holds two tin mugs of black tea.

Hiroshi stands, bows his head and says, 'Arigatō, thank you,' and takes both mugs, handing one to his love.

'What time is it, Dad?' Mary asks.

'Six thirty.'

'There's scones in the kitchen from Mrs Smith too, if you're hungry,' Banjo adds. Mary cannot believe how supportive and wonderful everyone is being.

Banjo brings out his banjo and starts singing 'Waltzing Matilda' and Hiroshi joins in softly, singing off-key but remembering the words from Mrs Smith's poetry book. Joan and the kids have appeared with the sound of the music so early in the morning and when Banjo is finished, Hiroshi gestures for the instrument, getting used to more strings, and tries to play a traditional Japanese tune. Everyone listens to every chord.

'It is a thank-you song,' he says over the music, looking at Mary, who cannot see anything for the tears flooding her eyes and cheeks. Her mother and father stand on either side, arms around their daughter, ready to catch her wounded heart at any minute.

The music stops when Jim arrives with another soldier from the POW camp. They will be Hiroshi's escorts out of Cowra and out of Mary's life.

At that moment, Mary hates Jim for being the one to do the job. She starts screaming. 'NO! He can't go anywhere. He's staying here with us, with me. Hiroshi, tell them. Tell them you want to stay.'

Hiroshi is standing beside her, not wanting to say or do the wrong thing. He loves Mary, he wants to be with her, but he must go home. He must see his family, they're the reason he stayed strong all those months. They're the reason he escaped the camp. He has tears in his eyes too. He can't bear to see Mary so distressed.

'I must go home, Mary, but –' He looks at Joan and then at Banjo. 'Can I take Mary with me? I want to marry her.'

'Yes, I will! I'll go with you.' Mary cannot believe he has said that straight out to her parents.

'Mary!' Joan and Banjo say.

Joan embraces her daughter. 'Darling, you can't go with Hiroshi.'

'Yes, yes, I can, I love him too. I *can* go!' She pushes her mother away.

The military men have moved in and are standing next to Hiroshi. 'You can't go, miss. All the Japanese will be going back together on boats.'

'I don't care, we love each other, and,' Mary clings to Hiroshi, 'we're going to get married.'

Banjo stands behind his daughter and puts his hands on her shoulders. 'Smith will never let you marry Hiroshi, Mary, never.'

Mary spins to face her father, crying so hard she struggles to get her words out. 'He can't stop me. I love Hiroshi, I know about his life and family and culture, and no one can stop me from being with the man I love.' She has made so much noise her sisters and brother are standing in the doorway crying too, not understanding what's going on.

'We have to go, sir.'

The soldiers usher Hiroshi towards the door and Mary becomes hysterical, clinging to him. 'No, no, no,' is all she can say. Her parents have to pry her from him. There is no goodbye, no further declarations, and no promises for the future. Mary doesn't know why Hiroshi isn't fighting to stay.

But there is no choice – he is lucky to be alive, to have survived the war, the escape and hiding at Erambie. He is grateful to be there, to have met Mary and to love her. But he has no say in the ending to their love story. He belonged to the Japanese Army and now the Australian Army. He will not put up a fight because he cannot win.

'Please,' he says softly and looks at Joan and Banjo. He extends a hand and Banjo shakes it, putting his free hand on Hiroshi's shoulder. 'Arigatō,' Hiroshi says and nods. He looks at Mary and cautiously moves closer to her, looking at Joan for permission. He receives a gentle nod and hugs Mary carefully. 'Watashi wa, anata wo aishiteimasu, Mary,' he whispers in her ear.

'Don't go, don't go, *please* don't go,' she sobs.

As he is escorted out of their hut, she collapses to the ground.

Mary feels her life has been sucked out of her. There is no spirit left and no energy to even walk around. She has made herself sick with heartache; she hasn't eaten for days, has been bedridden with anxiety and sadness. She cries continuously and Banjo and Joan are at a loss as to what to do. Mrs Smith shows the girl some compassion, making her a cup of tea before she does her daily chores when she returns to work after three days away.

Every shelf Mary dusts, every sheet she washes, everywhere she looks, she sees Hiroshi's face: his smile, the look of hope in his eyes the day she told him the war was over. The day she told him she loved him. 'Watashi wa, anata wo aishiteimasu,' she says to herself over and over.

In March 1946, Hiroshi is with all the other Japanese POWs from Cowra and Hay when he boards the *Daikai Maru* from Balmain back to Japan. He recognises some of the men. They share cigarettes and small talk, but they don't talk about the camp. He doesn't talk about Erambie, or about Mary. He suffers the effects of seasickness although he had not expected or thought about it until he boarded the boat. Many of the other soldiers are returning home with the ashes and belongings of dead soldiers and he is sharing a space with a number of men who have boxes covered in white cloth. Some of the boxes, Hiroshi knows, contain the hair and fingernails of soldiers who had died on the front. He wonders if any of the boxes belong to his friend Masao. He's heard that Masao was one of the two men shot by Alf Burke, who found a group of escapees when he was out hunting. Hiroshi's heart cries out for his friend.

Everyone is subdued and although rumour has it that the Chinese POWs from Cowra are fearful of being attacked on the boats by the Japanese, there is no real trouble at all. Hiroshi, like every other soldier, is filled with dread about what he will see when he gets home, and how his family will react. He walks miles and miles around the ship every day, making use of legs that had nowhere to walk when he was at Erambie. He recites poetry in his head for Mary and plans what he will say to his parents. Of a night, in the dark, when he is most alone and vulnerable, he cries. He is more afraid of facing his family than he was of facing the war.

When they arrive in Uraga Bay near Tokyo a month later, they are fumigated with the pesticide DDT. This is not the homecoming Hiroshi had hoped for – he is being made to feel like he is a virus about to cause damage to the country he went to war to protect.

It's cherry blossom season, but there are none in sight. The landscape is bare, trees are damaged; many look like they will never recover. It is clear to Hiroshi that fire bombings have destroyed much of the country, but in the distance, the mountains show some signs of colour. He wonders what he will find when he finally gets back to Shikoku.

His distress increases when he finds a plaque with his name on it at the Yasukuni Shrine – he has already been enshrined. His family doesn't know that he is alive. The letter never arrived. Or perhaps it was never sent by the Red Cross. He will shock his family when he walks into their home.

On the trip from Tokyo Hiroshi is sick with nausea. He prays his family will forgive him, that the shame will be forgotten when they see him. He prays that his father's face will not be riddled with disappointment but gratitude that his son has returned.

As he approaches his home, he is sweating more than when he ran into the dark of night during the escape. His legs feel like jelly and he wants to throw up. It is early morning, just as it was when he was found at Erambie, and he knows his family will all be present, probably having tea. He knocks hard on the front door and hears shuffling feet approach. The door opens and there stands his mother, as beautiful as he remembers.

'You are not a ghost,' his mother shrieks, looking her son up and down. She touches his legs to double-check he is real. When she realises the truth – that he is alive – she falls to her knees and howls. His father runs down the hallway, picks his wife up and with a single tear falling down his cheek, hugs his son for the first time since he was a child.

Epilogue

13 November 1964

JAPANESE AMBASSADOR FOR CEMETERY CEREMONY
Fifty Japanese consular officials and businessmen are to visit Cowra on Sunday, 22 November, for an inauguration ceremony at the new Japanese war cemetery.

Mary reads the first sentence of the article and immediately thinks of Hiroshi. She wonders what he looks like after all this time. She doesn't dare imagine what it might be like to see him again, that is not possible.

She is sitting on her back porch at her home in Lachlan Street, Cowra. There's a cup of tea cooling beside her and her new baby granddaughter is in her arms. Life in town is different to the one she knew growing up at Erambie, but when she married a white man, she had to leave.

251

Mary reads the newspaper every chance she gets, and the stories often carry her back to the bunker and her time with the man she will always love. When Hiroshi left, Mary pined for him for more than a year and then, finally, when she accepted he would never come back, she agreed to marry Raymond, the grocer's son who used to deliver food to the Smiths'. Mrs Smith told her it would be smart to marry a white man and move into town, and in her own way, Mary loved Raymond and he treated her well. She fell pregnant immediately with their first daughter, Amy, who has just had her own first child, Janie.

For some time now, Cowra has been buzzing with the news that the RSL has decided to build a cemetery for the Japanese soldiers and interns. Locals are surprised that Australians are being so chivalrous and generous towards a group of people once considered the most hated in the world. But the RSL men were tending the graves of the Australian soldiers and thought it only appropriate and respectful to look after the graves of the Japanese soldiers as well. They were men just like themselves, after all; men with families, men with hopes and dreams, and men with the courage to fight for their homeland. Men like Hiroshi. Many of the members of the RSL remember the well-kept graves of Australian soldiers in Palestine, and the comfort that brought to families, knowing that someone was caring for the grave of their son, brother, uncle, father. It makes sense to those who had fought in war to do what is right.

When Mary reads about the families of Japanese POWs who will be attending the opening, she hopes Hiroshi will be coming. But then she hopes he doesn't – what good can come of it?

Raymond is reading the paper at the table and says, 'It's senseless to go on with the hatred of war all these years later. I'm glad Cowra is doing this.'

It is Raymond's belief in justice that Mary loves. He knew about Hiroshi, as did everyone in Cowra by the time the soldier left, but he didn't care. He wanted to marry Mary and he knew that even if she carried a candle for the soldier, he had left and would not be coming back. Hiroshi was no threat. Mary knew that if she couldn't be with Hiroshi, she had still found a good man in the one she married.

On the morning of 22 November, Mary is awake before dawn, but she has hardly slept anyway. She is not expected at the hospital where she works as a ward assistant serving meals until the afternoon. As soon as she'd learned about the opening, she'd planned to walk to the site to look on from a distance. She knows that only Australian government officials and people in the military have been invited to the ceremony, but she can't stay away. What if Hiroshi is there?

When Raymond has left for the day she puts on her best frock and starts walking, nervous about what memories might come back and what she might do if she sees Hiroshi. Her heart wants to see him, but her head doesn't.

As she reaches the entrance of the cemetery in Doncaster Drive there are official cars, and media with big cameras, and

Japanese women in beautiful dresses. She wonders if Hiroshi married a woman like that. Could any of them be Hiroshi's wife? She stands back, scanning the crowds for his face, convinced that she could not forget it.

Inside the cemetery, Hiroshi stands, blinded by tears, overwhelmed by returning to the town that saved his life while others lost theirs. He reflects on the night of the escape, remembering the sounds, the lights, and the smell of burning wood as if it was only yesterday. Hiroshi is filled with the same regret he felt while hidden at Erambie. Hiroshi finds Masao's plaque and wonders if anything has been learned from the tragedy of war. He looks at other headstones and wonders why the men all behaved so recklessly when he knows so few wanted to go ahead with the breakout. Why did they cause so much trouble for the Australian guards who had treated them so well? Why, after arriving in Australia frail, injured and starving, had they all recovered their good health only to end up dead?

His heart aches with the memories, but he is there with a purpose: he has returned to Australia to pay his respects to his fallen countrymen. To Masao. To show there is no personal hatred for the country or its people; Cowra kept him alive and gave him hope for a better world.

He is also hoping to see Mary.

Under the clear blue sky and summer sun, Hiroshi looks out across the cemetery and notices a woman in a pale blue dress. She has dark skin and a thin frame; she has lips that he once kissed. He is frozen to the spot and overcome with the same emotion he felt when he first told Mary he loved her. 'She is here,' he says under his breath. The flame in his heart that he carried on the long boat ride home and for almost twenty years still burns as strong as it did the day he first knew he loved her. And now she is here, in front of him, looking for him. Now they can hold each other without fear of reprimand or judgement and, he hopes, without a government policy that says she can't marry him. 'She is here,' he says again.

While the ceremony is solemn and official, Hiroshi is full of happiness, as if he has just started breathing for the first time. He is focused only on Mary as he starts to move through the crowd. He hasn't taken his eyes off her for a second, hoping she will look in his direction and see him too. His heart is racing, his palms are sweaty and his mouth is dry. 'She is here,' he repeats, and he feels like the luck he experienced two decades ago is here again just for him and the woman he has never stopped loving.

Then Hiroshi watches Mary turn away without having yet spotted him. He can't see who she is talking to but by the time he gets to the gate, a man has his arm around her waist. Hiroshi stops still.

'I thought I'd find you here,' he hears the man say to Mary thoughtfully. 'It's time to come home.'

Acknowledgements

As history cannot be owned by one person, I thank all those who were part of pulling together the many stories of Cowra that became *Barbed Wire and Cherry Blossoms*.

First, my mum Elsie told me her own stories about growing up at Erambie. It was a wonderful writing journey to be on with her, listening, learning and retelling.

To those in Cowra who offered their knowledge, wisdom and time in helping me research and then in reading drafts, this book is for you. *Barbed Wire and Cherry Blossoms* could not have been written without the support of local Koori historian Dr Lawrence Bamblett; Lawrance Ryan and Graham Apthorpe from the Cowra Breakout Association; Marc McLeish and Aunty Norma Wallace (Newton) – who were all part of making as complete a story as possible, even though this is of course a novel.

To my tiddas Beatrice Murray and Jacki Beale, thank you for pounding the pavement with me on early mornings while I was in Cowra researching. I appreciated you trudging up Billy Goat Hill and back again and offering words of support all the while.

To Ann Weldon (Coe) for reading pages, and Aunty Hazel Williams for sharing the story about Claude Williams and the 'scary horse'. Thank you.

I'd also like to acknowledge the friendly staff at Cowra Library, and the volunteers from the Cowra Family History Group for helping load and reload the microfiche machine!

For information and insight into the Japanese stories around the Cowra Breakout, I thank Professor Mami Yamada for her time, knowledge and feedback on material. Thanks also go to Kylie Wallbridge for researching with me in Tokyo in 2015.

Heartfelt thanks to Dr Donna Weeks from Musashino University (Tokyo) for providing brilliant translations of Basho's haiku for the novel.

Much of the first draft was written while under the care and loving hospitality of my tidda Julie Wark in Barcelona, who also read drafts with a careful eye. I must also acknowledge Carles and the staff at Brunel's Café too, for filling me with appropriate fuel while writing in their space.

I did much of the editing of *Barbed Wire and Cherry Blossoms* at the State Library of Queensland and I thank all the staff at the Queensland Writers Centre for their support and literary collegiality. To my de-stressing swimming tidda Ellen van Neerven for listening to me whinge while I splashed – thank you.

And to Lisa Heidke – for the long phone calls about writing, researching, editing, planning and everything else that causes anxiety in the process.

To the publishing 'A team' at Simon & Schuster Australia, and to my editors Elizabeth Cowell and Kylie Mason. Thank you for helping me make this book the best it can be.

To my agent Tara Wynne, who I trust with my life – I've no words left to express my gratitude.

And finally to you my reader – I hope this book adds something to your own journey in life. I believe that understanding and appreciating who we are today requires us to understand and accept who and what we have been, collectively as a nation, in the past.

Anita Heiss

About the author

© Amanda James

Dr Anita Heiss is the author of non-fiction, historical fiction, commercial women's fiction, poetry, social commentary and travel articles. She is a regular guest at writers' festivals and travels internationally performing her work and lecturing on Indigenous literature. She is a Lifetime Ambassador of the Indigenous Literacy Foundation and a proud member of the Wiradjuri nation of central NSW. Anita is an Advocate for the National Centre of Indigenous Excellence and an Ambassador of Worowa Aboriginal College. She is an Adjunct Professor with Jumbunna Indigenous House of Learning, UTS, and currently divides her time between writing, public speaking, MCing, managing the Epic Good Foundation and being a 'creative disruptor'. Anita was a finalist in the 2012 Human Rights Awards and the 2013 Australian of the Year Awards. She currently lives in Brisbane.

Find out more about Anita on her website at
www.anitaheiss.com

on Twitter at @AnitaHeiss

and on her Facebook page

Book club questions

1. Life on Erambie Station was hard, with food rations and no electricity, constant restrictions and intervention in daily life. In what ways did the government benefit from enforcing these harsh conditions on Aboriginal people? Why would the POW compounds have better food and facilities?

2. Banjo Williams' decision to hide Hiroshi came at great sacrifice to his own family and the other families of Erambie. Do you think it was the right choice? What does this decision say about Banjo's ethics?

3. What would you have done if you were Hiroshi – stayed in the prison camp or attempted to break out? Is there shame in staying behind? Would you be able to survive on the run?

4. What are your thoughts on Mr and Mrs Smith? Was John Smith trapped in his role as the mission Manager or were there things he could have done to help out the residents of Erambie? Could John Smith have led a less harsh regime while still complying with government expectations?

5. The Japanese and Italian POWs were treated differently by the townspeople, with the Italians working and more integrated into life outside the camps. Were the Italians less discriminated against than the Japanese? Do you think any of these perceptions between the different cultures are still held in the broader community today?

6. Indigenous soldiers fought for Australia in the First and Second World Wars (and other conflicts) despite not holding Australian citizenship. Can you understand why people made this choice? Why/why not? Were these Indigenous soldiers treated equally in and after wartime? What sacrifices did they make for Australia?

7. Have you ever been to Cowra, in rural New South Wales? What were your experiences there?

8. What rights have Aboriginal people won since the 1940s? Do you think that all Australians are treated equally today?

9. Mary was only seventeen when she fell in love with Hiroshi. Did you fall in love as a teenager? How did it turn out?

10. Do you think Mary is truly happy in her decision to marry Raymond? Why/why not?

If you enjoyed
Barbed Wire and Cherry Blossoms
look out for *River of Dreams,*
a new novel by Anita Heiss,
coming in 2020